Loony Bin

Richard Leverone

Copyright © 2006 by Richard Leverone

All rights reserved. No part of this book shall be reproduced or transmitted in any form or by any means, electronic, mechanical, magnetic, photographic including photocopying, recording or by any information storage and retrieval system, without prior written permission of the publisher. No patent liability is assumed with respect to the use of the information contained herein. Although every precaution has been taken in the preparation of this book, the publisher and author assume no responsibility for errors or omissions. Neither is any liability assumed for damages resulting from the use of the information contained herein.

This is a work of fiction. Names, characters, places, and incidents either are the product of the author's imagination or are used fictitiously. Any resemblance to actual events or locales or persons, living or dead, is entirely coincidental.

ISBN 0-7414-3572-1

Published by:

INFINITY
PUBLISHING.COM

1094 New DeHaven Street, Suite 100
West Conshohocken, PA 19428-2713
Info@buybooksontheweb.com
www.buybooksontheweb.com
Toll-free (877) BUY BOOK
Local Phone (610) 941-9999
Fax (610) 941-9959

Printed in the United States of America

Printed on Recycled Paper

Published November 2006

To my wife,
Maureen

"To cure sometimes, to relieve often, to comfort always."

— Anon.

1

Within seconds, she had slipped into one of those moods I dreaded.

Tucked into our usual window booth at Ricco's on the day before the shooting, sharing a pitcher of Bud draft and waiting for our half-mushroom half-plain thin crust, Trisha began spewing out her day.

Fresh off her nine-to-five shift at Finney's Flowers, she was on a roll, and trapped with no alternative, I sat there, nodding like a mindless simpleton, listening to her vent.

She went on incessantly about Dora, the older woman she worked with. I had never met the lady, but within minutes, Trisha had me convinced Dora drove a broom.

Slamming into high, she shifted her wrath to her mother, Alice. Alice, Trisha complained, still treated her like a sixteen-year-old, constantly calling her and imparting unending bits of motherly wisdom like, "Don't forget to eat lunch," or "Try to save at least fifteen percent of this week's paycheck." Trisha was well into a rant of her outrageous car insurance bill when the pizza arrived.

The twenty-seven-year-old woman who shared my bed ceased whining long enough to pick out a large slice of mushroom, stuff a third of it into her small, round mouth, and without missing a tick, pick up where she had left off.

Desperate not to further stoke the ire smoldering deep within her, I ate and drank with my head lowered, avoiding direct eye contact. Six times she asked, "Do you understand what I mean?" And six times I dutifully answered, "Of course I do" into my beer.

Thirty minutes later, the volatile, Irish redhead was done. Finished. Catharsis complete. Thank the Lord for small favors.

Trisha shoved away her plate of partially eaten crusts, lit a cigarette, drew in a long haul, and exhaled a hearty plume. Pushing back in her side of the booth, she adjusted her petite, hundred-pound frame, flipped back a coil of hair, and snapped me a queer look. "You're awful quiet. What's bugging you?"

The day of the shooting, I arrived at work eight minutes early. The Monday five-p.m.-to-closing shift remained my favorite. The liquor store was slow the day after a weekend; I figured most people had imbibed enough during the weekend to last well into Tuesday, and felt the need to avoid the sauce at least for a couple days. Regardless, I liked the quiet; it gave me a chance to catch up on my reading.

When I walked into Chen's Liquors, Ming Chen, the sixty-six-year-old owner, stood at the register, cashing out the day's receipts. Except for my evening shifts on Mondays, Wednesdays, and Fridays, Chen worked the store every day from opening to closing. If the law allowed it, he'd be there all day Sunday, too, watching his little eight-inch black and white portable, selling beer, wine, liquor, cigarettes and lottery tickets. The old man personified the traditional Asian work ethic.

Chen ignored me when I stepped behind the counter and hung my jacket on the coat rack. He continued counting his cash and puffing on one of those cheap Chinese cigarettes that gave off an odor of smoldering rags. He purchased them somewhere in Chinatown. I could never figure that out; he owned a store stocked with a dozen brands of quality American cigarettes, yet he chose to suck those nasty unfiltered things from that soft paper package covered with Chinese print. The stench never left the store, and from time to time, a customer standing at the register would overtly sniff the air and ask what stank. Once, a middle-aged woman dressed to the nines and buying a forty-five-dollar bottle of Grey Goose, grabbed her change from a fifty, told me to try a bath and hurried out, cringing.

"You feed Cat first," Chen said, his face still in the register.

I nodded.

My first task of every shift was feeding the black feline named Cat. Chen kept a store cat, not as a pet—he showed no particular attachment to it—but rather to forestall an invasion of rodents. Cat, a mix of who-knows-what breeds, spent a good portion of her day in a collapsed heap of fur, sleeping in front of the broom closet. Old, fat and out of shape, I doubted Cat was capable of catching anything. Still, she remained my lone companion on the evenings I worked, and she managed to come out of her hibernation whenever I showed up.

I yanked open the broom closet door and retrieved the five-pound bag of Cat Chow from the top shelf. This, of course, brought Cat to her feet. Moments later, she started her customary feline jig, arching her ample back and rubbing herself across my ankles, purring.

As always, I teased her with the bag. "Is this what you want? Is this what you want, girl?"

This made Cat rub harder and meow louder. It was our little ritual.

"No feed too much. Cat fat," Chen called down the counter. Ming Chen was a man of few words, but I'm positive his concern was more with the cost of Cat Chow than that of Cat's portly physique.

Twenty minutes after Chen left for home, Leo stumbled into the store. It was just after eight; I remembered looking up at the Budweiser clock. Outside, a freezing rain had started to fall.

Leo came in bundled up in a soaked, dirty-green parka, his greasy unkempt hair dotted with sparkles of melting sleet, his hands shoved deep into the bulky parka's pockets.

Removing his right hand and running the back of it across his nose, he sniffed and said, "Hey, Matt. How's it going?"

"Leo, what's up?"

He shrugged and danced back and forth on the toes of his beat-up Timberlands, glancing up and down the store's single aisle.

Leo Tracy was a pathetic soul. At twenty-five years old, his scrawny body, tucked away in that filthy, rag of an oversized parka, looked used up. His sunken brown eyes, discolored teeth and twisted, many-times-busted nose gave him the appearance of an indigent street person. He had worked for Chen for just six weeks, covering Tuesday and Thursday evenings, before the old man fired him. That was a month ago.

Most nights Leo's register had come up short. At first, when he was five or six bucks under, the old man would throw fits, yelling and cursing in his native Cantonese. When the shortage touched twenty dollars, Chen stopped yelling and let Leo go.

Although never caught red-handed, Chen knew Leo was stealing from the till, and I knew he was helping himself to the merchandise. One evening I watched Leo slip a pint of Jack

Daniels into his parka when he stepped behind the counter to pick up his paycheck.

I was stocking the beer cooler, and when I turned to grab another case of Coors, I caught him. With one smooth motion, he swept a bottle off the shelf and right into the left pocket of his jacket. I almost yelled out but decided not to. What the hell, Leo probably walked away with half the store on the nights he worked, anyway. Chen called him a thief; I suspected some sort of drug habit. Besides, I had my own problems to deal with. I wasn't paid enough to play policeman.

"Slow night?" Leo asked.

"You're what, my third customer?"

Leo nodded, his eyes shooting back and forth, his foot shuffle slowed. He appeared nervous.

I leaned on the counter with both hands. "So, what is this, a social visit, or are you going to buy something?" I asked, glancing down the aisle to check on Cat. Well stuffed, the fat feline lay grooming herself in front of the broom closet. A second later, I heard the metallic click.

Leo sniffed once and said, "Neither. It's a robbery, Matt."

I turned and found myself staring down the black bore of a cocked .22 pistol. It took a moment to register. I instinctively raised my open hands between the gun and my face, and my heart took off in a gallop.

"Whoa, Leo, what the hell are you doing?"

"Give me the money, Matt. All of it."

"What? Are you crazy, man?"

Leo's hand shook. "Hurry up, Goddamn it."

Stunned, I punched open the cash register. I couldn't believe what was happening. I'd always feared an armed robbery, but not by Leo—not by someone I knew, someone who'd worked here just a month ago.

"There's less than forty dollars here," I said, running my hands over the cash drawer.

"Give it to me," Leo demanded. "Put it in a paper bag."

I pulled a folded bag from under the counter and shoved the bills into it. "Do you know how stupid this is?" I said, easing the bag toward Leo.

He grabbed it and motioned down with the gun. "Now the safe."

I shook my head. "Leo, this is bad."

"Hurry up, Matt. I'm not fucking around."

I lowered myself to one knee in front of the chipped, gray metal safe under the cash register and started dialing the combination. Leo knew Chen did all his banking in Chinatown and that he made his weekly deposit on Tuesdays. He knew the safe would be good for at least $4,500—the usual week's take. He also knew Chen had entrusted me with the combination because that's where he stored the extra lottery scratch tickets. Leo had never worked long enough to earn that privilege.

"Hurry up," he demanded, bending over the counter, waving the gun back and forth above my head.

"You want to point that thing in another direction?" I snarled, growing pissed.

I dialed in the last number and cranked the thick, heavy door open.

"Put it all in another bag." Leo's voice grew more agitated with each command. He had to be high.

I snatched a second bag, a larger one this time, and started stuffing it with cash from the safe. As I did, I thought about Chen and the part-English-part-Cantonese rant he'd spit when he found out. Holy shit, I was being robbed. By *Leo*.

With the bag full, I stood and placed it on the counter. Leo kept waving the gun, shuffling from one foot to the other. I don't know why, but I decided to try reasoning with his better senses.

"Keep your hands where I can see them," he said.

I raised my hands shoulder high. "Come on, Leo. You're not going to shoot me, and you're not going to get away with robbing the place. The cops will have you in jail in an hour. You'll do serious time for armed robbery, man."

Leo stopped shuffling. He seemed to be listening.

"Why don't I put Chen's money back, you walk out of here and we call it a night. No hard feelings and no one will be the wiser." I paused. "What do you say?"

Leo's movements seemed to calm. The gun stopped waving but remained in my face. He tilted his head and grinned ever so slightly.

"You don't know me at all, Matt."

The fool was starting to scare me. He had the look of a crazy man.

"Leo, I don't want—"

"You just don't understand, do you?" he said.

Those were his last words. Raised to my forehead, the gun detonated in a thundering crack.

2

He shot at me. The little bastard actually took a shot at me.

I was on my back, my shoulders resting on the first shelf behind the counter where Chen kept the extra paper bags. My head had hit the shelf above it, knocking pints and half-pints of brandy onto the floor mat. I heard Leo's footsteps hurry across the floor, then the sound of the door opening. Moments later, a cold draft carried street sounds into the store.

My ears were still ringing from the gunshot when a wave of rage spun through me. My first instinct was to get up, go after the scrawny little prick, and beat the living crap out of him. But when I tried, I couldn't. Nothing moved. Jesus. The bullet must have grazed me. Maybe I had some sort of concussion. I decided to give it a moment and then try again. I knew sudden movements with a severe concussion could prove dangerous.

Lying there, I realized I no longer felt the draft from the open door. Perhaps the wind blew it closed. But no, I still heard the sounds of passing traffic; the door had to be open.

I tried my feet again. Nothing. By now, Cat had wandered over. She licked my face, meowed, and moved out of my field of vision. I felt the draft again, but only where Cat had licked me. Everything else was numb. What the hell was wrong? It couldn't be that serious. If I'd been hit directly, I'd be dead.

Enough of this, I decided. I tried yelling. Nothing—not even a whimper. Why wasn't anything working? I felt no pain. In fact, I felt pretty damn good lying there, head on the shelf above the bags, feet buckled under me.

The last thing I remembered was staring up at the ceiling and the humming, florescent light bar. The view reminded me of the time I accidentally hit the record button on Trisha's video camera during a family wedding, and wound up filming twenty minutes of the church's overhead beams.

I watched the lights beneath the water-stained ceiling tiles of Chen's Liquor Store for what felt like hours. I thought I saw Trisha's face, and then a warm, comfortable darkness overtook me.

During my four-week coma, I remember bits and pieces of certain things—my body being jostled; distant, watery voices; flashes of light and odors . . . all kinds of odors. I recall Trisha's perfume, but I don't recall Trisha. I remember the smell of alcohol, the scent of soap and the aroma of food. But most of all, I remember nothingness—a black, timeless void, a poor man's death, a deep, dreamless sleep.

At some point, I regained a form of consciousness and my eyes opened to darkness. My body weighed a thousand pounds. Like the morbidly obese, I lay there, unable to move my limbs. My arms, fingers, legs, and toes each felt burdened with the force of a hundred steel weights.

As time passed, I tried to remember things, but my brain refused to cooperate. My memory seemed locked in a chamber just the other side of an invisible wall in my head. I had to get into that place and release the memories stored there. At one point, I tried to recall my name. I thought it might be Matt.

Time moved by in clumps. There were clumps of noise, clumps of light, clumps of voices and laughter. There were clumps of my body being moved—lots of them. I couldn't feel them move me, but I heard their grunts when it happened. The clumps were beginning to annoy me. None of it made sense.

Over time, voices became more prominent. I acquired an acute sensitivity to sound. Suddenly, everything was too loud. People spoke too loudly. People laughed too loudly. It was as though someone had turned the volume in my head to maximum. I wanted to cover my ears and scream.

My capacity to comprehend and reason progressed slowly. Soon I was able to distinguish day from night, one voice from another, cries of laughter from those of agony. The sounds returned to a normal volume, and I began to understand much of what was said to me. Blurred images replaced dark shadows as my vision gradually improved. And then—I'm not sure when—I remembered what had happened. *Leo shot me.*

That single cognition started bringing things together—not because of my ability to recall events, but because I could better grasp what was being said to me.

"Matt, it's Kathy. Remember me? I'm your nurse. You're in the hospital. I'm here to help you."

To this point, I hadn't understood where I was or who these other people were. Until now, the more I tried to reason, the more mixed-up I got. Most everything had confused me. Now I understood. Leo had shot me and I was hurt. My mind was beginning to click.

At about this time, I remember visits from family and friends. From Trisha. Sometimes they came in groups and circled my bed. Other times they came in ones and twos. Trisha, Ming Chen, Mom and other faces I knew but whose names I couldn't place. They all talked in upbeat voices, words of encouragement, but I can't recollect what they said.

My cognitive functions healed independent of my physical faculties, but the invisible steel weights remained, pushing my inert body hard into the bed. Despite my most determined efforts, my limbs refused to move. I could breathe and blink my eyes, but my swallowing was spastic, so they fed me through a stomach tube and suctioned me out when I chocked on my saliva. The remainder of the time, I lie motionless, locked a prisoner in my own body.

I'm not sure how long I spent in intensive care, because so much of the time I was either in a coma or semi-conscious, but one day it was decided all medical heroics on my behalf had been exhausted, and I was moved to a medical ward.

There I spent weeks receiving stimulation and physical therapy. During that time, a portion of my memory returned. The recollections came in spurts. I'd have vivid recall of an event of a year ago, and then another and another. The process was akin to learning to talk; the more I tried recalling events, the easier they came. One particular memory remained vivid: Leo pulling that trigger.

My mind continued to heal, but the rest of me refused to begin. I remained paralyzed. My food and liquid continued to come to me through a stomach tube, and I urinated through a catheter placed in my bladder. Like a newborn, I defecated into a diaper.

As my mind mended, a seed of bewildered anger grew with amazing intensity, blossoming into a raging hatred for Leo Tracy. Why did he do this to me? Why did he pull that trigger?

I became obsessed with revenge. I craved retribution, punishment for this person who had robbed me of my life. I wanted Leo to feel pain—a mental and physical anguish many times that of my own suffering. I wanted him to suffer a fate worse than being locked away in his own body, if that was possible. I wanted Leo dead, but not before he endured an agonizing cruelty, a hell on earth. Oh how I wished.

At regular intervals, a medical team visited the ward, strolling bed-to-bed discussing cases. During their first visit to my bed, the group fell silent, surrounded me in a semi-circle and waited. A doctor by the name of Weiss stepped forward and began speaking. I later learned he was the attending physician, a team leader in charge of the fledgling resident physicians. I learned about myself by listening to them.

"This is Matt Kenney," Weiss explained to the group. "Cerebral gunshot victim who spent twenty-nine days in a Level One coma. He now demonstrates blinking eye movements fifteen weeks post injury but is otherwise totally paralyzed. We're unsure of his level of awareness, if any. Neuro is working him up for locked-in syndrome."

"Locked-in syndrome?" a female voice asked.

After a pause, Weiss said, "Dr. Lee, please explain locked-in syndrome to your colleagues."

"Of course," a strong male voice answered. Clearing his throat, the young resident began. "Locked-in syndrome is a rare neurological disorder of devastating proportions. The syndrome is characterized by the complete paralysis of all voluntary muscles in the body. Some patients are able to control eye movements—otherwise, total and profound paralysis. The tragedy of locked-in syndrome is many of its patients are completely lucid in the shell of their body. They are able to hear, see, understand, reason, and think as coherently as you and me, but remain unable to express themselves."

"And what is the cause of locked-in syndrome, Doctor?" Weiss asked.

"Damage to the brainstem. Damage to the nerves that control muscle contraction. In this case obviously, massive damage and hemorrhage caused by a gunshot wound to the head."

"What's the prognosis?" the female voice inquired.

"The prognosis of a locked-in patient is grim," Weiss said. "Most patients never regain function. In Mr. Kenney's case, recovery is further impeded by a bullet projectile that sits precariously imbedded at the top of his brainstem. I don't envision him improving beyond his present condition."

Trisha stopped coming soon after my move to the ward. During her last visit, she sat next to my bed, held my limp hand, stroked my hair, and tearfully whispered to me, "Matt, it's time for me to close this chapter of our lives. It's time for me to move on. I have to do this. I hope you understand."

With her head in her hands, she cried a long while. When she finished, she got to her feet, said she was sorry, kissed my forehead, and walked away.

I'll never forget that crushing feeling of loneliness. My empty shell was now a vacuum. My one reason to hold on had just walked out the door. For the first time since it all had happened, I wanted to die. I wanted it to end. Pull all the tubes out of my body; stop all medication. Let me die with dignity. Let me go. Please, God, let me go. I cursed Leo Tracy.

My mother became my sole visitor. God bless her. Sixty-eight years old, and every day she dragged herself in and sat with her only child for two hours. If Dad were still alive, I'm sure he'd have come with her. Sometimes Mom talked, sometimes she cried, sometimes she sat quietly and watched the tiny television mounted on an adjustable arm next to my bed. But she was there every day, rain or shine.

Conversely, the hospital staff offered me little emotional comfort. Seemingly desensitized by an endless stream of the infirm, they operated with a cold efficiency. Nurses, therapists, the X-Ray technicians with that big portable X-Ray machine they wheeled around, the lab people who drew blood, came and went, speaking only when they had to.

"I'm going to roll you on your side, Matt."

"I'm going to change your IV line, Mathew."

"I'm going to take some blood, Mr. Kenney."

Sometimes they came and did their thing without breathing a word, like I was an inanimate object—a vegetable. Roll me onto my side, change my diaper, walk away disgusted.

Even Dr. Weiss's team started to ignore me. Most times they skipped me during rounds. With my locked-in syndrome status confirmed, there was little for the team of rookie doctors to learn from a static pile of flesh and bones. It was now up to the nurses and their support staff to keep me well; Weiss and his team had pushed on to the curable.

Four weeks later, I was moved again. My nurse came in and gave me the news.

"You're being transferred to Slater Hospital, Matt. It's a state-run, long-term care facility about an hour away. We've done all we can for you here. The people at Slater will take good care of you. I hear it's a nice place." She touched my arm and managed a fleeting smile. "The ambulance people will be here shortly. Good luck."

A poor economics grad student when Leo shot me, I carried the minimal college-offered health insurance. The policy covered acute hospital expenses, but carried no provision for long-term care, because the concept of long-term care for eighteen-to thirty-year-olds seemed absurd. Through default, I had become a ward of the state—an indigent—and I was on my way to spend the rest of my life in a state-run facility. I had a bad feeling.

3

I arrived at Slater late in the afternoon. The March sun had just settled behind a bordering cluster of tall pines, tossing long, jagged shadows across frozen lawns and darkening the brick-faced ambulance entrance.

With trailing white breaths, the ambulance crew rolled my gurney up the cold cement runway, past a melting bank of dirty snow and through a set of brown double-doors. The two men, one at each end of the gurney, talked football while guiding me through a series of long corridors. Their voices and the sharp rattle of wobbling wheels echoed off the stark-white cinder block walls as they pushed their quiescent cargo around corners, past doors reading *Private* and *Staff Only*, and to the end of a short corridor smelling of fresh paint.

With impassive efficiency, they transferred me from their gurney onto one belonging to the hospital, and then pushed it against the wall. They took a few moments to secure their property before heading back the way we came. I listened to their voices melt off into the distance.

I was left to lie in a dingy corridor for over an hour, studying the newly painted yellow wall and taking in the noise of the building. Over passing conversations of hospital staff, I heard a male voice off in the distance moaning the words, "Mother, please" over and over. Another voice, this one female and gentle, called out for help at regular intervals. *Welcome to Slater State Hospital, Matt*, I thought.

Finally, without a word, a male staffer dressed in white pants and a blue shirt wheeled me down a hallway and into a room. The dimly lit hole, with its peeling plaster walls, smelled of urine. Two other staffers, one a large black woman with a rich Caribbean accent, the other a pencil-thin Hispanic male, transferred me from the gurney to a bed, set up some IV poles, and left me with my head awkwardly twisted into the pillow.

Twenty minutes later, a middle-aged male nurse came into the room, straightened my head, said, "that should be better," set up an IV, injected a syringe into the line, and walked out. I was asleep within minutes.

I dreamed of Leo Tracy. He appeared in my room with a six-pack of beer, placed it on the bed table, pulled off a couple of cans and popped the top from both.

"Thought you might like a cold one," he said, placing one can on the table and taking a long swallow from the other. "I stole it from Chen's."

"Can't drink it," I said.

"Why the hell not?" Leo appeared insulted.

"I can't move. I'm paralyzed. You shot me."

"Come on, Matty. You're faking." He picked up the other beer and handed it to me.

I reached out and grabbed it. I felt the cool, wet can in my hand.

"See," he said. "There's nothing wrong with you."

I sat up, took a large gulp and watched the beer flow out from the hole in my stomach where the feeding tube had been.

A soft moaning woke me. Someone had turned me onto my right side. I figured several hours had to have passed, and it was now well after midnight. A pale light spilled into the room from the lowered hallway fluorescents of the quiet ward.

The sound came again from behind me, from the bed next to mine. Moans. Not the moans of distress, but of pleasure. A moment later, it clicked. I was hearing the intimate timbre of lovemaking.

Snapping wide-awake, I listened. I heard the rhythm—his thrusting grunts, her pleasure-drenched moans. She cried his name—Stephen. Behind me, a few short feet away, Stephen and his partner were dancing the horizontal shuffle on the room's spare bed. Unbelievable.

Within seconds, their vigor quickened and the pair's gasps deepened in intensity, metal bedsprings squeaking an offbeat cadence, the bed frame tapping off the hard wall. With all effort to mute their sounds abandoned, primordial groans of ecstasy filled the room and spilled into the hallway. Surely they'd be discovered. She called out curses with each blissful thrust, and he, like an animal acting on instinct, grunted something unintelligible.

Seconds later their passion erupted in a single culminated burst of climatic exhilaration that quickly tailed off to whimpers.

For a long moment, the room fell silent, devoid of movement. And then a murmuring of chuckles quickened to a chorus of unsuppressed laughter that slowly dulled back to quiet.

After a short while, I heard movement, the strain of weighted bed springs, the quiet ruffle of clothing, the snap of fasteners, and the zip of zippers.

"What about him?" the woman asked quietly.

"He came in this afternoon. Head injury. He's like a Level Three," Stephen said.

He walked around to my side of the bed, tucking in his white shirt, buckling his belt. He was young, twenty-five at most, tall and wiry. He bent down and, squinting in the low light, carefully studied my face. "His eyes are open, but that doesn't mean he's aware of what's going on."

"Well, if he is," the woman said, walking to the head of my bed and adjusting her pullover smock, "he just heard one hell of a show."

She placed her hand on my forehead, fixed my pillow and pushed back my hair. She had at least ten years on Stephen, but appeared well kept. "Did we wake you?" She flashed a devilish smile. Somewhere outside the room a telephone rang, causing her to stiffen. She rushed from the room.

Stephen watched her fade into the hallway. "Sorry about that, my friend, but Tina's kind of a noisy lay. Good and experienced," he whispered, "but noisy."

Stephen spent a few minutes with me, raising the head of my bed a bit, adjusting the IV poles before he leaned over and whispered, "Welcome to the Loony Bin."

On my first full day at Slater, a doctor examined me. He listened to my chest with his stethoscope, shined a penlight in my eyes, and stuck needles into my arm, watching for a response. I felt nothing, and even if I did, I had no means of responding, but I guess he knew that. He explained his methods to the assisting nurse and described the horror of locked-in syndrome.

"Mathew," he said to me, "my name is Dr. Wells. You're in Ward Three of Slater State Hospital. If you understand me, blink your eyes twice."

This wasn't the first time I'd been asked to respond to commands with my eyes. They had tried it in the ICU at Mercy. It didn't work. My blinking was strictly involuntary. I had no control over it.

"Go ahead, Matt, blink," the nurse said softly. She was an attractive, sweet voiced, middle-aged woman with emerald eyes and pinned-up, light-brown hair.

I tried and, as expected, had no control. I tried again. Nothing. On the third attempt, my right eye blinked several rapid winks. I was trying for one wink but got a bunch. I tried again. Same result. I had no control over the number of blinks, but some ability to make one eye act different from the other. Did this mean I was communicating? Dear, God, I *was* communicating.

"That's it, Matt. You understand me, don't you?" Dr. Wells said.

More spastic right eye action. Wells smiled.

"Excellent, Matt. Excellent," the nurse said. She patted my arm.

They conferred a few minutes and spoke at length about Julie, a therapist who would help me refine my eye movements. I was elated. A tiny portion of the inmate had just escaped from his prison.

Later in the morning, they moved me to another ward and suddenly I had a roommate—Roger.

Roger talked to me, but he also talked to himself. He was a fragile old man in baggy maroon pajamas, with scrambled silver hair and faded tattoos. Suffering some form of dementia, he spoke nonstop. He called me Bobby and promised to take me fishing at five tomorrow morning. By early afternoon, I was ready to strangle him. Mercifully, sometime in the mid-afternoon, Roger fell asleep and napped for nearly two hours.

While my roommate slept, two staffers came in and moved me from my right side to my back, then applied a cream to the exposed area. I was turned four times a day to prevent the development of decubitus ulcers—open sores caused by the constant pressure of lying still. The cream helped ward off the sores.

When on my back, I had a view of the wall-mounted television across the room. It was turned off, so I spent the time daydreaming of exacting revenge on Leo Tracy. Such vicious thoughts kept my brain busy and that was important. Otherwise, I'd go mad.

I envisioned my healed body cornering Leo in the back of Chen's store and effecting various horrible things to the man responsible for all this. In my thoughts, Leo had died a thousand hideous deaths by my hand.

Though my mental revenge gave me a pittance of solace, I knew my one recourse in bringing him to justice was learning to communicate. The ability to tell others what Leo had done to me was now my life's obsession. I needed Julie, the therapist.

When Roger woke, he started talking about someone named Norm. Within minutes, I learned Norm owned Norm's Bait and Tackle Shop.

Whether real or imagined, Norm turned out to be quite a character. Fat and bald, he had a twenty-six-year-old wife and a thirty-five-year-old daughter. He owned six hound dogs and had never fished a day in his fifty-eight years. He made whiskey in his cellar and sold it from under the counter on Sundays. Best of all, Norm was the town's retired chief of police.

Later, I discovered something interesting about Roger. While yapping nonstop, he crossed our small room and flicked on the television. And as if someone had flicked his switch, Roger clammed up in mid-sentence, walked back to his bed, and quietly watched the tube until dinner arrived.

Nothing proved more maddening than the smell of food. My nourishment came through a tube from a plastic bag. It sustained me, but in no way did it satisfy me. I longed for the taste of food, any food—the tartness of a fresh Macintosh apple, the sweetness of a piece of fudge, the creamy taste of chocolate ice cream. I wanted to drink a beer, eat a pizza, chew a piece of bubble gum. But in a single moment, I had been forever robbed of those simple pleasures—robbed by Leo Tracy.

Out of my peripheral vision, I caught glimpses of Roger stuffing his face. He slurped his drink and loudly chewed his food. I heard the clatter of his and other patients' tableware—people enjoying their supper. It never occurred to me how much of life revolved around meals until I was denied the delight of food and drink. Another nuance of normal living once taken for granted, now forever lost.

That evening, Roger fell asleep watching a movie. Rotated to my left side hours earlier, I spent the time watching Roger and listening to the TV until someone came in and shut it off. A short time after, the room lights were lowered.

From my prison, I listened to the evening staff chatting and laughing while they sat at the nurses' station just outside my door. The women talked about husbands, boyfriends, and life outside the confines of Slater State Hospital. Real people with real lives. People who got to leave the building after their eight hours, jump into their cars, and drive home.

Later in the evening, my nurse hung another bag on one of my IV poles. She spoke to me about the medication in the bag, but none of what she said made much sense. She left the room and, soon after, I drifted into a deep, dreamless sleep.

4

Roger woke me sometime after seven a.m.

When my eyes opened, he was inches from my face, talking fishing reels. He sat in the chair next to my bed and, like an industry expert, lectured me on the various brands—fly, casting, and spinning. He talked of how reliable the Penn and Quantum brands were, of the fact that the Daiwa was Japanese and he hated the Japs because they bombed Pearl Harbor, so he considered the Daiwa junk. The Shakespeare reels were his favorite, but not the spincasters—the open bale-spinning reels only. Having an open bale was important. According to Roger, it allowed full control of the cast when working a jitterbug.

Positioned to my right side, I watched him come to his feet and pace a gimpy gate back and forth, falling in and out of my field of vision. His loquaciousness turned from reels to monofilament line, and then to tackle boxes. *Another Rogerism*: plastic made the best tackle box because if someone happened to come along and kick it into the water, the thing would float.

Roger proclaimed Yukon Jack an unrivaled mosquito repellant. It didn't matter whether it was drunk or rubbed on— the eighty-proof Canadian sipping whiskey worked just as well either way. He boasted of always having kept a half-pint of it in the bottom of his plastic tackle box. I remember seeing bottles of the stuff on the shelf in Chen's but never sold any.

In the distance, I heard the clattering food cart working its squeaky wheels through the corridor, stopping at each room. When it squealed to a halt in front of ours, a huge black man wearing a white plastic apron, vinyl gloves and a blue hair net sauntered in with Roger's breakfast tray, absently humming some unrecognizable tune.

"Here you go, Captain," he sang.

"Thank you, Carlos," Roger mumbled, looking away as if threatened by the big man.

"You enjoy your breakfast, my friend," Carlos said in his Jamaican accent. He patted Roger on the shoulder and, a moment later, disappeared from the room and down the hall humming, following the noisy food cart to his next customer.

Food worked as well as television when it came to stifling my voluble roommate. Roger went at his breakfast like a man starving, clanking flatware and loudly chewing.

The sweet scent of maple-flavored bacon and fresh coffee wafted over from his tray. My sense of smell had become keener than ever. I cursed the countless times that, concerned about cholesterol, I had forced myself to skip the bacon at breakfast. Now I would kill for a single morsel.

I listened to him scrape the butter knife across his toast and envisioned the melting butter seeping into the fine crevasses of the bread. The spoon clinked against his cup while he stirred his coffee. Even their cheap, institutional coffee smelled like freshly ground, premium Columbian.

Slater State fell far short of the Sisters of Mercy, the general medical-surgical hospital where I spent my first weeks after the shooting. Here, no team of doctors made morning rounds, poking, probing and commenting in long, unfamiliar medical jargon, presenting opinions and conferring on diagnoses. Absent was any sense of urgency—the hustle of nurses, techs, and aides racing room to room drawing blood, hanging IVs, shuffling patients off to X-Ray, physical therapy, and the operating room. Gone were the busy hospital sounds, the overhead pages, the ringing phones, the alarms of complicated medical equipment.

Slater offered a different culture. The pace was slower, the staff more laid back, the building—with the exception of a few resident screamers—quiet. The smells were different, too. The faint odor of feces and urine replaced the clean, antiseptic essence of the ICU and medical ward.

From what I observed during my brief journey through the building, funding for maintenance appeared to be an issue. Slater was a state-run institution, so I assumed the operating budget was perpetually under-funded, the facility understaffed, and the employees paid a fraction of the wages their private sector counterparts enjoyed.

I knew of the state health facilities horror stories revealed by over-zealous investigative reporters, and on the 11 o'clock news had seen the footage of cockroaches, filthy bed linens, unsanitary kitchens, and unqualified staff running from the cameras while disheveled administrators stared blankly into glaring camera lights, claiming their patients received world-class care.

The recollection brought to mind a story I read in a magazine years ago about a paralyzed patient hospitalized in some squalid, third-world country watching helplessly as hungry rats gnawed at his flesh with impunity. My insides churned at the thought.

On the fourth day, I received an afternoon visit from my mother. As usual, she said little, spending most of her time watching television with Roger. Sitting next to me, she looked old and tired. The creases in her face had deepened, her eyes were sadder than ever, and her hair looked an ever-purer white.

Mom had to take three different buses to get to Slater, and the trip took more than two hours. Her tenacity amazed me. She did it for me. She was all I had left. I was supposed to take care of her when she got old, visit her in the nursing home when her time came, not the other way around. What a twisted turn of events.

Mom had to leave at three, and with a two-hour ride and three bus connections to make, I didn't blame her.

A half hour later, I met Julie. They had taken Roger out for an afternoon social activity, and I had started to nod off when she entered the room.

"Hi, Matt. I'm Julie." She stood at the foot of my bed and smiled broadly. "Your doctors believe you understand verbal commands." She continued toward me. "And they think your level of awareness is normal. That's why I'm here. I'm going to help you develop a system that will enable you to communicate with us. Okay?" She flashed that beautiful smile again.

Somewhere, Leo Tracy had to feel my warm breath on the back of his scrawny neck. Look over your shoulder, you bastard. It's me, Leo, coming after you. You're going to pay dearly for what you did. You're going to rot in some pit of a prison cell. I'll make sure of it, you dickhead. It's only a matter of time.

"I'm going to schedule two thirty-minute sessions each week," Julie said. "Unfortunately, that's all the state will pay for, but I'm sure if we work hard, we'll see some remarkable progress."

A shapely, raven-haired beauty in her late twenties, Julie's soft hazel eyes conveyed a comfortable confidence that put me at ease. For the first time, I felt a glimmer of hope. I watched her prepare herself. She stood at the head of my bed and flipped through my medical chart, carefully studying the pages. When she finished, she set the chart on the bed and gently placed her hand on my forehead.

"Matt," she began, "you've suffered a horribly destructive trauma to the brain. But I have experience working with others who have suffered similar injuries, and I've been able to elicit remarkable results. I'm very good at what I do, Matt, but positive outcomes require a lot of work. During this journey back, you're going to experience a level of frustration you never thought possible."

She peered deep into my eyes. "You must remember that no matter how futile and disappointing the therapy may become at times, you must never surrender. Never submit to the disappointment. Never quit. You'll have to work harder with me at this than you have at any other thing you've ever attempted in your life. We're going to retrain your brain to do things that used to come automatically, and each act will require a tremendous amount of mental effort."

She removed her hand from my head and smiled softly. "I know you can do it, Matt. You look like a fighter." She took a long breath. "Now, I'd like you to close your eyes for me."

I tried, and of course nothing happened. My involuntary blinking continued unabated.

"Come on, Matt. You have to give it all you have. Reach deep."

I tried again with everything I had. No response.

Julie extended her arm over my head, held it there a moment and then swiftly brought her open hand down toward my face. A few inches from striking me, she stopped. At that same instant, my eyes blinked. She repeated the action several times, and with each try, she forced the same response—my eyes quickly blinked.

She repeated the drill a dozen times, and then held the hand over my head. "Now, imagine the same motion is going to occur, Matt, but you just don't know when." She jerked her hand a fraction of an inch and my eyes closed. She repeated the exercise to a point where I closed my eyes, anticipating she was about to jerk her hand.

She lowered her arm to her side. "Imagine my hand is still there, and when I say 'now,' envision it coming at you."

"Now," she snapped.

My eyes blinked.

"Now."

Same result.

She repeated the command five or six times, and each time I reacted with a blink.

Julie placed the back of her hand on my cheek. "Excellent work, Matt. I'm very proud of you."

This angel of a therapist spent another fifteen minutes repeating variations of the same drill. Her half-hour was over before I knew it.

"I'm sorry, Matt, but that's all the time I can give you today. I've got other patients." She smiled her soothing smile and touched my hand. "You were great. I want you to practice what we've done here today and I'll see you Thursday. Bye-bye."

And in an instant, she was gone. My savior. My conduit to the outside world. Gone until Thursday. I inhaled through my nose, capturing the last bit of her lingering fragrance.

I heard Roger's voice growing in intensity as they wheeled his returning bag-of-bones carcass down the corridor. I couldn't decipher his words, but the timbre of his voice carried the usual authority of subject I now associated with my talkative roomie. I was becoming fond of Roger.

"Aluminum only. Fourteen feet with a four-horse. Evinrude makes the best four-horse. Johnson ain't a bad second choice."

With an aide pushing his wheelchair, Roger rounded the doorway.

"But it's got to be aluminum, Jessie," Roger explained as the aide brought his wheelchair to a stop behind me. "No maintenance. Just flip her over in the winter. Flip it back in the spring. Course, you got to sweep out all the leaves, spider webs and stuff. Spray her with the hose, mount your four-horse, and you're good to go."

I heard Jessie help his patient into bed, Roger rambling on about aluminum fishing boats and Evinrude outboard engines. On his way out of the room, Jessie stopped long enough to flick on the TV and, mid-sentence, Roger fell into his television trance.

That evening, I spent five hours with my back to the TV, rotated onto my left side facing Roger. I spent a good hour practicing Julie's eye exercise. I had her lovely image fixed in my mind, her kind voice softly instructing me.

At first, I had little command of my blinking, but as I concentrated on Julie and on gaining control, my ability to blink momentarily on mental order improved. I developed an exercise regime: ten minutes on, ten minutes off. Each time I started a new repetition, gaining control required a few minutes, but by hour's end, that time had shrunk to less than thirty seconds. By ten p.m., I was blinking voluntarily. Thrilled with my progress and mentally exhausted by my accomplishment, I slipped off to sleep.

5

A few hours later, I was roused from a dream in which I heard the far-off voice of a man calling the name *Forsythe*, asking over and over if I could hear him. Each time I answered "yes," but the man continued asking.

When I opened my eyes, I recognized Tina, the thirty-something sparkplug from my first night at Slater. She stood over me, checking my IV and arranging my bed covers.

Watching her work, I noticed that, unlike Stephen and the other nurses, she wore no nurse's pin. It was difficult distinguishing nurses from support staff; they all dressed the same.

"Oh, you're awake," she said, leaning over, straining her eyes in the dimness of the room. She continued adjusting the bed sheets.

"You were naughty the other night," she said playfully, "Listening in on Stephen and me. Shame on you."

She stopped, leaned close to my face, and lowered her voice to a whisper. "Did you like what you heard? Did I turn you on?" She giggled.

She stood over me with a wicked smile and placed her hand on my chest. Her eyes bore into mine as the hand slithered down the length of the sheet covering my broken-down body, stopping over my groin area. "Can you be turned on? Huh? I bet you can." Her smile widened.

My eyelids went into an uncontrollable blinking spasm. Christ, I didn't believe what was happening.

"Huh. Doesn't seem so," she said disappointedly, lifting her hand.

She glanced at Roger's bed—the old guy lay in deep slumber, and then took a quick look over her shoulder. Her lips twisted back into a mischievous smirk. She snorted a laugh, backed away from the bed, and pulled the front of her smock to her neck, exposing her braless breasts.

"What about now, Matt? Anything happening now?"

I stared in utter amazement.

Her eyes widened as if to ask if I approved. Though in her mid-to-late-thirties, she touted a pair of nicely shaped breasts—no sag and no stretch marks. A moment later, she tugged with one hand at the tie string of her scrub pants. I was about to get the whole show. Unbelievable.

"Tina," Stephen's voice echoed from somewhere beyond the nurses' station.

She froze. *Damn*, I thought.

"Yeah?"

"We've got to start giving the three a.m. meds." He sounded all business. "You do the north side; I'll do south. Let's go. We're already forty minutes late."

"Yeah, thanks to you," she responded sensuously, still holding the smock up. Her mouth formed a childish expression of disappointment. She opened her hand and the smock fell back into place.

Damn.

"Maybe some other time," she whispered, backing up and tying her scrubs. She waved her fingers before turning to leave the room.

I tried to stay awake, hoping Tina would return, but within an hour, I surrendered to a deep, dreamful sleep.

In my dreams, Tina did return, but she had aged into an old lady with wrinkles, black veins in her arms, and liver spots. Mercifully, she didn't offer herself to me. Instead, she adjusted my head, smoothed out my pillow, asked me if she still turned me on, and left the room.

In addition, I had that dream again. I sat in the ink-black darkness and heard the same voice as before: A male calling the name Forsythe and asking if I heard him.

The next day, after the others were served breakfast, my day nurse, Nancy, entered the room. Slightly favoring her left leg over her right, she made her way to my bed.

Nancy's bright, warm eyes effused a reassuring kindness. A pleasant, gray-haired woman well into her fifties, Nancy had long ago traded shapely curves and fashionable attire for that of a plump, dowdy, warm-hearted grandmother. She had seemingly stopped caring about herself years earlier. Others now claimed the tender portions of her boundless heart. A true altruist she was.

"I have a surprise for you, Mathew," she said, smiling and rubbing my arm. "Ramon and Charles are going to bring in the portable chair and wheel you down to the dayroom for a bit. It'll be nice for you to get out of this old room and away from—" she tilted her head in Roger's direction. He stood at the window, gazing out and muttering quietly.

"I know Roger is a dear, and God bless him," she whispered, "but you deserve a break." She stepped to the foot of the bed. "They should be here for you in about ten or fifteen minutes."

Nancy spent a minute adjusting my pillow and bedcovers, which was a huge waste of time considering Ramon and Charles were on their way to tear it all apart. When she was satisfied with my comfort, she grinned, said, "I'll see you later, Mathew," and shuffled from the room.

Ramon and Charles breezed in a short while later, and in less than a minute, they had me strapped into the portable chair and sitting up at a forty-five-degree angle. Charles, a balding, overweight man who smelled of cigars and talked from the corner of his mouth, wheeled me in the direction of the dayroom located at the far end of the ward.

On the way, I got a good look at my surroundings. The nurses' station, a small patch of corridor encircled by three-foot-high counters, sat in the center of the non-descript hospital ward. Three women and a man sat within the station's confines, working. A few patients wandered the long, green-tiled corridor. None appeared in particular need of rehabilitation, but then I was judging them based on my needs, and those had to be at the extreme end of the rehab scale.

In the dayroom, I noticed one man sitting on a worn sofa, watching a large TV pushed against the wall. Three others sat around a small table mid-room, playing cards.

Charles pushed the portable chair into a corner between a well-used, imitation leather sofa and the wall, facing me toward a large window that looked out onto a courtyard.

"Thought you might like a view of the outside world for a bit," he said. Stepping forward, he crossed his arms and gazed into the courtyard. "It's starting to snow. They said we're supposed to get eight to ten inches. Just what we need for the third week of March." He chuckled. "Monday's the first day of spring."

Charles stood with me for a few moments, silently watching the first snowflakes float to rest on the brown lawn. We watched a young woman hustle across the courtyard's diagonal walkway, hugging the collar of her unfastened jacket against the back of her neck, white snowflakes clinging to the surface of her dark brown hair.

"Well, back to work," Charles said, expelling a deep breath. "I'll check back in on you later. Enjoy the show."

I listened to his footsteps traverse the room and dissolve into the hallway. Watching the storm grow in intensity, I thought of the nor'easter of two winters ago when I met Trisha.

A driving wind had delivered the snow horizontally at three inches an hour, closing all the roads and stranding us at the Greyhound station in Albany.

As strangers seated on the same waiting-area bench, we started chatting and were surprised to learn we both attended the same school—Boston College. With a sudden sense of BC Eagle camaraderie, we kept each other company, laughing and joking about our predicament.

During the night, the stories of our lives unfolded. Trisha sat on the wooden bench facing me, with her wool-socked feet tucked beneath her. We talked until sometime after two in the morning, when the cold of the drafty bus station forced us to huddle against one other. A short while later, she unwittingly nodded off against my shoulder. I remember the warmth of her body pressed against my side and the smell of lilac shampoo in her soft, light auburn hair. I didn't dare move.

By dawn, the storm had passed. We did our best to wash off the night in the station's tiny restrooms, ate breakfast in a nearby diner and together caught the first bus to Boston.

Soon after, our relationship hit the fast track. Within two weeks, we were sleeping together, and a month later we moved in together. Trisha soon firmly established herself as the relationship's decision-maker. The only female of seven siblings, she had long ago learned to stand her ground. And although she was strong-willed and sported a hair-trigger temperament, she proved every bit a sappy romantic with an insatiable need for affection. When I delivered, she turned into putty.

I missed Trisha sorely. I missed her wit, her charm, her stubbornness. I missed her company. But I didn't blame her for leaving. It was the right decision. I didn't want her if I couldn't have her. She was gone and as much as it broke my heart, I wished her only the best.

The penny poker game behind me broke up with an argument. Someone named Jeff was accused of cheating. I heard the sound of coins hitting the floor, followed by a toppled plastic chair sliding across the off-white tile. Two of the three players left the dayroom in a huff, swearing never to play cards with Jeff again. I listened to a mumbling Jeff collect his scattered winnings, return the chair to the table, and disappear in a fade of jingling coins.

By now, the courtyard lay under a thin blanket of white powder, and the storm was swiftly ramping up. The wind quickened and fine white flakes whirled in eddies across the courtyard, whistling against the window frame. The angry sky darkened, squeezing out daylight and casting the world into an ominous, twilight-like spectacle.

With the outside world a gloomy gray, the lighted dayroom bounced off the windowpane. I saw my reflected image in the glass, and it shocked me. I didn't recognize myself. I had lost weight—lots of weight. My cheekbones and chin protruded from my face like that of a cadaver. I looked like a freak twisted in my chair, my stick-thin, lifeless arms limp at my sides. I was sickened at the sight.

The horror of what I viewed quickly turned to a deep, fervent loathing for Leo Tracy. *Look what he did. Look what that good-for-nothing bastard did to me.*

I began to weep, and for the first time since the incident, a river of tears poured from my eyes, washing my cheeks and falling onto the thin white blanket covering my upper body.

The tears were a purification, a cleansing purgation rinsing away every misfortune to befall me since that fateful evening at Chen's. They washed away the pain of losing Trisha, my confused fear, any hope of ever recovering from this nightmare. But tears could not dilute my hatred of Leo. They refused to wash away the abhorrence I felt in my heart for that man, the malignant rancor coursing through me. Only the taste of sweet vengeance would satiate the gnawing hunger growling deep within me. I wanted Leo dead. I wanted to kill him with my own hands.

Movement in the window's mirror reeled me back. A young man, who had sat in silence behind me since I'd entered the room, rose to his feet and came toward me. He came within a few feet of my chair before pausing, then watched me study his reflection in the window. Perhaps twenty-two, heavy, and average in height, he wore regular street clothes; I wasn't sure if he was a patient or a visitor.

He continued closer. Gripping the handles of my chair, he pulled me from the window. I didn't recall Ramon acknowledging him when he wheeled me in, so I doubted he was staff. I grew anxious. *Who was this guy? What did he think he was doing?* He turned me toward the door and started to push.

6

"We're on a mission," the stranger said.

We exited the room and he turned my chair right, maneuvering me away from the ward and in the direction of the far end of the building.

Who was this person? What mission?

We rounded a corner and darted through a long, deserted tunnel of corridor. The speed at which my chair moved was disturbing; the cinderblock walls sped by at a frightful rate. Two-thirds of the way through the tunnel, he jerked me to a stop, turned my chair to the right and, with alarming force, crashed the chair through a door.

A portion of my left metal footrest caught the door jam and broke off, bouncing with a ringing *clang* across the cement floor before coming to rest against the wall. My left leg dangled inches above the floor. The door slammed behind us. We were in a ground-floor stairwell.

Who was this fool? What the hell was he doing?

He stopped the chair. Straight ahead, stairs ascended to the first floor. Adjacent to the ascending staircase, a three-foot-high, chain link gate, with an attached sign that read "No Admittance," blocked the entrance to stairs that descended to a below-ground level. To the right, an alarmed crash-bar fire door passed into the courtyard.

He pushed me within three feet of the gate and stopped. A flimsy latch bar, secured with a padlock, attached the swinging portion of the gate to the concrete wall. The stranger walked to the front of my chair and gave the padlock a flick. Looking over his shoulder, he turned his spooky brown-eyes toward me. He studied me a moment before a sick smile cracked his pockmarked face, revealing a row of crooked, yellow teeth.

He returned his attention to the gate, raised a boot, and gave the meshed barrier a shove. It rattled. He walked back to my chair, grabbed the handles and said, "Desperate times call for desperate measures."

What was that supposed to mean?

He backed the chair up to the doorway, stopped, and with a force that sank me into the foam cushion, ran my chair across the short span of stairwell and crashed it hard into the gate. The metal barrier vibrated fiercely in its steel frame. The jolt snapped me forward, sliding my body under the nylon restraints and partially down the length of the chair.

Jesus. What the hell was this madman trying to do? My left foot, having received a portion of the impact, began to bleed. A wave of fear rolled through me. I was alone in an isolated corner of the hospital with a psycho case trying to shove me down a flight of stairs, and I didn't know why.

He backed the chair across the stairwell. "Second time's a charm," he grunted.

Jesus, he was going to do it again.

With a frightening crash, he again smashed my chair into the gate. The sound of vibrating metal filled the stairwell. The sudden stop jerked me further forward in the chair, leaving my right arm hanging over the chair's armrest and my left foot dragging on the floor. One more attempt might knock me from the chair or, at the very least, crush my left leg.

The stranger reached from behind, grabbed me under my armpits, and pulled me back into the chair. Adjusting my blanket, he said, "Don't want you falling off."

Wonderful. Suddenly, this crazed psychopath is concerned with my well-being?

With an eerie calmness, he turned the chair and backed me in the direction of the fire door. He hit the crash bar and pushed open the door, sounding the built-in, battery-operated alarm. He pulled me out into a wind-whipped alcove, turned the chair, and gave it a shove. I rolled about ten feet into the raging weather, slowing to a halt on the snow-covered walk. A moment later, the door banged shut behind me and he was gone. I sat there alone, strapped to my chair and facing the mouth of an ugly, late March nor'easter. It took a few seconds to comprehend the seriousness of my predicament. *I think he's trying to kill me.* I began to panic.

The wind whipped me with waves of twisting snow, punishing my face with blinding cruelty, howling off the building's walls, screaming with an icy fierceness. In a short period, the storm had escalated from a picturesque flurry to a dangerous whiteout. I would last no more than half an hour out here.

Within minutes, a freezing sheet of snow covered my face, hair and blanket. Over the storm's fury, I heard the muted wail of the door alarm. *Would anyone hear it before the battery died?*

Across the courtyard, the building was barely discernable through the heavy, driving snow. My snow-layered chair now blended with the backdrop of the building's white facade. I was becoming invisible to anyone who happened to glance across the courtyard from one of the windows.

The shrieking door alarm began to weaken, its battery slowly draining. The only clue I was out here was about to disappear; my chances of being discovered were quickly diminishing.

While I sat there, propped in my portable chair, unable to feel the storm's rage and waiting for the inevitable, I heard the voice.

"I'm right here in front of you, Matt. Can you see me? Can you hear me? Matt, I'm here."

It was Forsythe again. *Forsythe, I'm here. I hear you. Help me. I'm going to die out here. Please.*

"Matt, can you hear me? I'm here to help you."

Yeah, I hear you, Forsythe, but you're not real. You're in my mind, the product of a damaged brain. You don't exist. You can't help me.

The voice faded into the storm's bluster. I could no longer see across the courtyard; visibility had lessened to thirty feet. A small snowdrift had formed in front of my chair.

How do I prepare to die? Is there a checklist? Should I pray, asking God for mercy? With the exception of a few weddings, I hadn't attended church in years. *Would God even take my call? Why should he?* Good, holy, church-going people were at this same moment inundating the good Lord with pleas for help. *Why in the world would he listen to me?*

The snow, which minutes ago melted the moment it hit my skin, was now accumulating, burying each arm in two long, icy mounds. Flakes collected on my eyelids, obscuring my vision. Breathing through my nose became difficult. The storm was burying me alive.

I began to feel a detached calmness, and my fear gradually dissipated. A comfortable, welcomed repose was taking over. I felt the warmth of a place just beyond me. My eyes grew heavy, my mind numb. Sleep beckoned. I no longer heard the storm's angry rage. Slowly, the white confusion turned to a shade of gray, and then to black.

A sudden jostling stirred me. I tried to understand the confusing motion while I slowly regained my senses. I was moving backward, away from the storm at a quick pace. The chair shook violently as it backed over the threshold and into the alcove's protection.

"Son-of-a-bitch, Robbie. Goddamn it."

Ramon's angry voice drew me completely back as he pulled me through the fire door—its alarm still sounding, albeit weakly. The metal door slammed hard in front of me shutting out the blizzard's rampage. Ramon spun me around, pulled me through the stairwell door and into the warm corridor. He yanked off the snow-covered blanket with one hand and spoke into a hand-held radio using the other.

"I got him."

"Where?" A voice crackled back through the speaker.

"The boiler room corridor. Robbie pushed him outside. He's covered with snow, but I think he's okay."

"I'll be right there."

Ramon clipped the radio back to his belt and started scooping handfuls of snow off me.

"You're going to be fine, my friend," he said. He wiped the snow from my face, hair, and arms, and started my chair in the direction of the ward.

Ahead, Charles rounded the corner full throttle, clutching a fistful of white towels.

"Ah, for Christ's sake," he said when he reached me. He tossed Ramon a towel and they both began wiping the storm from me.

"Where's Robbie now?" Ramon asked, drying my face and hair.

"Locked in his room," Charles said. "The little fuck's going to Building Two for this one. He could have killed this guy. I don't know what I was thinking, leaving him with Robbie lurking around. Vinny, Jeff, and Mitch were playing cards; I thought he'd be okay with them around. They must've broke it up and left Robbie alone in the room with him."

"Don't beat yourself up, man," Ramon said in a conciliatory voice. "You didn't know. Robbie should've been put in Building

Two weeks ago. Let's get this guy back to his room." Ramon started me toward the ward.

"They're going to love this incident report," Charles moaned.

"Hey, wouldn't have happened if we'd had help. There're only two of us on today, man. We can't be everywhere." Ramon patted my head. "Tell that to this guy. Right, Matt?"

Back in the warm safety of my room, Roger napped blissfully. Charles and Ramon changed me into dry pajamas and explained the details of my abduction to a stunned Nancy and an angry nursing supervisor named Charlotte. Apparently, I wasn't the first patient kidnapped by Robbie, a long-time Slater resident with a behavioral disorder.

From what I could discern, Building Two, Robbie's soon-to-be residence, was a lock-up for patients who offered a threat to themselves and others—in other words—the mental cases. Listening to the discussion of Robbie's history, I concluded the kid was certifiable.

Sometime after lunch, a tall, attractive female in a long white lab coat came into my room and began to examine me. She looked to be Asian, though her height and facial features suggested a Caucasian influence somewhere within her lineage. Nancy joined us a minute later, addressed the woman as Dr. Woo, and stood at my bedside, observing.

With long fingers and perfectly manicured nails, Dr. Woo took my temperature; the electronic thermometer displayed the result in seconds. After listening to my chest with her stethoscope, thumping my mid-section with her fingers, examining my eyes and ears with a penlight, and bandaging my leg, she spoke to me in perfect, native-born English.

"Mathew, do you understand me?" Her eyes widened. "Blink if you do."

I tried a single blink but, once again, I produced a spasm of three or four rapid flickers.

"Good," she said. "Now, do you understand what happened to you this morning?"

Again, I let go a blinking barrage. She smiled and laid her hand on my forehead. "Poor thing. You must have been so frightened." She turned to Nancy. "He seems no worse for the wear. I'll order vitals every two hours until midnight. He should be fine."

Nancy nodded approvingly.

Dr. Woo moved to the foot of the bed. "When does Julie see him again?"

"Tomorrow," Nancy said.

"Has Robbie been sent over to Two yet?"

"Dr. Myers is writing the orders as we speak."

Dr. Woo and Nancy stood beyond the foot of my bed and mumbled in quiet conference for a few minutes before wandering out of the room.

Ten minutes later, Nancy returned with an injection and shortly thereafter, two ward staff turned me onto my left side. Beyond my sleeping roommate, the nor'easter slammed its icy wrath against the room's window, its whistling fury clearly audible above Roger's wheezing snore.

I envisioned myself in the midst of it, still in the courtyard, enveloped in growing snowdrift, waiting for the end. I thought of Ramon. He'd saved my life, and I couldn't even thank him. Next, Robbie and his cold, yellow-toothed smile flashed into my mind. The image of an emotionless madman frightened me.

The day's events began to take their toll. My body seemed to triple in weight and my thoughts became scrambled. A short while later, physically and mentally drained, I lapsed into a deep sleep and dreamt of Trisha.

7

I woke on my right side before dawn. The black-and-white wall clock hung outside my door, next to the nurses' station, read four-forty a.m. I had slept thirteen hours; the effects of Nancy's injection still fogged my mind.

It was Thursday, and in less than twelve hours, I'd be working with Julie again. A sense of anxious anticipation filled me like that of a child on Christmas Eve. *How long before Julie and I exchanged our first message? How long before the world understood the senselessness of Leo's violent, unprovoked act?*

The wheels of my mind spun wildly. I imagined the trial. I, a pitiful soul, propped up and strapped to my chair, spewing "testimony," Julie at my side translating each blinking eye response to an outraged prosecutor's questions.

I imagined a sympathetic jury on the edge of their chairs, soaking in every word, each blink of my eye further sealing Leo's fate. I envisioned court officers dragging Leo from the courtroom, guilty as charged, handcuffed and shackled.

When my eyes opened again, I heard Roger's voice. I had drifted back to sleep for a few hours, still victim to whatever sedative Nancy had injected me with.

In the distance, I heard the clangs and rattles of the meal car and the accented voices of the kitchen workers manning it, progressing through the corridor, moving room to room with breakfast trays.

What was it this morning? Bacon and eggs or pancakes? Maybe waffles. Yeah, that's it. How about waffles? Did they serve waffles here? I pictured a plate of steaming Belgium waffles, covered with strawberries and smothered in whipped cream and fancy chocolate shavings, the way they looked the last time I ordered them at Gil's House of Pancakes less than seven months ago. Not that it made a difference; my breakfast now consisted of the same off-white liquid delivered via plastic tube three hours every day.

I listened to Roger ramble on about a bass fishing tournament to no one in particular, but in his mind, I'm sure he held a captive audience of adoring fellow anglers. He claimed to have won the tournament by landing an eight-pound large mouth off Kimball Cove, using his secret weapon—a top water lure he called the Scorpion.

He worked his way over to the near side of my bed, pacing back and forth next to me, animating his presentation with waving hand gestures.

"The secret to working the Scorpion is in the line. Nothing heavier than six-pound test," he sputtered rapidly. "And none of those fancy colors. Never use anything except clear monofilament line. The fish ain't stupid. You gotta know how to work her. She's no good if you don't work her right."

Apparently, his secret weapon lure bore feminine attributes.

"You gotta run her just below the surface, letting her pop the top and stop her for just a second, and then pull her under again. Just keep doing it that way and that big old bass will think she's wounded and say, 'There's supper,' and *bang*! He'll go for it."

The food cart suddenly loomed at the doorway. A skinny black man carried a breakfast tray to Roger's side of the room. Roger stopped and followed the man with his eyes for a moment before turning his attention back to me.

"She comes in two colors, green and yellow. Large mouth love the yellow. Won two tourneys with the yellow. I've got lung cancer. They're taking me to radiation starting today. Next time we go out, I'll let you try out the yellow. If you don't bag at least a five-pounder, I'll buy you a beer." With that he fell silent, turned, and moved to his side of the room.

I listened to Roger prepare his breakfast. *Was he serious? Cancer? Was the poor old guy lucid enough to understand if he had cancer or what it meant?* Strange how he slipped the fact in, buried in the lines of his story.

I began to wonder just how much Roger understood. How much of life was reality to him and how much was played out in the recesses of his mind? Did he really believe his own stories? Perhaps the tales did occur in one form or another sometime in his life—glory days recalled with keen fondness. Or maybe he made them up as he went along, believing every word as gospel.

Roger spoke with a full mouth. "Smoked two packs a day for forty-six years. Unfiltered Camels."

He had never spoken while eating.

"Now I have cancer and I'm going to die."

He spoke the truth. Late in the morning, two paramedics in blue uniforms came and took Roger away. This was to be the first of thirty radiation treatments at Angel of Mercy Hospital, twenty miles away. His frightened eyes probed me for a reassurance I was unable to deliver as the paramedics rolled an uncommonly quiet Roger from the room.

Minutes later, Nancy and Charles came in, turned me onto my back, and applied the ulcer cream. On her way out, Nancy clicked on the TV. I watched the noon news, and then soap operas until Julie showed up at three and turned the TV off.

She wore her hair pulled back and shot me a confident smile when she entered the room. "Hi, Matt. How're you doing today?" Julie placed her hand on my arm. "Ready for another session?"

She studied my face a moment before I understood she was waiting for a response. Trying for a single blink, I managed two. The reaction came easier than it had previously.

"Good," she said. A smile conveyed her satisfaction. She grabbed my hand and, seconds later, her smile abruptly turned to surprise, and then split into a broad, open-mouthed smile. "Matt, you're squeezing my hand."

I didn't know it, but I had reacted to her hand grasping of me by squeezing her fingers. I tried it again, and her wide-eyed gaze froze on our two hands.

"Matt, this is remarkable." She tilted her head. "Try it once more."

I concentrated on my right hand and her face lit up. "Excellent," she said. "This is excellent. I'm so proud of you." She reached over and took my left hand. "Try this one. Try and squeeze this one for me."

I watched her face glow with anticipation and focused every thought on my left hand. I mentally pressed her clutched hand in mine, bearing down with every last ounce of cerebral energy, but her facial expression registered failure.

"It's okay. I'm sure it'll come." She straightened. "Let's try something." She took hold of my right hand again. "Can you squeeze my hand twice? Try to squeeze it two times."

Again, I focused on my right hand. Watching her high cheekbones, the sweet curve of her slightly parted mouth, her clear, resolute eyes, I directed my hand to tighten—once, and then twice.

Her glow flattened a bit as she moved her gaze up and held my eyes. "This is good, Matt. Very good. Your grasp is weak and spastic, but it's a good sign. It means your brain is recovering; you're regaining function."

While I gloried in my small victory, Julie moved to the bed table and jotted notes into a chart. I was regaining function. Julie said it; my therapist said it. My brain was recovering. This was good, but how good? How much recovery would I achieve? I had been shot in the head, paralyzed by a bullet. What about the portions of my brain that were missing, the chunks of gray matter blown away? How important were those neurons and synapses? What function did they play? *Stop it. Remain positive.*

During the remaining twenty minutes, Julie worked me through a series of blinking eye exercises. By the end of the session, I blinked on her command most times, but was able to control the number of blinks only a small percent of those times. In order to communicate with the world, I needed the ability to articulate yes and no answers. I had to learn to control my blinking: once for "yes," twice for "no." It sounded simple, but at the moment, it seemed impossible.

Julie made a few more notes and then turned to me. Stroking my forehead, she said, "You should be encouraged with what we accomplished today. I'm speaking through experience. The progress we've made in just one week usually takes at least three months with your type of head injury. Make sure you remain positive, Matt. Don't you go disappointing me. I want you to keep practicing what we've done today, okay? Do the exercises I showed you, four times a day."

Julie made one last entry on the chart before she picked up her jacket and handbag. "I'll see you Tuesday, Matt." She grasped my arm. "Keep the faith." She grinned, wiggled a wave, and then turned away, vanishing into the corridor.

For a long time, I lay there thinking, staring at the ceiling, feeling heartened. A warm exuberance flowed through me. I had studied the committed encouragement in Julie's face; her eyes mirrored hope and her words bespoke genuine optimism. I wondered how the dark-haired beauty managed to trek from one brain-damaged patient to another, day after day—from one Matt Kenney to the next—with such infectious optimism. What gave her the drive? What did it take for a person to show such unwavering dedication? I wondered if she had time for a normal social life: a boyfriend, fiancé, or husband? I did manage to steal a quick glimpse of her ring finger. It offered no evidence of a commitment.

I'm convinced Julie believed in herself, in her abilities. I had to believe, too. Someday, Julie's skills would flush me from this shell of living death and allow me to proclaim Leo Tracy's guilt to the world.

The afternoon sun settled low in the sky, casting long, ragged shards of light through the window, brightening the room with a late-day yellow glow.

I watched a small black spider move across the ceiling above me. The insect scurried a few inches, stopped, scurried, stopped. It made a track around the sprinkler head above me and settled against the metal ring supporting the fixture.

Spiders used to give me the willies. I hated them. I avoided the basement of my mother's house because I knew the musty smelling hole, with its field stone foundation and dirt floor, was teeming with spiders. Spiders of all shapes, sizes and colors. Spiderville. Every floor joist, corner, and crevice hosted dusty, woven webs of the repulsive arachnoids. Spiders owned my mother's basement.

When I was nine, my best friend, Barry Parsons, showed up at my house one day with a large brown spider he had caught and placed in an empty peanut butter jar. Spiders didn't bother Barry in the least, but they petrified me, and he knew it. With holes punched in the lid to offer his new-found pet fresh air, I reluctantly followed Barry into the backyard in search of something to feed it.

"Here's a juicy black ant," Barry said, pointing at the ground. He shoved the jar at me. "Here hold it."

My skin crawled as I clutched the jar at arm's length. The brown spider stuck stubbornly to the clear glass side.

"Got it," he said, proudly pinching the ant between his thumb and forefinger, its tiny legs wiggling for all their worth. Barry wore a sadist's grin. "Unscrew the top."

I remember the uneasy feeling knowing the barrier of safety between the jar's ugly creature and my outstretched arm was about to disappear—and by my own doing, no less. The hair on the nape of me neck stood on end.

Barry stood patiently, his fingers grasping the spider's next meal.

I removed the lid, and with a nervous twitch, accidentally dropped it to the ground. It rolled over to Barry and bounced off his foot. He gave it a gentle kick. All this took less than two seconds, but when I returned my eye to the jar, the spider had vanished. For a moment, this confused me, until I realized the brown spot on my shirtsleeve was Barry's big, ugly spider, with two of its eight legs pointed outward.

With an ungodly howl, I threw the jar to the ground, where it shattered, thrust my arm toward Barry, and screamed, "Get it off! Get it off!" I couldn't push my arm any further from my body, but I continued trying.

With an easy swoop, Barry wiped the creature from my sleeve and proceeded to buckle over in a convulsing fit of laughter.

"Is it off? Is it off?" I yelled, too panicked and afraid to look myself.

"Yeah, it's off," sputtered Barry from his knees. "You should see your face." Tears rolled from his eyes. "It's only a little spider, Matt."

A wave of anger wove through me while Barry made sport of my foolish phobia, but then I felt something out of kilter, something warm on my leg. Barry stopped laughing. He looked up at my right leg in wide-eyed amazement, pointed, and then fell into another fit of laughter. I looked down. I had peed my pants.

The spider above my bed began to move again. Scurry and stop, scurry and stop. *Today's entertainment: A black spot plotting a slow, tortuous path across a pealing plaster ceiling.*

I no longer fretted about or feared spiders. I didn't care if, at this very moment, this spider spun itself down from the ceiling, landed on my chest, and crawled all over me. In fact, I dared it to. *Go ahead, creep all over me. Who gives a damn? I couldn't feel you, anyway.*

The spider worked its way past the area above Roger's bed and to the point the ceiling met the wall above the window. I then lost sight of it. I strained my eyes hard to the left, attempting to catch one last glimpse of the little black dot, but no luck.

I felt a sudden trace of emptiness, a speck of loneliness. *Where had it gone? Where will it end up?* A simple spider had brought me brief pleasure and a fond memory. I couldn't believe I'd developed an attachment to a bug running across the ceiling—a spider no less. This is what my life had come to.

When the beams of sunlight began to fade behind the building, something strange happened. The room started slowly turning fuzzy, and I began to hear watery, distorted voices. Female voices. At first, the voices were unintelligible and distant, but they gradually grew clearer.

"Mathew. Mathew can you hear me? Do you understand me? I want you to get up. I'm going to help you to your feet. You need to get to your feet and walk. I'll help you. Don't be afraid. You can do it."

I had a sensation of movement.

"Don't be scared, Mathew. I've got you. That's it. I'll help you."

How could this happen? I'm paralyzed and lying on my back in a bed.

The sensation continued a few moments longer. It felt like a roller coaster ride, up and down, back and forth. I never cared for roller coasters; they made me nauseous. This ride was making me very dizzy—dizzier than I'd ever been—until I felt myself falling backward, and the voices became anxious and shrill. A few seconds later, they faded into a watery blackness. The room quickly refocused back to normal.

8

On Friday morning, a small throng of hospital staff visited my room.

They congregated at the door and, for a few minutes, mumbled amongst one another before moving in my direction and surrounding the bed.

The group consisted of a doctor, three nurses (including Nancy), three therapists, and two administrators (in suits) I'd never seen before.

The doctor, a short, pudgy, balding man with a ruddy face, stood at the foot of my bed and in a monotone, talked about me as if I wasn't there. He briefly presented my case, talking in terms obviously unfamiliar to some in the group.

Nancy spoke next. She stood at my side, held my arm, and described my status, including the small degree of progress I'd made with Julie. I felt most comfortable when Nancy spoke.

The majority of observing eyes exhibited pity. One of the suits couldn't bring himself to look at me, choosing instead to fix his gaze elsewhere in the room.

A back-and-forth ensued between Dr. Pierce, as the others called him, and Nancy, but their medical parlance sounded Greek to me.

The team moved to the foot of my bed, exchanging comments, and then migrated to Roger's side of the room. Nancy stayed back a moment. She adjusted my sheets and pillows, squeezed my arm and flashed her trademark crescent smile.

"You're doing great," she whispered before moving to join the others.

Roger sat in silence on the edge of his bed facing me.

"Mr. O'Dell is a seventy-six-year-old, long-time delusional resident diagnosed three weeks ago with bilateral, non-small cell lung cancer with nodal metastases," Pierce explained to his audience. "Yesterday, he started a six-week course of radiation and chemotherapy at Angel of Mercy. As long as he's able, we'll transport him daily, but I foresee an admission to Mercy."

"How long before they'll need to admit him?" one of the suits asked.

"His blood work will dictate that, but I'd estimate three, maybe four weeks. But then again, you can never tell. He may hang tough the entire time and remain right here."

"Mr. O'Dell," Pierce said. "Do you have any questions about your treatment?"

From my position, flat on my back with the head of the bed slightly raised, I saw Roger bow his head sadly.

"No," he murmured.

Pierce patted his back and moved away.

"You're going to be fine," one of the nurses lied.

"Why don't you sit back and rest, Roger?" Nancy suggested. "We'll be done in a minute, and then I'll turn on the television for you. Okay?"

Nancy cranked up the head of his bed to a sitting position. She helped Roger swing his feet around and fussed with him for a few moments. Meanwhile, the remaining team moved to the center of the room and continued its discussions in hushed tones before spilling into the hallway. Roger stared impassively in the direction of the television.

"Do you need anything, dear?" Nancy asked.

Roger shook his head.

"Well, don't hesitate to buzz me if you do."

She fussed a little longer than needed with Roger; she seemed inclined to make her patients as physically and emotionally comfortable as possible. As I watched the kind-hearted woman go about her business, I hoped that, when her time came, Nancy's own caregiver would show her the same kindness and compassion she gave others.

When she finished with Roger, Nancy rushed across the room, flicked on the TV, adjusted it to a home improvement program, and hurried out the door.

Metastases. I knew what that meant; the lung cancer was spreading. Roger was dying and, delusional or not, he knew it.

I felt guilty. My lungs were perfectly healthy—at least as far as I knew. But my lungs were being wasted in the body of someone who did nothing more than lie motionless day after day, one degree from dead. *Let me have Roger's lungs and give him* mine. Who the hell wants to live like this? It's not fair. This entire joke we call life was so Goddamn unfair.

After lunch, Ramon took Roger to the recreation room to play cards. He needed a change of scenery. I decided my second message to Julie, after I dime out that slime, Leo Tracy, of course, would be to get someone to take Roger fishing. Imagine that— Roger on a fishing trip. He wouldn't shut up about it for a month.

Sometime after one, Mom came in. She looked good, and I wanted to tell her. She had a spring in her step, and she brightened when she saw me.

Mom pulled a chair up to the bed. She spent ten minutes combing my head with her hairbrush and telling me about my cousin Rudy's new job, operating a tow truck for Interstate Towing. She was quite excited.

"Interstate has the contract for all state highway towing in the county," she said. "Anytime Rudy tows a disabled car, he makes fifty dollars. Your Aunt Beth said during the last snowstorm, Rudy made five hundred dollars in twelve hours. Can you believe that? *Five hundred dollars.* That's almost half my monthly Social Security check. If you get better, maybe he can get you a job there."

Mom beamed as she patted my hand. Aunt Beth's oldest son had finally landed his dream job.

Truth is, Rudy never was the brightest bulb on the family tree. I figured it was only a matter of time before the stupid klutz yanked the front end off of a sixty-thousand-dollar Mercedes and found his sorry ass back among his friends in the unemployment office.

At one time, when we were in the sixth-grade, Rudy took me out back to Uncle Jack's tool shed to show me how to make a smoke bomb. He broke the heads off two-dozen wooden matches, stuffed them between two bottle caps and fastened the whole mess together with masking tape. According to Rudy, when the contraption was hurled to the floor, the matches would ignite, spewing out a sulfur-stinking plumb of dense white smoke as it rolled along.

I watched Rudy prepare his prototype. He raised the tightly taped bomb over his head and slammed it to the shed's wooden floor. As promised, the device instantly burst into a hissing trail of smoke, bouncing around the shed's confines and filling the small wooden building with pungent, white smoke. As we ran out the door coughing, the bottle cap bomb bounced into a bucket of paint thinner and *"whoosh,"* Uncle Jack's tool shed was history. My genius cousin, towing cars. God help us.

But who was I to talk? Sack-of-rocks dumb as cousin Rudy was, he was the one pulling in five hundred bucks in a single night, while I filled space in a state-owned hospital bed with a hole in my head.

Mom continued to rattle off the events of her week. It was the usual stuff—lunch at the Senior Center, a doctor's appointment, a visit with Aunt Beth. She was speaking of how well her cat, Ginger, had been behaving when she suddenly buried her face in her hands and burst into tears. She cried hard without looking up. I felt helpless, watching her silver head shutter while she quietly sobbed. As proud as they come, mom would melt in embarrassment if anyone else witnessed her crying. I wanted so much to reach over and wrap my arms around her.

After a minute, she removed a tissue from her bag and mopped the tears from her puffy face. The small amount of mascara she wore clogged the corners of each eye. She looked at me.

"Oh, Matty," she moaned, her head shaking and her lips quivering. "I try to be so brave when I'm here. I've got to at least be as brave as you. How do you do it, dear?" She stroked my face. "It's so hard seeing you here like this, all . . . twisted and—" Tears poured from her eyes again, and she patted at them with the tissue. It took a minute, but she managed to compose herself. "Please get better and come back home."

She reached over and patted my face with her crumbled tissue. I was crying; for the second time since this horrible nightmare began, I cried.

9

After a week of radiation and chemotherapy treatments, Roger became violently ill. He ate little, and whatever he managed to force down came right back up. I felt sorry for him; a harmless old man in his twilight years, groaning in agony, vomiting bile into a green plastic basin. When he wasn't puking his guts up, he slept, sedated by anti-nausea medication. I missed his ramblings.

Like clockwork, the ambulance crew came for him at nine-thirty. When Roger saw them, he curled up in his bed and groaned. "No. I don't want to go. Let me die. Leave me alone."

His feeble protests were useless. Within ninety seconds, the two-person crew had him strapped onto the gurney and out the door, his objections quickly subdued by the ambient ward noise.

Ten minutes later, Nancy bounded into the room with another IV bag.

"Good morning, Matt."

How that woman remained so upbeat all the time, in such a dreadful place, amazed me.

"I have another bag of your medicine here."

I watched her hang the bag on the metal IV pole, unwind the ball of tubing, and place one end of it into the needle stuck into the back of my hand. She opened a valve in the tubing line that released the medication, and watched the solution flow into me for a few moments.

All my IV bags were small, brown plastic bags with a yellow label attached to the top front that I couldn't read. In contrast, Roger's IV bags were clear plastic and looked like any other IV bag I'd ever seen. *Why were mine brown? What were they pumping into me?* I wasn't in pain, and my nourishment came through a stomach tube. *What could it be?* What ever it was, I'd been receiving it since my arrival at Slater. I wanted to ask Nancy, but of course, I couldn't. I trusted her, though; if she had no problem giving me the stuff, I guess I needed it.

After fiddling with the tubing—wrapping it away from the bed to keep it from snagging—Nancy nodded contently.

"There you go." She took a moment to smoothen my hair back with her fingers and fidget with my sheets before she moved on.

Later in the morning, Ramon and Charles showed up with the portable chair. Just the sight of that chair stirred in me a frightening flashback of sitting helplessly in the howling nor'easter.

"Don't panic, my friend," Ramon said. "We're only rolling you out into the hallway for a little change of scenery. You can watch the rest of us work." He leaned over me. "Don't worry, crazy Robbie is locked in his room over in Building Two." He winked.

Once I was secured to the chair, Charles rolled me into the hallway and parked me in an open area across from the nurses' station, next to a mumbling old lady slumped in a wheelchair.

"Matt, meet Margaret," Charles said, gesturing. "Margaret, this is Matt. You two have fun, and no funny stuff."

Grinning, Charles trod to the nurses' station, took a seat, and picked up the ringing telephone.

Margaret never moved. She remained on my left, collapsed in her wheelchair; as she mumbled away, her sounds were partially obscured by a janitor in the closet behind us, running water into a bucket. When the janitor finished, Margaret fell silent for a few moments, and then started up again. I listened closely. She wasn't mumbling incoherently, as I'd first thought; she was praying softly, reciting the Rosary.

"Hail Mary, full of grace, the Lord is with thee . . ."

I listened for a while, watching her from the corner of my eye. A frail, broken old lady, was making her peace with God. But something was different about Margaret—her dress. It was blue and reached all the way to her feet. Something hung from her neck. At first, I couldn't place it. Then it struck me. A crucifix. Margaret was a nun.

I considered this for a long moment, and before I knew it, I had managed to conjure up the unpleasant memory of Sister Mary Elizabeth of St. Luke's Elementary, the meanest nun to ever walk the planet. The palms of my hands, a frequent target of her ubiquitous wooded ruler, throbbed in phantom pain at the very thought. I recalled how her mere presence made me shudder in my seat. Looking back, I wonder what event in Mary Elizabeth's life compelled her to serve God and terrorize elementary school children.

For the next ten minutes, I watched the mundane activities of the ward staff and listened to Margaret quietly pray. I wondered if perhaps I should be praying, too. *But pray for what? A recovery? Fat chance.*

As a kid, I prayed all the time, scared into it by the constant threat of being cast directly into Hell and consumed for all eternity by raging fire. Not a day passed in which Sister Mary Elizabeth and her flock at St. Luke's didn't remind us of such a fate. Perhaps this would be a good time to start again.

With my attention drawn back to Margaret, I noticed her tone take an ominous change, and then I heard, "Matt. Mathew."

Disconcerted, I shifted my gaze to the corners of my eyes in an attempt to see her more clearly. Margaret was speaking to me.

"Can you hear me? I want to help you."

Seconds later, everything in the hallway began to shift. The nurses' station slid across the floor and Margaret faded into a watery image. The entire area became dark—as if someone had suddenly lowered the lights.

"Matt, I'm here to help you." Margaret continued, but her voice had changed to the pitch of a young female. "You have to get up. You have to walk. I'll help you."

And then her voice changed again, this time to a deep pitch. A man's pitch.

"Let us help you up. Grab my arm. Don't be frightened. You can do it." Margaret spoke in Forsythe's voice.

Everything became confused and the entire area started spinning. My stomach twisted into a ball, and I became nauseous. I felt myself fall forward just before all turned to black.

I awoke on my left side.

Facing Roger's empty bed, I had no idea what had happened, and because my back was to the hallway clock, no concept of how much time had passed. I didn't remember being put back in bed. *Where was Margaret? What was happening to me? Why did I keep hearing voices? Who was Forsythe, and why did he want to help me? Why were the voices coming from Margaret? Was the old woman possessed, or was I losing my mind, crazy from the gunshot damage?* That last question scared me; my mind was all I had left.

Julie's session lasted close to an hour. She wound up spending twenty-five minutes of her own time with me.

"Sometimes the state-allotted half-hour is just too little," she complained. "I can see so much eagerness in your eyes. I'm not packing up just because our thirty minutes is expired; not today." Julie—angelic and selfless.

My progress encouraged her and fed her altruism. If I concentrated intensely on a task and then fiercely pictured the action in my mind, going through it several times, I found I was better able to elicit the correct response for something as simple as blinking my eyes. And though I felt I responded to each of her eye blinking commands perfectly, in reality the outcome was still too spastic to serve as a communications medium. But hope remained—hope was my impetus for living, for hanging on; hope of someday looking Leo Tracy in the eye and simply asking, *Why?*

More good news. Strength was gradually returning to my hands. By the end of the session, I had weakly squeezed Julie's finger—twice with my right hand and once, albeit barely noticeably, with my left. In addition, over the past several days, I had developed an occasional twitch in my arms, legs, and head. Out of nowhere, my arm would spasm once or twice, or my head would jerk a fraction of an inch to one side. Julie called the movements *tics*.

"Tics indicate nerve healing," she said, patting my hand.

Was my damaged mind actually healing like a big scab of regenerating synapses and neurons, rewiring the connections that made up that neurological stew called the human brain? The prospect renewed my spirits.

After Julie left, Fran, one of the evening nurses, came in and applied cream to my back and buttocks. Fran was an attractive woman somewhere in her early thirties. When she applied the cream to my rear end and rubbed it in, it turned my thoughts to Tina. At twenty-eight years old, I was now incapable of being sexually aroused, regardless of the stimulus.

The ambulance crew brought Roger back just before dinnertime. He looked thin and brittle when they helped him from the gurney into his bed. The treatment was taking its toll; since he'd started treatment ten days ago, his weight loss was profound. His eyes were flat and hollow, and the unshaven skin of his face hung like a damp cloth on a rack. He had lost all enthusiasm.

Without a word, the two men helped Roger between the sheets of his neatly made bed. With his back to me, he let out a quiet groan and then fell still, his bedcovers rising and falling with each exhausted, wheezing breath.

After the ambulance crew took its leave, Fran came in and spent time with Roger, starting an IV and trying her best to make him comfortable. When he spoke, I heard a desperate weakness in his voice. I felt terribly sad for Roger. I wished I could go over to him and say, *It's okay, Rog. I'm here. I'll take care of you, and when you're feeling better, we'll go on the mother of all bass fishing trips. I promise.* But Roger was in worse shape than I was. Neither of us was going anywhere.

I spent the remainder of the evening on my right side, trying to watch a movie on television while Roger slept. Sometime during the eleven o'clock news, I nodded off.

Shortly after midnight, my eyes blinked open. I had fallen asleep on my right side, but awoke on my back; I couldn't remember being turned. In the past, that particular effort, requiring the strength of two people, usually woke me.

Roger snored peacefully as I turned my gaze out to the hallway clock. To my surprise, the clock was missing—all that remained was its wall fastener. *Strange. Who needed a large wall clock in the middle of the night?*

I listened to Roger's breathing, trying to figure out what was different. I heard no voices and detected none of the usual hallway activity. The ward was eerily quiet. Too quiet.

While staring at the tangle of ceiling shadows formed by the seeping hallway lights, I caught a glimpse of movement from the corner of my eye. I turned my gaze just in time to catch a brief image sweep past the open doorway. A chill ran through my numb body. *Leo.* Leo Tracy had just passed my room wearing that same dirty, oversized parka. *Impossible*, I thought. *Just the low lights playing tricks on my weary mind. How ridiculous—Leo Tracy wandering the halls of Slater Hospital unchallenged in the wee hours of the morning.*

Less than a minute later, a silhouette stood at the doorway, further darkening the dim room. For several seconds, the form stood motionless at the room's threshold. My heart broke into a galloping thunder when the familiar outline started in my direction. Leo Tracy was ten feet away and closing.

He stopped at the foot of my bed and checked on Roger with a long glance before moving within twelve inches of my face. A pungent, musty odor emanated from his damp parka. He studied me a while, running his gaze up and down the bed.

"How you doing, Matty?" he said in his familiar, squirrelly voice. He wore a sick grin. "Been looking all over for you." He gave me a sad, curious look and then his eyes brightened. He held up his right hand. "Brought you something." A syringe, the plunger pulled back, hung between two of his fingers.

"No more pain, Matty. No more misery. I'm going to finish what I started. I owe it to you." He turned to the IV bag.

My breathing grew labored and erratic. Leo was going to kill me by injecting something deadly into my IV. *What was it? Where'd he get it? Would it be quick or a slow, agonizing death? Where was the staff—Stephen and Tina?*

He grabbed my IV bag with one hand and raised the syringe. *God help me.*

"Don't care much for trout fishing out of a stream."

Leo spun around in startled surprise.

"Did it a few times using a fly rod. Too much work," Roger said. He stood at my feet, back straight and hands by his side, looking strong. "Wouldn't rule out trying it again, though."

Leo shot me a look, his eyes and mouth wide with astonishment.

"You there, Matt?" Forsythe's voice echoed from somewhere outside the room.

I looked toward Roger and then back at Leo, but Leo had vanished.

A beat later, Stephen stuck his head in the doorway, glanced at both beds, and turned away.

The wall clock was back in its place. Roger stirred in his bed and resumed his rhythmic snoring.

10

At five-fifty, the first slivers of dawn seeped through the window and crept across the cold, bare wall. For four hours, I had lain wide-awake, staring at the ceiling, too confused and too frightened to sleep.

Real as it all seemed at the time, I knew Leo had not visited the room, and Roger had never left his bed. I was hallucinating. *First voices, now visions. How long before reality and delusion became one?* I wondered. *Was I going mad, losing the only faculty spared me by Leo's hand—my mind?*

I strove to determine the cause and meaning of all that had recently happened—the voices, the sensations of walking and falling, Margaret, visions of Leo, and Forsythe.

Who was Forsythe? For days, I had tunneled to the far reaches of my mind trying to recall a person by that name, and each time, I came back empty. *Who was he, and why did I keep hearing his voice?* To the best of my knowledge, I had never known a Forsythe. But the name sounded comfortably familiar, ringing an easy resonance. Maybe I knew a Forsythe as a child, or as an infant, the name somehow instilled years ago.

Then again, I had a bullet hole in my head. My thought processes and senses had been altered—they had to be. Julie claimed my brain was healing, and perhaps the voices, visions and spasms were all part of the mending process. Regardless, the hallucinations were coming with frightening regularity.

The sound of Tina pushing the medication cart into the room suddenly distracted me. The cart was for Roger, who now relied on an around-the-clock regimen of pain and nausea medication, spaced every four hours.

Tina looked tired as she prepared the meds. Shift change came at seven, less than an hour from now. To my way of thinking, working the graveyard shift carried more disadvantages than benefits, and this morning Tina wore the downside in the form of a weary mask.

Out of my vision, I heard her footsteps shuffle behind me.

"Roger. Roger," she repeated. "I have your medication."

Roger moaned. Half awake, he complained in a weak, shallow voice, "Pain."

"Swallow this; it'll make you feel better." A moment later, "Now take a sip."

For nearly a minute, Roger broke into a chain of lung-rattling coughs. When he finished, he groaned in agony. "I need more pain pills."

"I've already given you your pain medication. You can't have any more for four hours. Try to sleep, okay?"

He broke into another extended coughing fit, wheezing in a desperate effort to grab a breath. Mercifully, after what seemed an interminable period, he quieted.

When Tina finished, she made her way back to the med cart near the doorway. I watched her fidget over the cart with something she held in her hand. She looked back at Roger, glanced at me, and then leaned forward in the direction of the doorway, as if watching for someone. A moment later, she slipped a small plastic package into the pocket of her smock.

In the poor lighting, identifying the object was difficult, but not impossible. It was a package of tablets. Tina was stealing medication—Roger's narcotic pain medication.

I listened to another series of agonizing groans from Roger. The poor guy was lying in pain, consumed by his disease and denied pain medication by a caregiver, who was stealing it for herself.

A bolt of anger surged through me. *How could you do this, Tina? Listen to him; he's dying. Being eaten alive by his cancer, wilting in horrific pain. Give him the medication, you horrible bitch. Ease the poor bastard's suffering.*

I wanted to leap from my bed, slap her face, and snatch the medication from her pocket. *Oh, please, God, allow me to move just this once.* I tried with all I had to move—harder than I had ever tried for Julie. The fervency of my effort made my brain ache. I was boiling with anger and frustration, seething to the point where my head was about to explode. And as Tina began to move the cart and her stolen stash to the door, it happened.

"Aarrgh." The first sounds registered from my lips since the shooting.

Startled, Tina spun on her heel, her face registering disbelief.

I had blurted an utterance born of pure rage and contempt—it was so unexpected, it surprised even me.

Tina hurried to my side, her jaw slack. She stood there a long moment and studied me before holding her hand to her mouth and softly chuckling.

"Son-of-a-bitch," she whispered with wide-eyed amazement. Then she shook her head, turned back to her cart, and pushed it from the room.

By seven-thirty, Nancy and a second nurse, Cheryl, were attending to Roger. He was a mess. Writhing in pain, he had soiled the bed. With my back still to them, I listened.

"When was his last dose of pain med?" Cheryl asked.

"Tina gave him eighty milligrams of oxycodone at six."

"It's not touching him."

"Roger," Nancy said in a loud voice, "are you still in pain?"

Roger responded with a sickening groan.

"We've got to get the dose increased," Cheryl said. "He's hurting."

"I can't believe 80 milligrams isn't doing it."

"Check the chart and make sure he got his last dose."

Nancy moved to the medication cart and flipped a chart open. "Yup, 80 milligrams. Signed off by Tina at five-fifty-five this morning."

"Incredible," Cheryl responded.

I never felt so helpless. I wanted to scream. Roger never got that dose—nor probably the one before it—thanks to Tina, the cold-hearted, pill-stealing pig who worked the midnight shift. I had witnessed a crime and now knew of *two* perpetrators walking about freely. I was helpless to do a thing about either.

Exhausted, I eventually succumbed to a deep sleep. A few hours later, Nancy and Ramon jerked me awake. They moved me about the mattress, working collectively to change the bed linen, an every-other-day occurrence.

When they were finished, Ramon helped Nancy rotate me onto my stomach, the position I disliked most. It limited my range of vision, reducing my view to the plain green wall opposite my bed. I couldn't watch television or see out into the hallway without straining my eyes downward, to the point where my vision blurred and my head pounded.

When Ramon made his exit, Nancy began applying ulcer cream to my back and sides. As she worked the cream into my skin, I listened for Roger, but heard nothing. While I slept, the ambulance crew had taken him for his treatment. I wondered how long before he didn't come back. How long before he was too sick to return to Slater. *How much more could the old guy take?* I felt a deep sadness for him.

"It's a beautiful spring day, Mathew," Nancy said. "It's supposed to make it into the mid-seventies this afternoon." My body shook as she worked in the cream with a strong hand. "Soon we'll be able to get you outside for a while. The hospital grounds are beautiful in April. We have a bunch of cherry trees, and when they're in full bloom, they're gorgeous. As soon as I'm finished here, I'll crack the window and let in some fresh air."

The smell of a sweet, fresh breeze from the open window filled the room. After months of sniffing stuffy, stale air, it was exhilarating. I felt renewed hearing the dulcet tones of birds perched nearby, the sounds of passing automobiles, the normal noise of an outside world unencumbered by a paralyzing injury. *Weird, how well the world carried on without me. A testimony to my life's thus far minute contribution.*

It was the second week in April, and that meant major league baseball was in full swing. A year ago yesterday, Trish and I were sitting in first base box seats, watching the Red Sox pound the Cleveland Indians.

I loved the Sox, having become a life-long fan since the day my father took me to my first game at Fenway Park, in celebration of my ninth birthday. A cloudless, deep blue sky covered the ballpark that warm June afternoon. We took the train to North Station and then rode the Green Line to Fenway. Before the game, Dad bought me a baseball and took me down to the area next to the Sox dugout, where we hung out until Carl Yaztremski walked in from batting practice.

"Hey, Yaz. Sign my kid's ball? It's his birthday," Dad yelled.

Yaz looked up, stopped, and raised his hand. Dad flipped him the ball and then a pen.

"How old are you today?" Yaz asked me.

I was too struck to answer.

"He's nine," my father said.

Yaz scribbled his signature on the ball and tossed it back to me. "Happy birthday, kid." He threw Dad the pen and disappeared into the dugout.

We sat fifteen rows up from first base. Dad bought me two hot dogs and a bag of peanuts that Saturday afternoon. We lost to the Orioles 7-4, but Yaz hit a double off the left field wall. Dad said it was my birthday gift from the slugger, and though I knew better, I pretended for weeks that Yaz hit that double for me.

I missed my father. He left mom and me way too soon, dead of a heart attack at the age of thirty-eight. A foreman at Spindles Machine Company, he was playing basketball with plant coworkers during their usual Wednesday night game. He had just retrieved a missed shot off the rim when he dropped to the floor. In a way, I was glad he was gone. I wouldn't want him to see me this way.

Sometime after lunch, Charles and Ramon came in and flipped me onto my back. On the way out, Charles flicked on the television.

I spent a portion of the afternoon watching an old black- and-white movie starring people I had never heard of. By the look of the automobiles and the style of clothing, I placed the era of filming to sometime in the 1930s. The plot was stupid and the acting poor, but it beat staring at the ceiling for two hours. Later, I dozed off watching a game show. Sometime later, I awoke to the early-evening news and the rattle of the meal cart.

I glanced at the hallway clock; it read ten minutes after six. Roger usually returned from treatment by three, but his bed still sat empty. An hour later, I watched one of the evening staff strip his bed down, place the linen into the dirty linen cart, and push it all into the hallway. The room suddenly held a vacuous silence. With a hollow feeling in my gut, I glanced over at the bare bed. Somehow I knew I would never see Roger again.

11

For me, most days ran seamlessly into the next. The exceptions were the weekends. Saturdays and Sundays crawled by, each seeming twice as long as a weekday. The staff, leaner on weekends, ran busier. Sometimes six hours passed without anyone poking his head into the room.

I learned that Roger, too ill to return, had been admitted to Mercy. With no one to share my room, I hungered for human contact—a face, a voice, a touch. Even the spiders had abandoned me, fleeing the confines of my hospital room for the warmer spring offerings outdoors.

This Sunday morning was like all other Sunday mornings—quiet.

Just after noon, Mom showed up. She remained my one faithful visitor, slogging her way in by bus every Sunday, bringing with her the latest news of Aunt Beth and my shallow-brained cousins. Sometimes she'd bring the Sunday paper with her and read while I watched the ball game. Today she felt like talking.

She got right to the meat of things. As predicted, Rudy was again amongst the unemployed. Big surprise. Mom said Aunt Beth claimed some kind of management shake up at Interstate Towing resulted in layoffs, but I'd bet you dollars-to-doughnuts my idiot cousin got himself fired.

More good news. Aunt Beth's daughter, Sue Ellen, a sometime-cocktail waitress, was expecting her third bastard child. This time the proud father-to-be was her tattoo-infested, live-in biker-boyfriend of five months. Wonderful!

Cousin Jerry, Beth's youngest, still had eighteen months remaining before becoming eligible for parole. Jerry, a veteran of the Gulf War and the one we held so much hope for, was doing eight years at the House of Correction in Ayer for selling cocaine within one hundred yards of a school zone. Not exactly your consummate Mensa candidate.

Aunt Beth had a penchant for raising losers. This, of course, was more the fault of my philandering Uncle Jack, who never drew a sober breath in his adult life or held a steady job for more than a year. When he died—drunk—in his rolled-over pick-up truck twelve years ago, he left his family nothing but debt, forcing Aunt Beth to raise my three cousins on part-time cashier jobs and public assistance.

Still, Mom and her younger sister remained inseparable— both widows left to raise families on their own. Fortunately for us, my father had a couple of small investments and a decent life insurance policy when he died. However, Mom never splurged. Instead, she denied herself life's creature comforts, opting instead to squirrel away most of the money for my education. Though she never spoke of it, I knew she funneled Aunt Beth cash on a regular basis.

Mom spent more than three hours with me this Sunday, gossiping, reading some of the paper aloud, and watching a few innings of the Sox-Yankee game before finally kissing me good-bye and starting her long journey home.

The television kept me company the remainder of the afternoon. As usual, most of the programs seemed geared to the lowest common denominator—all flash and no substance. *Television, the great national babysitter, filled the void of my worthless life with trash.* Most repugnant were the foolish weekday afternoon shows, named after the host, in which an endless chain of human refuse played to the audience and camera. *The boob tube—a label well deserved.*

I missed reading. I missed books, magazines, and newspapers. I missed seeing with my mind rather than my eyes. Nothing portrayed a story better than the mind's eye. If I had to credit the nuns at St. Luke's with a single accomplishment, it had to be their unyielding insistence that their students read—a developed habit that followed me to adulthood.

Without the opportunity to read, the one portion not imprisoned by locked-in syndrome—my imagination—remained my sole means of escape. By closing my eyes and shedding off the real world, I was whole again, back to wherever I wished. I spent an ample amount of time casting myself back to my early teen years, a time when the world and its seemingly infinite offerings beckoned.

Lying there, I thought back to the summer of my fifteenth birthday, and my first paying job. Bobby Fossa and I worked for Fitzgibbons Landscaping, mowing lawns for four dollars an hour. Sixteen years old and the owner of a new driver's license, Bobby drove the pickup truck that pulled the equipment trailer. I rode shotgun.

Driving the lawn tractor, running the push mower or power trimmer proved easy work, especially when Jimmy Fitzgibbons wasn't around. He tended to get unnecessarily fussy about things. Jimmy checked on us once or twice a day between his jaunts to and from the dog track, but most of the time we were on our own.

Jimmy gave us a certain number of jobs each day, usually six or seven depending on the size, and when we finished, we were done for the day. Sometimes the last job ended at three, sometimes not until six. Regardless, we earned eight hours pay.

Bobby and I worked well together, each complimenting the other, racing through the jobs as though we were competing, finishing them as quickly as possible.

Working in shorts and bare-chested most the day, Bobby and I gained perfect tans that year. Girls liked that.

One hot and humid Friday we were over an hour behind, working our last yard late in the afternoon. The house, a large colonial on a heavily wooded lot with over an acre of lawn, sat back fifty yards from the road. The owners had bucks.

I remember dripping with sweat, trimming the bases of what had to be twenty large maples. When I finished the last tree behind the house next to the pool, I collapsed in the shade beneath its canopy to catch my breath and wait for Bobby to load the tractor onto the trailer.

Listening to the light breeze whip its way through the leaves of the tall backyard maples, exhausted, I started nodding-off.

"Nice tan."

Looking up, I saw her—an attractive woman in her late twenties. She stood with one hand on the pool's open stockade fence gate, wearing a white bikini top and a red towel wrapped around her narrow waist that reached mid thigh, exposing a pair of delightfully long legs.

I pushed the gas trimmer from my lap and drew myself up. "Comes with the job." The sounds of Bobby positioning the tractor onto the trailer echoed from out front.

Her wet, strawberry-blonde hair, ran straight back behind her ears, and the beads of water clinging to her skin sparkled like diamonds in the late afternoon sun. Tall and thin, but chiseled as an athlete, the nipples of her perfectly proportioned breasts bulged prominently against her wet swim top.

"I didn't think anyone was home."

"I've been out here swimming laps the whole time," she said.

"Wouldn't have heard you over the noise of the gas engines."

She gestured toward the trimmer. "Looks like hard work."

"It's not so bad."

She nodded. "Oh. While I've got you here, I wonder if you wouldn't mind taking a look at this gate latch. I've been after my husband all summer to fix it, but he never seems able to find the time. He's on the road most weeks. Salesman. Medical devices. I'd hate to have some neighborhood child wander into the pool because of a broken latch."

I left the trimmer at the tree. Up close, I noticed her bronze skin covered in goose bumps. Her sharp blue eyes studied me, forcing my gaze away and directly onto her erect nipples. She quietly chuckled, no doubt enjoying the tantalizing effect she had on me.

Embarrassed, I tried the latch. "Ahh. Looks like all it needs is a shot of oil. Have any WD-40 or anything like that hanging around?"

She flashed a helpless smile and shrugged. "In the garage?"

"Would you like me to take a look?"

"Maybe later," she said. "You look terribly hot. Would you and your friend like to take a swim? Cool off a bit?"

"Umm, no bathing suits," I said with a nervous laugh.

"I wouldn't worry about something as simple as that. We're all adults here, aren't we?"

Shocked, I uttered, "Yeah, I guess so." *My God*, I thought. *Was she talking skinny-dipping?* I looked around the secluded lot. We could definitely get away with it. My heart rattled in its cage. I think an older woman was asking me to get naked with her.

Bobby gave two short blasts of the horn. She looked in the direction of the house.

"Sounds like someone is in a hurry," she said, her tone laced in disappointment.

"Yeah, I've got to go. Got to get the truck back or our boss will have a fit."

"Sure you have to leave right now? I've got some cold beer and a little bit of weed left inside. We could have a little party. You me and—" she motioned with her head toward the front of the house.

Excited, I began to tremble. Nothing like this had ever happen to me. "Maybe I can come back later and oil this latch for you."

"I'd appreciate that." She shifted her weight from one sensuous leg to the other. "By the way, what's your name?"

"Matt."

Another short blast from Bobby.

"You better get going, Matt. Your friend's getting impatient."

"I'll see you later, then."

She grinned. "Hope so."

I hustled over to the tree, grabbed the trimmer and scooted for the front of the house. Before rounding the corner, I looked back and noticed the towel slung over her shoulder.

"Bye-bye, Matt."

"What, are you fucking crazy?" Bobby said, guiding the pickup through the four-way-stop intersection.

"I'm telling you, Bob, she all but asked me to take my clothes off. Oh, man, she was hot. And those boobs, damn. I thought her nipples were going to bust right through her top."

"She's married, asshole. Forget it. You trying to get yourself shot? What if her husband came home. Happens all the time. They call them passion killings. A guy comes home and catches his old lady in the sack with some stranger and, boom! Forget it, Matt."

"All she wants to do is party with us a little, smoke a little pot, drink a few beers, maybe take a swim in our birthday suits. What's the harm?"

"Yeah? Well, you can party without me. I'm not going near the place except to mow the lawn. She's got to be screwed in the head, married and coming on to guys our age. She'd probably tell her husband just to make him jealous, and then you have him coming after your ass. Let *him* oil the goddamn latch. I'm telling you, Matt, forget it."

I sat in disappointed silence. Bobby, the logical one, always thinking things through. Why couldn't he get half as excited as me? Live a little for Christ's sake, take a chance, have some fun. But I knew he was right. I was playing with fire. A woman twice my age, hitting on me. He was right. Let her husband oil the latch.

We did that yard four or five more times that summer, but I never again caught another glimpse of her. I often wondered what would have happen if I returned that night? Fantasies fifteen-year-old boys daydream about.

Later that evening, while lying on my stomach and staring at the wall next to my bed, I listened in on the conversation emanating from the nurses' station. Jennifer, one of the weekend part-timers, recounted the events of a house party she'd attended Friday night. Her description of the hot tub activities was getting interesting when her story was interrupted by the telephone.

After a short conversation with someone on the other end, she hung up. I heard her say, "That was the ICU at Mercy Hospital. Roger O'Dell died this evening."

12

Julie hurried into the room fifteen minutes late. With the somber news of Roger still fresh, her chirpy demeanor did little to console me. I couldn't help thinking of Roger. For some reason, his passing struck too deep. Not since my father's sudden death had I been so affected by the news of someone dying.

Like so many when they lose someone close, I started wondering about our reason for existence. *Why did some people win life's lottery, having every possible good fortune befall them, while others seemed doomed to endless struggle? Was this God's plan, or random fate? Did a true order to the universe exist, delineating our predetermined destinies like some sort of giant galactic roadmap, or was destiny a simple toss of the dice? Why was I wasting away in a hospital bed, while beyond these walls, others, who never performed a decent act in their lives, thanklessly enjoyed another day of perfect health?* Like so many things, it made no sense.

Julie grew frustrated working with me; I wasn't in the mood for therapy. She left a half-hour later, the disappointment of my regression obvious in her expression.

Later that afternoon, Nancy hobbled into the room accompanied by a young, large-boned woman in her late teens, dressed in a poorly fitted blue uniform.

The woman's shoulder-length, brown hair wreathed a round face that hosted hazel eyes, bright rosy cheeks, thick lips, and a recessed chin that disappeared into her neck. My first impression, unkind as it seemed, was that the young men weren't exactly beating this one's door down.

"Matt, this is Monica. She's a second-year nursing student doing a rotation here."

"Hi, Matt. How are doing today?" Monica said, her voice deeper than I expected.

Nancy continued. "I've gone over your chart with her, so she's familiar with your case, and she'll be spending time with you over the next two weeks."

Monica nodded.

"It's such a lovely day out there," Nancy said, "we're going to have Charles and Ramon put you in The Buggy and Monica's going to take you out onto the grounds." Her eyes widened. "How does that sound? We're getting you out of this God-forsaken place for a spell."

Parole was the word that came to mind. For the first time since my involuntary sojourn in the snowy courtyard nearly two months earlier, I was leaving the confines of Slater's Building One.

Too much time had passed since I'd last viewed puffy clouds dotting a cobalt sky, or let the sun's radiant warmth bathe my face, or breathed cool, fresh air. Monica was taking me outside, and she immediately became the most beautiful woman in the world.

Charles and Ramon strapped me into The Buggy—a hybrid unit with the padded, reclining back of the portable chair and the large, maneuverable wheels of a wheelchair.

When they finished, Monica wheeled me out of the room, scooting me past the nurses' station and down the hall, negotiating The Buggy as if she did it every day.

"Charles suggested we go out the south entrance," she said. "It empties into the gardens and the lawn. He said it would be a little warmer on that side of the building."

I didn't care if we were headed for the parking lot—I was getting out of there for a while, and that's all that mattered.

We whipped by the dayroom, with its large television blaring. Through the doorway, I caught a glimpse of four bodies seated around a table in the middle of the room, the card game seemingly devoid of the acrimony I'd been audience to during my last visit.

"It's a gorgeous day out there, Matt. I noticed a wall of forsythias in full bloom along the drive coming in. They're always the first flowering spring bush, and such a beautiful yellow. The buds on the maples are starting to open and the cherry trees look like they're about ready to blossom."

We zipped across the back foyer, out the automatic sliding doors and into the early afternoon sunshine. The bright daylight blinded me, forcing my eyes shut. After months indoors, adjusting to intense sunlight would take a minute.

"I brought us these," Monica said, moving to the front of the chair. She slipped on a pair of cheap, plastic sunglasses. When she placed the second pair on my face, the world turned amber. "How's that? They look good on you." She smiled approvingly.

Yeah. I bet they did. But what the hell? They worked.

Monica guided the chair down the back entranceway, across the asphalt drive and to a brick walkway that ran along a ridge overlooking the sprawling landscape.

In the distance, groundskeepers piloted two large riding mowers across emerald green lawns, the machines' engines humming in melodious unison. A light southerly breeze carried a faint mingling of freshly cut grass and exhaust fumes.

About fifty yards to our left, a young woman tossed a Frisbee to a black Labrador retriever. The large dog barked with delight, chasing the plastic disc as it sailed a few feet above the lawn. Across the spacious yard, a half-dozen people strolled leisurely along paved walkways that bordered the hospital property. Overhead, a single crow glided by, squawking its redundant verse. Close by, a flower garden sprouted fledgling green shoots amongst the brown ruins of last winter's final killing frost.

Monica halted the chair beneath a row of large, heavily budded maple trees and next to a gray, slatted, wooden bench.

She turned me to face the lawns. "How about we sit here a while and check it all out."

She sat on the bench next to me. "This is my second rotation this month. I spent the last two weeks in a surgical ward at Mercy Hospital." She looked off in the distance. "It was interesting, but not very much fun. This place seems much better. It's definitely prettier with these awesome grounds. Quiet and peaceful. It kind of reminds me of where I go to school. Sort of Ivy League like." She turned to me, held up her hand in a stop motion, and laughed, saying, "Not to imply that I attend an Ivy League school. I was about two hundred points short on my SAT's and twenty grand light in my savings account for one of those babies." She turned her gaze back onto the grounds.

Monica wasn't a looker, but she carried herself in a self-assured way—a well-grounded young woman comfortable in her own skin. Pleasant and talkative, she provided gracious company.

She carried on a one-way conversation while we watched the mowers work their way closer, cutting a path left to right, right to left. I learned her mother was a nurse's aide. Her father, a supermarket produce manager, had died when she was ten years old. Monica had a fiancé—Jason—a self-employed software engineer. Learning this earlier might have surprised me, but I quickly realized this affable woman had a ton of personality. Looks weren't everything.

After weeks of observing those who cared for me, I wanted to ask her, *Why nursing, Monica? With an obvious cache of smarts and such an amiable disposition, why not a less demanding profession? A job where you get to go home at five every day. The type of work where weekends and holidays are your own. Are you sure this is what you aspire to do—shove catheters up people's urethras and wipe their asses? Wouldn't you rather dress in business attire, sit at a large desk in a big office and pencil lunch appointments into a day planner?* But then, where would I be if she, and others like her, made that choice? Who then would care for the wounded, the ill, the dying? *Thank God for the Nancys and Monicas of the world.*

Monica relaxed, tossing her head back and running her arms out along the top of the bench. "Oh, that sun feels *so* good. Can't wait until beach weather. I *love* the beach, Matt—stretched out on a blanket with a good romance novel. That's what I call relaxing."

After reflecting on her words a moment, she leaned in my direction and managed a sad half-smile. "I guess relaxing on the beach is the last thing on your mind." She touched my face. "You poor thing. What sort of monster would ever do this to another human being?"

Leo, I screamed to myself. *Leo Tracy. And for no reason. The bastard shot me because I didn't understand. Understand what?*

Her piercing gaze studied my face, hazel irises penetrating my corneas like a laser beam. "I can see the anguish in your eyes," she said. She placed her hand on my forehead. Her head tilted. "You know who did this, don't you?" She continued to stare. "The person who shot you—he was someone you knew. A friend. Someone you . . ." She hesitated a moment, closed her eyes, and shook her head.

A queer draining sensation gushed from me, as if Monica had opened a tap and sapped me of all strength, the energy running like a warm liquid from my forehead to her hand. I felt an abrupt, unexpected, relaxing sense of relief. It was then I understood Monica possessed something special.

She removed her hand, straightened to her feet, and combed her hair back with her fingertips. "Why don't I take you for a scoot around the grounds? We'll head over there," she said, motioning to one of the bordering walkways. "I'll get some exercise and you some fresh air."

Monica fell quiet for a long period, leaving the thumping of my wheels passing over the concrete walk's expansion grooves, our lone audible companion. We wheeled along, parallel to the facility's long entrance drive, at a brisk clip.

Did Monica actually see my thoughts? Did she really possess a gift of clairvoyance? She did say *he*. He *"was someone you knew." How did she know it was a he?* This was the stuff right out of supermarket tabloids. I wondered at the possibilities. *What thoughts ran through her mind at that moment? What insights did she have? Had she caught a glimpse of Leo pulling that trigger? Did she know who he was, or was it merely a guess by a homely, fat, weirded-out chick?*

"It started when we were very young," she said in a quiet voice. "I had an identical twin sister, Roberta. We called her Robbie. For as long as I can remember, we knew each other's thoughts. It wasn't mind reading—we didn't have the ability to read each other word-for-word, but somehow we just knew things. I knew when she was sad and why. And without me speaking a word, she understood why I sometimes came home from school angry or upset. General kind of stuff, but accurate enough for us to understand we had something the other kids didn't: a paranormal gift."

Monica stopped the chair for a gray squirrel. It had scampered out from a clog of juniper bushes a few feet ahead. The animal stopped dead in its tracks, checked us out for a second, and then shot back into the safety of the heavy brush.

She gave The Buggy a shove and resumed. "There was a fire one night. A space heater set too close to the window ignited some curtains. In the blackness, my father found me. We could hear Robbie crying out but couldn't find her in the thick smoke. Dad got me out and tried to go back in after her, but the house exploded in a flashover just as he got to the door. He was blown back, knocked unconscious. He suffered second and third-degree burns on his face, arms, and chest."

She quieted for a few steps. "In the morning, they found Robbie exactly where I envisioned her—under her bed. I guess she panicked and crawled in there. The flames never reached her. She died from the smoke."

I counted the bumps of three expansion joints before Monica continued.

"I thought my special ability died with Robbie and kind of forgot about it for years. And then one day, when I was eleven, this horrible kid at my school bus stop, Teddy Monday, started teasing me. When he tried to push me to the ground, I grabbed his arm. In an instant, I felt a chill from the evil coursing through him—a true and deep-rooted malevolence. I immediately knew he had killed the two dogs, the Duggan's Springer Spaniel and Donny Fuller's beagle, both found mutilated in a cornfield behind our housing development a week earlier. I told Donny, and the next day his father confronted Teddy, telling him I witnessed the killings. Teddy broke down and confessed to doing it."

Reaching the end of the walk where it intersected the main road, Monica flipped the chair in the opposite direction and headed us back toward Building One, some two hundred yards in the distance.

"The police came to my house that night to talk with me. They called it an interview. I was scared to death. My mother sat next to me, chain smoking her Marlboros like she always does when she's nervous."

Monica quietly chuckled. "You should have seen the look on the two detectives' faces when I told them I didn't actually witness the wretched deed, but instead saw it when I touched Teddy's arm. They made me remain at the table while they took my mother into the next room and suggested I might be complicit in the crime, since they expected I was altering my story to hide that fact that I may have taken part. Fortunately, my mother was able to account for my whereabouts at dancing school the afternoon of the crime."

Halfway back to Building One, Monica stopped at the edge of another slatted bench, this one painted hunter green. She stepped to the front of the chair and knelt down to adjust my leg wrap. The white cotton sheet, bound tightly around both legs to keep my dormant appendages from shifting, had begun to drag on one side of the chair.

"That should be better," she said, tucking the maverick section under the deadweight of my right leg. She peered up at me with a sliver of a smile, and then rose high enough to slide onto the edge of the bench. Bending down, she plucked a single dandelion that had escaped the lawn tractor's ruthless blades, held it to her lips, and twirled it by the stem.

"Two months later, I had to testify against Teddy Monday before a judge. I was eleven years old and on a witness stand testifying for the prosecution. Teddy had retracted his story and was looking at eighteen months in juvenile detention. A lot of people were very upset about those dogs. But within minutes of starting his cross-examination, Teddy's lawyer had me reduced to a wailing heap of rubble, with the credibility of a delusional psychopath and a suspected deep-rooted hate for my childhood peers. Later, a defense rent-a-shrink, looking to be in dire need of psychiatric help himself, confirmed the defense's accusations in flowery psychobabble. But destroying a terrified, introverted eleven-year-old wasn't enough; that bastard of an attorney wasn't quite finished. He was determined to make an example of me."

I watched a single tear traverse Monica's left cheek. It ran to the corner of her mouth before she patted it away with the back of her hand.

"He put my mother on the stand and proceeded to whittle her to her dispirited core. He claimed I was a danger. He insisted she was responsible for my aberrant behavior, suggesting that, as a full-time working mother, she lacked the time and commitment to raise a troubled young daughter on her own."

Monica hesitated. Blinking back tears from her welling eyes, she grit her teeth and continued.

"He threatened her with the Department of Social Services. The prosecution immediately objected, of course, but the intimidation tactic worked. Frightened of losing her only remaining child, my mother lied. She said I made the whole thing up, and that I had a habit of fabricating bizarre stories and telling lies. She promised to get me help and to cut back on her work hours."

Monica opened her fingers, dropped the dandelion to the walk, and ground it into the concrete with the sole of her shoe.

"When charges against that monster-in-waiting were dismissed, I promised my mother, no matter what, to never again get involved." She turned toward me. "I mean to keep that promise."

Monica got to her feet, and continued us toward the building.

"By the way," she said, "last year, Teddy Monday killed and mutilated a nineteen-year-old prostitute. He's serving life at Cedar Junction in Walpole."

Numb with disbelief, I watched the approaching brick façade of Building One loom larger while the essence of Monica's words slowly sank in. She planned on keeping it all to herself. Whatever sixth sense she possessed, I wasn't to be a beneficiary. Any knowledge she had acquired of the robbery was doomed to the corridors of her mind, where they would eventually fade from memory. I felt like I'd been kicked in the gut. I wanted to vomit.

She wouldn't have to testify on my behalf, I reasoned. All she needed to do was to drop the dime. Make an anonymous call to the police, let them know Leo did it, and hang up. Given some time, a good detective could connect the dots and put the whole thing together. Then that little rat-bastard could take his turn rotting in some shithole of a prison cell.

I boiled in a stew of anger, frustration, and self-pity. *Why not this one time, Monica? Look what he did to me. It was worse than murdering me. He had mutilated the living. How can you know and remain silent?*

In front of the building's open automatic doors, Monica stopped the chair, leaned forward, and grabbed my arm.

"I'm so sorry, Matt," she said, and then wheeled me into the building.

13

Jabber from an afternoon talk show, hosted by a has-been sitcom star, poured from the television set, but it failed to interest me. Once again on my back and surrounded by the four miserable walls of my room, I stared at the dismal ceiling.

Nancy had gathered Monica fifteen minutes earlier to work on progress notes at one of the nurses' station computer terminals, which was just fine with me. I wanted to be alone and wallow in self-pity, seething that this gifted woman had refused to help me.

The more I thought about it, the angrier I became. I felt the resentment strengthen. After all, the object of my continuing vegetative existence was to one day see Leo Tracy brought to justice; to see him pay for destroying my life. Monica held the power to make this happen, but she refused. And then it struck me. *Who the hell would believe her?*

Whom did I think I was kidding? Without a stitch of evidence, the authorities would dismiss her accusations as nonsense. Some young woman with a crackpot background was at it again, they'd say. "Touching people and reading minds? Give me a break!" She'd be summarily dismissed as some sort of whack job. Did I really believe the cops would drag Leo off based on some absurd paranormal vision? They needed tangible proof. The gun. A witness. At least an accusation by the victim. An anonymous phone call to the cops? Forget it. They probably hung up on a dozen whacko calls a day.

Thoroughly disappointed despite a rare overdose of fresh air, I dozed off to the sounds of yet another TV game show.

I dreamt of Monica. In my dream, she had transformed into a ravishing beauty; long and lean, with flowing hair that tumbled out behind her as if caught in a gentle slipstream. She stood above my bed with her hand held out, and when she touched my face, I saw *her* thoughts.

Her mind beheld a frightened young girl in a courtroom, dressed in a frilly white blouse and plaid jumper. Tears cascaded across her porcelain complexion as her eyes darted back and forth in frenzied confusion.

An older gentleman, with neatly trimmed white hair and wearing a three-piece suit, stood facing her, his hands on the rail of the witness box. The man bellowed harsh words, blistering the flesh of her face. When her skin began peeling away, dropping to the floor and exposing facial bones, the image changed.

Now, my bed and I lay in the center of the hospital's south lawn. Monica stood next to me and seized my wrist.

"Walk," she said. "Get up and walk, Matt."

She helped me to my feet and the world instantly rolled into a sickening spin. When my legs crumbled beneath me, her strong arm pulled and held me upright until everything straightened. And then I walked. I felt the cool, wet grass between my toes and sucked in the scent of a freshly cut lawn.

When she released her grip, I stumbled slightly, and then quickly regained my balance. My legs felt strong, like my old legs. I walked, lengthening my stride, cutting a track across the lawn. Seconds later, I broke into a jog and then a full-throttled sprint—my newly restored calf and thigh muscles rippling under the exertion. I crossed the grounds, fleeing the property. I ran through field after field with the strength and stamina of a marathoner. Over my shoulder, Slater Hospital dwindled to a dot.

I journeyed past farmhouses, barns, grazing cows, and rolling hills. I ran along the shores of a dark green lake, and then followed a well-worn path carved through a thick forest until it broke into a large meadow, redolent with the fragrance of a million wild flowers.

In the distance, I noticed a cluster of brick structures and ran toward them. I dashed through the meadow, overtaking a pack of whitetail rabbits and racing past two grazing doe.

Closing in on the buildings, I observed what appeared to be a woman standing in front of one of them, her arm extended out to her side. Something about the buildings struck me as familiar.

A jolt of panic ripped through me when I recognized the edifice. I was running in the direction of the hospital. Nancy stood beside my bed, holding out her arm as if to say, "Time to come home."

I tried to stop, to turn back, but my pace only quickened. I had no control.

No. No. I can't go back. A deepening panic gripped me.

Both legs grew weaker as I approached Nancy. She looked like she was carved of stone. When she spoke, she did so in the voice of Forsythe.

"That's enough exercise for now, Mathew. You did very well. Why don't you rest now?"

My leg muscles began to burn, then cramped with terrible pain. When I glanced down, a wave of nausea enveloped me. My legs had atrophied into two stick-thin appendages. A moment later, my knees buckled and I tumbled, completely paralyzed, onto the bed. Smiling, Nancy methodically pulled the bedcovers over my withered body and started rolling the bed toward the rear entrance of Building One.

I awoke with a sour taste in my mouth. Beads of sweat had formed on my upper lip and were running to the corners of my mouth. My vision was blurred from perspiration. I was sweating as if I had actually made the run I'd dreamt of. It all seemed so real; the wind in my face, the smell of flowers in the meadow, the thrill of freedom. Another vivid dream and more words from Forsythe. *What did it mean?*

The hallway clock read seven-thirty. I had slept three hours. Monica, Nancy, and the day shift had punched out and I heard the evening staff clowning around at the nurses' station.

The television remained on and the silly afternoon game shows were replaced with flashy, early evening, Hollywood gossip programs.

I started watching a segment about a nightclub that catered to the stars, but I thought of Monica. I wondered what she would say to me the next day. Maybe, knowing what she now knew, she'd change her mind, have an attack of conscience. I was doubtful.

The next day was Tuesday; that meant Julie. Once again, she looked to be my sole conduit to the outside world. I'd work hard for her. Together, we'd amaze everyone.

One of the evening nurses trotted in, hung another brown IV bag of mystery medication, and left without saying a word. I fixed my gaze on the bag and again wondered.

A short while later, two ward orderlies turned me onto my right side, where I spent the evening listening to the TV until they turned it off sometime after ten p.m. The last time I remember looking at the clock, it was midnight.

It poured Tuesday morning.

An occasional clap of thunder obscured a steady patter of water bouncing from the sill of the open window, and a warm, damp breeze rustled the drawn drapes, allowing a vague smell of wet concrete into the room.

Monica popped in just before eleven. She spent about ten minutes with me, talking about the crummy weather and explaining she had to spend the day with Mr. Bradbury, an Alzheimer patient down the hall. She didn't refer to her disclosure of the previous day, and I had the feeling she never would.

Avoiding all physical contact, she adjusted the bedcovers, promised to check in on me at some point during the day, and left the room. Later on, I saw her wheel an elderly gentleman, whom I assumed to be Mr. Bradbury, past the doorway. I managed to catch a quick glimpse of them as they whipped past, the old man emitting a sick wail.

Julie showed up ten minutes early. She slipped off her light jacket and threw it over a chair.

"I certainly hope you're in better spirits today than you were last week," she said. "Remember what I said about frustration? You've got to commit to working through it. Otherwise, it'll only set us back."

Julie continued the lecture for another few minutes, but I didn't mind; I deserved all her wrath. I'd make it up to her by exceeding all expectations. To hell with Monica. Julie, always my salvation, would be my ticket out of here, and I'd become Leo Tracy's worst nightmare.

Five minutes into the session, I was stunned at my regression—it was as if I'd never had a minute of therapy. I couldn't fathom what had happened. My blinking was sporadic and involuntary, and I was unable to squeeze Julie's hand. I had lost all rapport with her.

"You're not concentrating, Matt. Come on. Don't do this." Her voice was noticeably angry. "Concentrate."

I tried—harder than I've ever tried at anything. Nothing. I had no control whatsoever. What little I had gained the past few weeks was now lost.

An overwhelming wave of angry frustration washed over me, snapping the tenuous structure of my spirit, casting me deep into a pit of despair. I was trapped at the bottom, looking up. At the opening, I saw Julie's face. It registered my hopeless discouragement.

For the second time in as many sessions, Julie left my room drenched with disappointment. Suddenly, I didn't care. I was comfortably seeping in a profound sense of indifference. Propped up in bed and without the means to kill myself, I watched television until another worthless day of my hideous life dissolved to black.

14

By morning, the persistent rains had ceased. Brilliant sunlight poured through the window, displacing the oppressive gloom and brightening the plain, quiet features of my decades-old room.

Some time after nine, the ward's peaceful tranquility was broken by an unusual bustle of energy. Staff, beds, and equipment swept past my room, and purposeful voices bounced about the hallway. In a single ten-minute period, I spotted the faces of a half-dozen unfamiliar nurses, orderlies, and aides. Something out of the ordinary was going on. The commotion intrigued me. Staff moved other patients—some in wheelchairs, others quite ambulatory—around the ward.

Thirty minutes into the mid-morning clamor, Nancy and a second nurse, whom I'd never laid eyes on, escorted a man in his early-to-mid-twenties into my room. Clad in hospital-issued pajamas, a New York Yankees baseball cap, and white tennis shoes, he carried his belongings in a green, New York Jets overnight bag.

"This isn't my room," he said, shuffling in and gazing curiously in my direction.

"This will be your room while they're renovating our ward, Kenny," said the nurse I didn't know. "You'll only be here a few weeks."

"I want my own room. I don't want him here," Kenny said, pointing to me.

The feeling was mutual. I didn't need another roommate, especially one with his pleasant disposition.

"This is Matt, Kenny," Nancy said, touching my arm. "He can't move or speak, but he can see and hear just fine, so don't hesitate to talk to him. I'm sure he'd enjoy it. Matt's a huge baseball fan. You two can watch the games together."

"I hate baseball," he snarled.

"Kenny," his nurse said, "I hope you're going to be a gracious guest. Matt is sharing his room with you, and I expect you to behave like a gentleman while you're here."

"I'm not staying here."

Hands on her hips, Kenny's nurse eyed him straight on. "Well, it's either here or Building Two," she said. "Would you like to spend three weeks in Two instead?"

Kenny lowered his head.

"What do you say, Mister? Here or Building Two?"

"Here," he mumbled into his chest.

"Good," his nurse said, "because if you cause any trouble, you'll be in Two so fast, your head will spin. Understood?"

Kenny nodded.

"Good. Now unpack your stuff and put it all in the drawers over there," she said, motioning toward the small bedside dresser.

Reluctantly, my new roomy went to work under the cross-armed, steely-eyed observation of his own nurse Ratched.

When he finished, Kenny propped himself onto his bed, donned a pair of headphones that ran to a small, black, plastic device he'd fished from his bag, and pushed the appropriate buttons. Satisfied, Ratched issued one last admonishment before she and Nancy disappeared into the ward confusion.

On my back with the head of my bed cranked up, I studied Kenny. His head bobbed to the tinny beat of music seeping from the headphones. Thin and gangly, he looked healthy enough to me. What type of rehab did he require? Perhaps he'd also suffered a head injury, albeit a less serious one than mine. He did seem slow in responding to his nurse. Yeah, that had to be it—some kind of head injury.

Kenny sat for a long while, his only movement a gentle, rhythmic bobbing of his head. He appeared absorbed in his music, his eyes focused on the opposite wall. I watched him from the corner of my eye; his haunting manner made me uneasy. Kenny was a far cry from old Roger.

I blinked in surprise when he abruptly snapped his head in my direction. It was as if he had read my mind. He held his blistering gaze on me for what seemed an eternity before removing the headphones and placing them on his bed.

With his stare riveted to me, he slid off the bed and to his feet. His probing brown eyes, like those of a curious child, widened as he approached. Pressed against the side of my bed, he examined my face. Without expression, he tilted his head to one side and then the other. My heart quickened. *First Robbie, and now this weirdo.*

Kenny raised an index finger and pressed it to my cheek, pushing my head to the right. He repeated his experiment a second and third time, his eyebrows arching with intrigue. I was a freak show, and Kenny was getting his jollies in the oddity laid out before him.

He withdrew his hand and, taking a step back, he wagged his finger. "I know you. You came here with Forsythe," he said.

With that, he retreated to his bed, slipped on the headphones, and returned to bobbing in rhythm to the music.

His words disturbed me. *How did he know?* And then I wondered: Did what I'd just experienced really happen, or was it yet another illusion? I was confusing reality with the imaginary. It was my head injury. The hallucinations were worsening. Kenny never left his bed; he never touched me. My damaged brain was sending erroneous signals. Anything to do with Forsythe was false; I knew that. It had never happened.

Soon after the ward commotion calmed, Monica entered the room, followed by Ramon pushing the Buggy. Monica walked directly to Kenny, and Ramon parked the Buggy at the foot of my bed.

"Hi, Kenny. My name's Monica."

Kenny continued gazing at the wall, head bobbing away, ignoring Monica's existence.

Asshole, I thought.

"I hope you don't mind, but I'm going to steal your roommate for a while," she said.

Kenny responded by rolling onto his side, his back to the three of us.

Monica turned to me and shrugged. "How about you, Matt? Want to go out and work on our tans?"

Great idea. Anything to get away from Mr. Personality for an hour or so.

She started to pull back the bedcovers and stopped. Leaning over me, she cocked her head and said, "Ramon. Take a look at these red marks on Matt's cheek."

With our plastic sunglasses on and adjusted, we pushed our way through the rear doors of Building One. The warm, late morning sun was busy drying scattered puddles left by the previous day's downpour. A brisk southerly breeze carried the odor of damp asphalt.

A few staff members and patients were walking the grounds surrounding the great south lawn, but in all, it remained a quiet weekday morning on the property of Slater Hospital.

Monica guided The Buggy toward a set of benches beneath a row of large, budding oak trees. The normally gregarious nursing student remained silent. For the moment, this didn't concern me; I was busy thinking about Kenny—the roommate from hell.

He did come to my bed and poke my face; it wasn't a hallucination. But did he really speak? "You came here with Forsythe." That part couldn't have happened. How could he know about Forsythe, when I didn't even know who the hell Forsythe was? The name was a figment of my imagination—a product of my head trauma. Still, it was enough to unsettle me.

As we neared the target benches, Monica finally spoke. "Boy, am I glad to get out of that madhouse for a while. We moved twenty-three patients from Three South into our ward in an hour. You're one of the lucky ones. Most of the other rooms on the ward now have three patients. Fortunately, the Two South staff came with their patients—some sort of renovation of their plumbing system. It's going to be a circus for the next few weeks."

We parked in front of the benches. Falling silent once again, Monica drifted in front and to one side of me, gazing out at two women standing near the middle of the lawn about two hundred feet away. She raised her hand to her brow for a few seconds before cupping both hands around her mouth and shouting, "Kathy!"

Both women's heads turned our way. Monica waved excitedly.

"Monica," the taller woman replied, waving back, her voice dampened by the long expanse of grass.

Monica leaned over me, her eyes bright with pleasant surprise. "It's Kathy Reid, one of my nursing schoolmates. I'll be right back." She took several steps onto the lawn before turning to me and saying, "Don't you dare move." She beamed a wide smile and then hurried in the direction of her friend.

I watched Monica set a hasty, yet less than blistering, pace across the grass. Agility was not one of her finer suits. She looked awkward bustling away, her manner clumsy and uncoordinated.

When she reached Kathy, they hugged and began exchanging pleasantries. Though well out of range of their gabfest, I did manage to catch an occasional shrill of laughter.

A minute later, Monica pointed me out and Kathy waved. I hoped she didn't think me rude for not waving back. Kathy gestured toward her companion, and Monica shook the woman's hand. I reasoned she was either a patient or another nursing student.

With their backs to me, Monica and Kathy talked a while, briefly escaping the toil of uncompensated labor. No problem. I was fine sitting in The Buggy, listening to songbirds and catching some rays.

The sun's warmth washed over my face. I couldn't feel the heat, of course, but I did sense a contrast between shade and direct sunlight each time a cloud passed. The experience was quite pleasant.

A minute or two into my sunbath, The Buggy jerked. When my eyes opened, I was being pulled backward toward the benches. With their backs still to me, Monica and Kathy remained steeped in conversation more than two hundred feet away. Kathy's companion looked off in the opposite direction.

The Buggy stopped next to the edge of the first bench and the person pulling it took a seat facing me. My heart shot to my throat. *Leo Tracy.*

He reached over and turned my head in his direction.

"Hey, Matty. How's it hanging?"

A spruced-up version of Leo stared back at me. Clean-shaven, fresh haircut, a blue, long-sleeved, cotton turtleneck, khaki pants, and brown loafers. I even caught a hint of cologne. He looked like a job interview candidate.

Leo eyed me up and down. With my heart punching against my breastbone, he spoke. "I wondered what happened to you. Lost track after they took you to Mercy." His tired eyes studied me further. "Of all people, who should I run into the other day but Trisha," he said. "She came into Chen's, bought a bottle of Merlot, and filled me in on you."

I couldn't believe what I was hearing. My fear was ebbing. Now I was angry.

"Yeah," he said, nodding, "old man Chen hired me back. Can you believe it? I even got my old shift—Tuesdays and Thursdays.

But I've cleaned up my act, man. No more stealing." He held up open hands. "Well, not as much, anyway."

My breathing and heart rate slowed to normal. I was trying to figure out if Leo was real or an illusion. I looked for signs. From the corner of my eye, I saw Monica and Kathy still standing with their backs to us, the third woman now seated on the grass, leaning back on her elbows. That appeared real enough.

I looked back at Leo. This Leo was more vivid than the previous ones, and this time he moved me, pulling my chair backward. I sensed the motion before I knew who it was. *Can an illusion do that?*

If this was the real Leo, why was he here? If I was him, this is the last place I'd be. How did he know I couldn't finger him? He wasn't privy to the type of rehab I was undergoing. For all he knew, I could be singing like a bird and naming names. Wasn't this a stupid, unnecessary chance? Then again, Leo never impressed me as one to spend too much time thinking things through. Maybe this was the real Leo.

He pulled a pack of cigarettes from his pants pocket and slid one out. "You know, Matt, you're the first thought that flashes through my head every morning when I wake up, and the last thought before I fall asleep at night."

He produced a book of matches, lit the cigarette and inhaled deeply.

"I think about you when I'm drunk, when I'm high. Shit, even when I'm cranking some bar whore, I have to fight off the image of your face." He took another long haul and held it a while before exhaling.

"As far back as I can remember, my old man smacked my mother around," he said. "Never once did he show either of us an ounce of affection. He was just plain rotten mean, twenty-four-seven. When I was about eight, he started getting meaner. He'd come home late from work three or four nights a week, totally shit-faced, and beat the crap out of my mother because supper was cold, or he didn't like what she'd prepared, or for no particular reason at all. When he finished with her, sometimes he'd try coming after me, but she never allowed it. She'd throw herself in front of him. Grab his leg, bite him, scratch him—anything to keep him from getting to me. And that just further enraged him. He'd beat her mercilessly. I'd run to my room, hide in the closet, and listen to Mom's cries as that son-of-a-bitch wailed on her. He'd beat her until passing out from either the booze or plain exhaustion."

Leo gazed at his cigarette and shook off the white ash.

"One Wednesday, I woke up after midnight to my mother's screams. This time I had enough. I went to my closet, grabbed my baseball bat, and charged into the kitchen. He was on top of her, hitting her with his fists. I could hear the punches land. Brutal blows that penetrated her raised hands. I never got to swing that bat. When Mom saw me, she screamed, 'Run, Leo.' The old man turned and clocked me with the back of his fist. That's the last thing I remember."

He took one last drag of the half-burnt cigarette and flicked it away. It traveled a good fifteen feet before hitting the grass.

"When I woke up, he was gone. Mom's face was covered in blood. I ran upstairs to the Murphys' apartment, yelling hysterically and beating on their door. They never answered—didn't want to get involved in the fracas they heard several nights a week. Every bastard in that building knew my mother was getting beaten most nights, and no one did a thing.

"I think old Mrs. O'Connell downstairs finally called the cops, because they showed up about fifteen minutes later, but it was too late." A short pause. "She was dead."

Leo went quiet for a long moment and looked off across the lawn at the women. "What do you reckon they're talking about?"

By now, I was quite convinced the real Leo Tracy sat next to me. More evidence—the timbre of his voice, the inflection of his words, his characteristic cigarette gesticulations.

"When the old man went to prison, I was sent to live with my uncle. The apple didn't fall far from the tree on my father's side of the family. Uncle Riley—or *Pickles*, as everyone called him—was a small-time hood who only took me so he could collect the monthly benefit check the state sent for my care. I saw little of that money. Because Pickles was a blood relative, the state rarely sent a social worker by to check up on things."

By now, Monica had noticed Leo sitting next to me. She looked our way, curious, while continuing her chat. When Leo gave her a wave, she reluctantly waved back. Figuring all was well, her attention went back to her friend.

"I soon found out a dirty little family secret. Pickles was a raging homosexual. I never got the full story on his nickname, but I can imagine. Anyway, the place was always full of his faggot fiends. Unfortunately, two of them had an affinity for young boys. My uncle never did anything to protect me. He was either too busy running numbers, fencing stolen goods, or entertaining a host of boyfriends. Consequently, these two pedophiles, Jerry and Ricky, had their way with me for almost six months. I tried to fight them at first, but it was no use. They were bigger and stronger, and there were two of them."

Leo took a deep breath and wiped away what looked like a tear.

"I ran away, but Pickles found me within a day. He didn't want to jeopardize that monthly check. When he dragged me back, he threatened to kill Jerry, Ricky or anyone else who dared put a hand on me. I guess he meant it because no one ever touched me again, and within a week, those two pedophiles vanished.

Leo looked at me sadly. "Those scars never heal, Matty."

He turned away, as if embarrassed by his admission.

"I was thrown out of more schools than I can remember, not that it mattered. I was lucky if I showed up twice a week for class. I was getting drunk every night when I was fourteen, and high every night at fifteen. I quit school at sixteen and wound up running errands for Pickles' gang for drugs and cash. When Uncle Pickles died from AIDS, I was on the street, without a skill or an education. I was seventeen."

Leo readjusted himself, facing me directly. Bending over, inches from my face, he continued. "It's been part-time, nowhere jobs ever since, and that's when I can manage to dupe some fool into hiring me. But worst of all, it's the ghosts of Jerry and Ricky. Those images are seared forever in my mind." He looked off. "I hope those two filthy bastards are burning in Hell."

Leo raised his hand and pressed a pistol to my temple. "Now you understand," he said.

Everything happened so fast, my mind blurred. For the second time, Leo held a gun to my head. He was here to kill me, the last bit of housekeeping in his otherwise perfect crime. Leo would disappear into the woods behind us before Monica, Kathy or anyone else realized what had happened. I choked on my last breaths.

"I want you to know I'm really sorry, Matt. I'm sorry I fucked your life up. I'm sorry I didn't kill you back at Chen's." He was crying, tears rolling down his face. "I'm sorry I made you suffer all these months. I really am."

I heard and felt the hammer click back. Leo's hand shook, the gun shook, and because it was pressed hard against my temple, my head shook. Terrified, I watched him from the corner of my right eye. This was it.

"It's payback time," he said in a quivering voice.

Leo paused a moment, shoved the gun barrel into his mouth, and pulled the trigger.

Over the explosion I cried, "Noooooo!" and shot up in bed.

15

My scream filled the room. For several moments, I sat erect and panted—each exhaled breath entwined in a moan of pure terror. Less than three feet from me, Leo had just blown his head off.

A nurse raced into the room, screeching to a halt ten feet from my bed as if she'd hit an invisible wall. Her eyes were wide with amazement, her lips parted in surprise. When my thoughts gelled to coherence seconds later, I realized I was sitting up in bed.

"Oh, my God," she whispered, still aghast.

A second person shot into the room. He stopped just inside the doorway. The two exchanged stunned glances.

"Get Dr. Moss in here," the nurse said calmly.

The man bolted from the room and the nurse moved closer, measuring each step as if approaching a dangerous animal.

I was awash in confused panic. *How'd I get here?* My heart pounded frantically; surely it would rupture at any second. My breath shuddered, and bile filled the back of my throat. *What the hell was happening?* My eyes welled from the fear, and I began to sob in blubbering wails.

"Matt. I'm Liz," the nurse said softly, coming closer. When she reached me, she took my hand. "Everything's fine." She began to giggle, and nodding, she said, "Everything's just fine."

I felt her gentle touch and my wailing calmed.

"Liz." The word softly escaped my trembling lips, astonishing me. I had spoken. "Liz," I repeated.

"That's right. Liz," she said. A cautious smile spread across her face.

Moments later, a middle-aged woman wearing a long, white lab coat barreled into the room, followed by three other people, including the person ordered by Liz to fetch the doctor. My eyes darted from person to person.

"How long?" the lab-coated woman asked Liz.

"About five minutes."

"Someone page Eric," she ordered.

"He's on his way," a reply came from the gathering crowd.

"Matt, I'm Dr. Moss. I know you're confused and agitated. I'm going to give you something to calm you down a little. Okay?" She tuned to a nurse who had followed her in. "A milligram of Ativan."

A moment later, Dr. Moss produced a syringe and pumped its contents into my IV line.

I was overwhelmed by the speed in which things were happening. My thoughts had become a cocktail of fear and bewilderment. *What happened to Leo? How could I be sitting up, talking and feeling?* I was supposed to be paralyzed. *Oh, God no*, I thought. *This is another illusion.*

If it was an illusion, it was becoming an extended one.

Someone else fought his way into the room, already occupied by a half-dozen people or more.

"Everyone out but Liz and Dr. Moss," said a man in his middle forties, dressed like Dr. Moss—long lab coat over street clothes. He worked his way to my bedside.

Within ten seconds, the crowd had dispersed and the room fell quiet. Still sitting up with my hands on my thighs, I studied the man, standing at an arm's length from me, and we locked gazes. Somewhat distinguished looking, he carried an air of sophistication, but not of arrogance. Under his white coat, he wore a dark blue shirt, matching tie, and light gray, pleated wool trousers. He had thick, wavy brown hair, an easy smile, and inquiring blue eyes. He was a handsome man in some respects, but not in a Hollywood way. He observed me with a quiet reassurance for what felt like hours. I felt I knew him.

"How you doing, Matt?" He smiled briefly. "Do you know who I am?"

I shook my head, but immediately recognized the voice.

"My name's Eric. Dr. Eric Forsythe. I'm your doctor here."

I shook my head again.

"Go ahead, Matt. Speak. You can speak, can't you?"

I nodded. "Yeah," I managed to utter. "I . . . think so."

"Of course you can."

"Doctor?" I whispered.

"That's right. I'm you doctor. Do you remember me?"

The effects of the sedative were kicking in. I had gone from panic to a state of complete relaxation. I tried to form my words, but my mouth wasn't cooperating. "You're the neurologist?" I managed to get out.

"No, I'm not a neurologist, Matt."

"But I was shot, paralyzed. Locked-in syndrome. Leo shot me." My words were as slurred as a drunk's. "Where's the neuro . . . neurologist? I'm in rehab." My thoughts were becoming unglued.

"I want you to try and rest for a while," Forsythe said. "We'll talk more later."

He eased me onto my back. Every muscle in my body had fallen limp.

"Forsythe," I whispered. "Leo did it."

"Rest," he said placing his hand on my brow.

"Leo," I managed one last time.

The room gradually faded to dark. My final blurring vision was of the clear tubing running to the brown IV bag that hung at the corner of the bed.

"How do you feel, Matt?" I opened my eyes to Liz's face. Her long black hair hung inches away while her hazel eyes explored mine.

I felt I had slept for days, but in reality, no more than three or four hours had passed. Still groggy, I took a moment to collect my thoughts, trying to sort reality from fantasy. I lifted my hand and held it in front of my face. A reality check.

"Ready to get out of bed?" Liz asked.

I lowered my hand and, holding her gaze, said, "Walk?"

"Yeah, walk. You remember how, don't you?"

The very thought petrified me. Sure, I could move my hands, even speak, but walk? What if my legs crumbled beneath me? Maybe I was wrong about the gunshot damage. Maybe I was only paralyzed from the waist down. I didn't dare try my feet. *Please don't make me do this.*

"Come on, Matt. The doctors want you up and moving around." She pulled back the bedcovers. "Don't worry. I'll help you like I always do."

"We've done this before?"

She smiled and nodded.

"When?"

Liz placed her hand between my shoulders and said, "I'd like you to sit up. C'mon."

With a push, I was up, and surprised at how little effort it required.

"Now swing those gams around," she ordered, pulling on one knee.

I sat on the edge of the bed, my feet dangling inches above the floor. It might as well have been a mile. The dreaded next move sent my heart bounding to my mouth. I felt my legs, but would they work? Liz placed her hands under my armpits. No time for contemplation.

"Just slide your butt off the edge," she said. "Go ahead. I've got you."

An instant later, I stood, my legs easily supporting my weight. They didn't crumble, buckle, or turn to rubber. Liz eased her hands from under my arms, but held them inches in front of me.

"Good job, Matt."

A nervous laugh escaped me. I felt the grin spread across my face. A mild wave of dizziness rolled through, causing my left leg to give, but Liz grabbed me and held me steady. This all felt familiar.

"It's called postural hypotension. It'll pass in a few seconds," she said.

And it did. My leg straightened and the strength returned. Once again I stood unaided.

"Ready to take a little walk?"

"I don't know," I said with another nervous chuckle, "I think—"

"Come on." One hand slid back under my armpit and she eased me toward her. "You can do it."

Before I had a chance to protest, I had taken two steps and stopped.

"See. There you go," she said. Her voice perked with delight. "Come on. Keep moving."

I wanted to quit and take a moment to relish my accomplishment, make sure this wasn't another dream, but Liz pressed me to continue. Placing one foot in front of the other, she guided my way, and I moved toward the door. At some point— I'm not sure when—she removed her hand, and for the first time since Leo Tracy shot me, I walked.

Dr. Forsythe pulled a stool up to the side of my bed and sat. "Heard you had a little exercise."

Resting comfortably in bed with my head cranked almost vertically, recovering from my first stroll in almost six months, I responded proudly, "I walked to the nurses' station and back."

"How do you feel?"

"Are you kidding, Doctor? I feel fantastic."

"Call me Eric," Forsythe said.

"Okay, Eric. I'm a little tired, but so what? It's been a while since I used my legs."

Forsythe stared at me for a long while, his gaze focused. "So. Tell me what happened."

"What do you mean?" I asked, unsure of the question.

"What happened to you? How did you get this way?"

Why would he ask a question like that? I wondered. *He was my doctor. He had to know.* "You mean the shooting?"

"Yeah," he said quietly. "Tell me about the shooting."

"The first one?" I asked.

He hesitated a moment. "Yeah, the first one."

Now I understood. Of course he knew about the shooting. He wanted the circumstances behind it. At last I could tell my story—the truth. Not that it mattered any more; Leo was dead—his brains decorating the south lawn.

"What did they do with Leo?" I asked.

Eric shook his head. "Tell me about the first one."

"All right," I said, curious he wasn't concerned with the disposition of Leo. His suicide had to have caused a firestorm of cops, emergency medical people, and heaven knows who else. A mountain of paperwork for someone, at the very least.

I eased into a narrative of the night I was shot, telling him everything to date, including the dreams, delusions, and voices, and culminating with Leo's self-inflicted demise. When I finished, Forsythe took a moment, as if considering everything I said, and then pushed himself erect. "I'll be right back."

He returned less than a minute later with a manila envelope.

"You say Leo Tracy shot you in the forehead?" he said, returning to the stool, the envelope in his lap.

"That's right," I answered, again unsure of his motive.

"Can you show me where?"

When forced to think about it, I realized I wasn't sure. I only remembered the gun being pointed above my eyes when it went off.

"I don't know." I placed my index finger in the middle of my forehead. "Right about here, I guess."

Forsythe studied the area. "Right between the eyes."

I adjusted my finger. "A little higher."

Biting his bottom lip, he examined the spot. "I see nothing unusual there."

"What?"

Forsythe opened the envelope and removed a small mirror, the type most women carried in their handbags. "See for yourself," he said.

Skeptical, I took the mirror. Sure enough, I saw no evidence of a gunshot wound—no scar, no mark of any kind.

Bewildered, I said, "I don't understand. He shot me at point-blank range. It knocked me back into the shelves. I was in a coma and intensive care for weeks. The bullet caused locked-in syndrome." I lowered the mirror and stared at Forsythe.

"I'm going to ask you a series of simple questions," he said.

"All right."

"What's your name?"

"Matt Kenney."

"How old are you?"

"Twenty-eight."

"What is your occupation?"

"I was a grad student."

"Where?"

"Boston College."

"Where are you now?"

"A hospital," I said.

"Which hospital?"

"Slater State Rehab."

"And why are you here, Matt?"

"I'm recovering from a gunshot wound to the head. Or at least I thought I was."

"How long have you been here?"

I thought for a moment. "I don't know. Since March, I guess."

Forsythe, nodding, drew his gaze across the room, shifted on his stool, and looked straight at me.

"Matt. You were never shot. You're not twenty-eight. You're forty-seven. You're not at Slater Rehab. You're at Slater State Psychiatric Hospital. You've been a patient here for nineteen years, eighteen of which you've been in and out of a catatonic stupor. For eighteen years, you've lived in a delusional world that doesn't exist. Matt, you're a refractory schizophrenic, the most severe case I've seen."

Reading my blank expression, he nodded, adding, "I'm your psychiatrist."

16

My breathing stopped. Eric Forsythe's words flooded my head with a million thoughts; the first, a question of whether this was all some mammoth hallucination, another figment of a severely injured mind. If so, this one played like real life, but so did the last six months. When I tried to think back beyond six months, something existed, but most of that memory was murky and scattered. However, that was before the injury, if there ever was one. With the lines between real and imaginary growing more vague, I wondered if I could accurately differentiate between the two.

"I'm unsure what's real and what isn't," I said.

Dr. Forsythe crossed his arms. "I'm here to help you with that. I won't pretend this is going to be easy. Quite frankly, I'm sailing uncharted waters here. Your case has baffled and frustrated better clinicians than me. Until now, no form of therapy has proved viable for you, and believe me, we've tried some pretty unorthodox procedures."

"So what happened to me? I feel totally lucid, except that I feel I've been dropped into the middle of some foreign world."

Forsythe rose to his feet and took the pocket mirror from my hand. "We'll talk more later, Matt. I don't want to overload you at this point. As time goes by, you'll begin to remember bits and pieces."

"Even though I was in a trance?"

"A stupor," he corrected. "And yes, certain things have subliminally made their way into your subconscious."

"Really?"

"You'll see." He tapped my knee with the file folder. "We'll talk later," he said again, and made his exit from the room.

For a long time, I sat staring out the window in a state of amazed disbelief, trying to comprehend the revelations Forsythe had just laid out. I was a forty-seven-year-old schizophrenic, with no recollection of nearly half my life. *One night at age twenty-eight, I went to sleep, and woke up at age forty-seven.* The thought twisted my gut, but I had to consider the bright side. I guess Leo never existed. I was never shot, never paralyzed, never a locked-in syndrome patient—if such a condition even existed. I could feel, talk and walk. With the exception of some moderate physical weakness, I felt good. I felt normal—no voices, no visions. *Had I come out of the stupor, as Forsythe called it, for good? Was I cured?* My head swam with a million questions.

Sometime later, I heard a familiar sound, the clatter of the food cart working its way through the ward. My stomach had finally come alive. I was starved.

The smell of food was exquisite.

A tiny aide with bottled-blonde hair carted in my meal: a plastic tray with a carton of milk, coffee, red jello, and a brown plastic cover over the main dish. She placed it on a table that swung over the bed. The name "Amy" was embroidered on her uniform.

"Macaroni and cheese," she said, placing the meal on the Formica tabletop. "Don't touch it until the nurse comes in," she warned, waving a finger. "They want to observe you." With the admonition delivered, Amy scampered from the room on miniature legs, shoving her cart on to the next patient.

I felt like a cheating grade-schooler when I raised the plastic cover a tad and peeked underneath. A whiff of steam escaped, carrying the aroma of baked cheese. I closed my eyes and inhaled the essence of my first conscious meal in a long time.

"You're supposed to wait for me."

I glanced up to see yet another unfamiliar face marching into the room—a tall, wiry female with frizzy red hair and wide-set eyes.

"I was waiting," I said innocently.

"Yeah, I bet." She pulled the dish cover off and placed it on the table. "Yum. Mac-and-cheese. My kids could eat this stuff breakfast, lunch, and dinner. How about you?"

"I'm not so sure about breakfast."

"Well, we won't make you eat it for breakfast, then." She pulled up the same stool Forsythe had used earlier. "I'm Debbie, one of your nurses," she said. "I just want to watch you eat. We've been feeding you ourselves for quite a while, Matt. Just want to make sure you don't choke, poke your eye out with the fork or anything stupid like that."

She made it sound like a joke, but I knew she was serious. I hadn't fed myself in years, but to me, it felt instead like a few months. I didn't worry too much about poking my eye out, but I was ready to inhale the dish, if necessary.

I managed to devour the meal without incident. Debbie watched carefully, ordering an occasional "slow down" and "take your time."

We chatted during the meal. I asked her a couple of questions about my condition, but she refused to answer, saying Dr. Forsythe would cover everything with me in due time. When I asked about her kids, she opened up.

Jessica and Megan were the twins, ten-years-old and going on sixteen. They wanted their beautiful, light-brown hair dyed blonde, rose tattoos on the smalls of their backs, and nose rings. She said they watched too much MTV and VH1, and claimed the non-stop hip-hop blaring in their room unnerved her. I nodded, with no idea of what any of it meant.

Twelve-year-old Justin, on the other hand, had a completely different demeanor. "He's very laid back, like his father. Sometimes you have to place a bomb under his butt to get him moving. But don't get me wrong. He's a great kid, and once he gets his paw into something, there's no limit what he'll achieve. Right now it's radio-controlled racing cars. Did you know those things go as fast as a real car?" Debbie shook her head in mock disgust, the way all proud mothers do.

After dinner, she took me for another walk. I did better this time, hoofing to the dayroom and back. During our stroll, I told her about Nancy, my imaginary nurse. She listened without comment, nodding and supporting me by the arm when she feared I might stumble. I saw a lot of Nancy in Debbie.

At ten the following morning, Liz walked me to the elevators. We rode the number two car to the fourth floor and marched the short distance to Dr. Forsythe's office. She knocked, and a voice, deadened by the solid wooden door, summoned us in.

Inside, Eric Forsythe sat at his desk with the phone pressed to his ear. He motioned me to a blue upholstered chair across from his desk and returned his attention to the telephone conversation.

"He'll be with you in a moment," Liz whispered. "I'll see you later." She stepped from the room and pulled the door shut.

I quietly eased my way to the chair and sank into its soft cushions. Forsythe flashed me a quick smile. Consumed by his call, he doodled on a note pad, drawing small concentric circles and scribbling in the spaces while he spoke of a presentation he was scheduled to give.

The small office was unkempt. The beat-up cherry-wood desk was heaped with papers, charts, journals, Styrofoam coffee cups, and notebooks. A thin layer of dust covered everything. The rug was worn and filthy, and the window looked as if it hadn't been washed in a decade. A maple bookcase overflowed with even more journals. Textbooks of all sizes were stuffed into its four sagging shelves.

Above the bookcase hung Forsythe's academic achievements: An undergraduate degree from Harvard, a medical degree from Dartmouth, a psychiatric residency at Bellevue, and certifications in internal and psychiatric medicine. There were other framed awards and accolades, and a few pictures of Forsythe shaking hands with people I didn't recognize. No doubt they were other bigwigs from Shrinkworld.

When Forsythe finally ended his phone call, he apologized for the delay, then opened a thick chart set in front of him and started fingering through it.

"That my chart?" I asked.

"One of them," he said without looking up.

One of them? "How many are there?"

He didn't answer. When he found what he was looking for, he removed it and closed the chart.

"How do you feel today, Matt?"

"Like Rip Van Winkle."

Forsythe smiled and leaned back in his chair. He studied me with a look of smug satisfaction.

"I heard your voice when I was, you know . . . when I was in my delusional world," I said.

He tilted his head. It appeared more a gesture of affirmation then surprise.

"I remember you asking if I could hear you. Sometimes your voice came from the mouths of other people."

"You did hear me," he said. "I *was* speaking to you. You began responding to my voice when you started coming out of it."

"Coming out of it? The stupor?"

Forsythe lifted one of the covered Styrofoam cups, folded back the cover tab, and took a sip.

"Six months ago," he said, "I submitted an application to enroll you in the first-phase clinical study of an experimental antipsychotic drug. Atrazipine, or AU-811 was presented at a conference I attended in New York City last fall. The drug is an analogue of Clozapine, an agent that didn't work for you, but one that's served to clear psychiatric facilities across the country of hundreds of once hopelessly institutionalized schizophrenics. Clozapine and another drug, manrazipine, remain the gold standards in the treatment of schizophrenia. Although AU-811 is a close cousin to both drugs, it appears to work completely differently. AU-811 is extremely difficult and expensive to produce. Consequently, Portland Pharmaceuticals, the drug's manufacturer, offered just forty slots in its phase-one trials."

Forsythe took another sip of coffee. "I'm sorry, Matt. You want a coffee or something?"

"I'm fine."

He waved the paper he had fished from my chart. "In February, our application was the thirty-eighth approved."

"Looks like we just made it."

Forsythe snorted a chuckle. "Yeah. Lucky."

He placed the paper face down on the chart and folded his hands.

"Four weeks ago, forty catatonic, schizophrenic patients in facilities across six countries started receiving intravenous AU-811. You're one of thirteen in the U.S., and the only one in the state. All patients were started on four milligrams every other day. A week later, the dose was upped to six milligrams. Unfortunately, because of AU-811's narrow therapeutic margin, eleven patients had to be dropped from the study in the first ten days."

"*Therapeutic margin?*" I said.

"The therapeutic margin is the difference between a dose that delivers a therapeutic benefit and one that's toxic to the patient. All the patients pulled out of the study—twenty-six so far— showed signs of renal insufficiency."

"What's that?"

"Kidney damage. AU-811's major side effect is renal damage."

"What about my kidneys?"

"So far, your renal function's fine," he said. "All your lab test results are normal. You remain one of nine patients in the U.S. still enrolled in the study."

I nodded with a degree of apprehension.

"For week three, the protocol called for another dose adjustment. Everyone was upped to eight milligrams, and twenty-one hours later, a patient in Baltimore came out of an eighteen-month stupor. Within a week, twelve more patients in the study came out. You were number fourteen, Matt."

I was sitting up, leaning in the direction of Forsythe's words, afraid I might miss something. I fell back into the chair, sinking into its marshmallow-like firmness. A myriad of questions streamed through my head, but all I managed to muster was, "The miracle of modern medicine."

"The psychiatric community is buzzing at the prospects of this agent. All results thus far are still very preliminary, of course, but we're optimistic; this could be one of the greatest breakthroughs in psychotropic medicine ever." Forsythe sounded elated.

I began sorting through my questions. "Is the result permanent?"

"These are the first human studies involving the drug, Matt, so, frankly, we don't know. It's learn-as-you-go, but I have to tell you, the most stunning result thus far is the degree of lucidity patients exhibit once they're out. It's as if"—he knocked on his desk—"their disease has been totally eradicated. Look at you."

"A cure?" I said.

Forsythe hiked his eyebrows as if to say, "Perhaps."

"What about the side effects?" *As if I gave a damn, considering the alternative.*

"We'll take blood three times a week and monitor your renal function. I think you'll do fine. We've lost no one in the last six days. No one who's made it to eight milligrams has had to drop out."

Forsythe slid my chart aside and wiped some speck from his desk. "Now let me ask *you* something. What do you remember prior to the time you thought you had been shot?"

I tried to concentrate. "There are memories, but I'm not sure if they're real. Big chunks of my life seem to be missing."

Forsythe leaned forward, placing his arms on the desk. "How about high school? Can you remember anything about high school?"

I tried concentrating, harder this time. A kaleidoscope of images flashed by, but none stirred a memory of high school.

"There's stuff there, but I'm just not sure."

He closed his eyes and nodded. "Tell you what we're going to do," he said, pushing back in his chair. "Every morning at ten, you and I are going to meet right here and talk for an hour. Call it a debriefing if you like—a debriefing back into a normal life. We'll both get to know a lot more about you."

"Sounds like a plan." I gave Forsythe a nervous smile. I guess he didn't want to hit me with everything at once, and that sat fine with me.

17

As Forsythe walked me back to my room, he spoke with surprising candor of Slater's dreadful condition and the tight purse strings he and his colleagues were forced to operate under. With the exception of a current facelift on the fifth floor of Building One, little money had been freed up for improvements of the hospital infrastructure in the last twenty-five years.

Forsythe took it as an affront that the public had forever considered the nation's mental health woes as a subject to be swept under the rug, though almost every family in America was touched at one time or another with a mental health crisis.

The politicians were no different, he said. They'd rather see their names attached to more popular health legislation, like AIDS prevention and prenatal care. Those were terms—with no lack of fanfare—that resonated with their constituencies, they thought. Those were the programs targeted for priority funding. Unfortunately, he said, State spending for the mentally ill had not improved much since the snake pit days.

By the time I reached my room, I was tired. My thighs burned. Although I'd received physical therapy throughout my catatonic period, my legs remained weak. When Forsythe saw my level of consciousness improving two weeks before I came out, he ordered a more aggressive PT routine that included walking me short distances in my room. Still, my legs suffered from years of under-use. He later explained the newer PT regimen most likely caused my sensations of dizziness, motion, and nausea I experienced during my stupor.

While in bed resting, staring mindlessly at the ceiling, my thoughts slipped back to the spider episode. I wondered if I ever did have a childhood friend named Barry Parsons with a spider jar. I was still freaked out by spiders.

I wondered about my family—my real one. *Was it the same family I knew in my delusional world? Had my mother visited every Sunday?* There was so much I didn't know. The thought of being suddenly dropped into this existence overwhelmed me. Worse than that, it scared the living crap out of me.

After resting for about ten minutes, I got out of bed and walked to the room's small bathroom to take a leak. I found the light switch, flicked it on, and suddenly stood face-to-face, with an image in the mirror. A stranger looked back at me.

When I had peered into the small pocket mirror a few days before, I was more concerned with finding a bullet wound than taking a good look at my face. *How long had it been since I viewed a mirror image of myself?* To be honest, I held no mental impression of my appearance. But the person I saw in the mirror was older looking than I expected, with well-worn creases in the forehead, baggy circles under deep-set brown eyes, thin lips, and a long chin. My hair showed more gray than its original brown, and my well-trimmed beard was mostly white. All that aside, I wasn't an unattractive person. My teeth were straight and white and my smile was pleasant.

"Everything all right, Matt?" Liz's voice slipped in through the half-closed door.

"Yeah, fine."

"How'd it go with Dr. Forsythe?"

"Good. We're going to meet every day."

"You're very fortunate. He's excellent—an absolutely brilliant man," she said. "Carlos left your lunch on the table."

"You want to watch me eat again?" I asked, still gawking at the mirror.

"Promise not to poke your eye out?"

"Promise."

"Good, because I've got better things to do. I'll be at the nurses' station if you need me."

"Thanks," I said and pulled the door shut.

After lunch, I walked to the dayroom and watched a rerun of the previous night's Red Sox game on a local sports network. As the game progressed, I noticed something peculiar. Many of the player's names were familiar, though most were toddlers when I fell off the face of the real world nearly twenty years ago. Forsythe was right. I was recognizing some of my surroundings. I must have been planted in front of the television during Red Sox games and somehow absorbed the information.

I gazed around the room and found the card table pushed off to one side. I got up and walked to the window—the same window through which I'd watched a snowstorm a few months earlier. *Or had I? Was there a storm? Did a nut-case patient push me into the courtyard and leave me in a raging blizzard? How much of my memory was real and how much a part of my made-up world?* I was curious to find out. Suddenly, I couldn't wait until ten the next morning.

At the bottom of the third inning, Liz came in, wheeling a stainless steel IV pole.

"I've got something for you." She held up a brown IV bag and tubing.

"The AU-811," I said.

Liz nodded. "Your miracle drug."

The next morning at five minutes of ten, I knocked on Forsythe's door. He was hunched in front of his computer screen, tapping away at the keyboard, a pair of Styrofoam coffee cups within easy reach.

"Good morning, Matt," he said sprightly.

"Morning."

He flicked back the sleeve of his shirt and glanced at his watch. "Ten all ready?"

"I'm a few minutes early."

He returned his attention to the monitor. "I'm going over another research protocol here. I'll only be a minute."

"Take your time," I said.

Forsythe worked quietly, pausing to jot an occasional note on a yellow legal pad set to one side of his keyboard. Over half-framed reading glasses, he studied the monitor screen, pecking at the same key with his right index finger.

On the corner of the desk, I noticed a framed photo of an attractive blonde woman in her early thirties, sitting between two little girls, each with light golden hair and wearing a white dress. With radiant smiles, the three shared a red Victorian-era sofa beneath what looked to be a large coat of arms.

"What're your girls' names?" I asked.

Forsythe looked up.

I gestured with a tilt of the head toward the photo. "They're beautiful."

The corner of his mouth curled up slightly. "Christy and Jenny," he said. "And my wife, Jill."

I smiled approvingly.

A minute later, Forsythe pushed aside the keyboard, opened the top desk drawer, pulled out a small stick of gum, removed the wrapper, and popped the gum into his mouth.

"Nicorette," he said, chewing. "I quit smoking almost a year ago; now I'm addicted to the gum. I don't know which is worse."

I hesitated a moment. "Dr. Forsythe?"

"Eric."

I nodded. "Eric. What about my family—my mother and father?"

He stopped chewing. "What do you remember about them?"

"My father died of a heart attack playing basketball when I was ten."

"Tell me about him?"

"He was a great dad. We did things together."

"Like what?"

"I don't know. We played catch in the backyard, shot hoops, went to Sox games—stuff like that."

"How did he and your mom get along?"

I shrugged. "Fine."

"What was your dad's name?"

"It was . . ." My mind blanked. I couldn't remember Dad's name. It was on the tip of my tongue, but it just wouldn't come. I stared blankly at Forsythe. His eyes widened further. "It's . . ."

"How about your mom? Tell me about her."

"She's your typical, doting mother. She visits me here on Sundays." I hesitated. "Doesn't she?"

"How old is she?"

"Sixty-eight, I think."

"When was she here last?"

I tried to think. It should have been last Sunday, but did she show? My thoughts were jumbled. "I'm not sure. A week ago?" A feeling of dread overtook me. I shot an anxious look across the desk. "Is my mother okay?"

An awkward silence filled the office. I saw Forsythe steal a quick glace at his family photo and squirm, adjusting himself in his chair.

"Your mom is deceased, Matt."

My building dread erupted into a wave of desperate grief. My mouth went slack with a dry, sour taste. "When?" I managed to mutter.

"Thirty-six years ago."

I felt like someone had hit me on the side of the head with an iron pipe. My tongue tried to form the first syllable of the words "thirty-six." I was dumbstruck. *Thirty-six years.* My mother died a young woman. She never lived to become the loving, elderly mother who read the paper to me on Sundays. It had all been in my sick mind.

"How?" I said.

Forsythe bit at his bottom lip, glanced away for a second, and then clamped onto me with a strong, fixed gaze.

"Your father," he said. "Your father killed her—beat her to death."

Every drop of blood drained from my face. My gut wrenched and my bowels twisted. This was all too familiar. Stunned, I snorted, "What?"

"You father killed her, Matt. Your father—Leo Tracy."

18

As the office walls collapsed around me, I writhed in shocked disbelief. Shaken and unsteady, I pushed myself straight in the chair. Flashes of the Leo Tracy from my imaginary world played and replayed in my head, the derelict in the filthy, oversized parka. My mind raced through a string of possibilities, but nothing added up. *Had my thoughts distorted the truth to such a degree?*

"Leo Tracy?" I said, struggling with the words. "My father is . . . Leo Tracy?"

Forsythe responded with a single, closed-eye nod.

"I don't understand. My name's Kenney, Matt Kenney."

"I'm afraid not. You're Matthew Tracy, born the third of February, 1959, in Brookline, Massachusetts, to Leo and Karen Tracy. You're Matt Kenney only in your delusional world."

I sat there, my head throbbing, unable to respond.

"Look," Forsythe said. "I understand how hard this is. These revelations are going to keep coming. Some, like this one, are going to floor you. There's an entire lifetime out there that belongs to you—good stuff and bad. Much of it will come to you on its own. The rest I'm going to have to help you with. We still don't know what effect, if any, AU-811 has on repressed memory." Forsythe drew a deep breath. "Maybe we should stop for today."

"No," I barked, and then immediately calmed myself. "It's only been ten minutes."

He nodded. "We can keep going."

I tried to wet my lips. "What happened to my father?"

"He was convicted of first degree manslaughter—spent twelve years in prison. He moved to Cleveland and remarried. He died of liver disease eight years ago."

I thought of the perfect father my mind had created—the one who got Yaz to autograph my birthday ball. Though he never existed, he was the dad I missed. I felt no sense of loss for my real father, the one I couldn't remember—the one who'd killed my mother.

"I don't recall siblings. Are there any?"

"You're an only child."

At that point, I began to weld with anger. Suddenly, I wasn't sure I liked what was unfolding before me—my real life in the real world. I was alone, my mother dead, my father a murderer. Christ, even my name was different. I wanted to run away from it all. Get up and escape the office, and run until I collapsed from exhaustion. I didn't want to hear the truth—not *this* truth. I shot to my feet, seething. Forsythe recoiled in surprise.

"Matt," he said calmly, "sit down."

I glowered at him as if it was all his doing.

"Sit," he said again, his voice more stern.

I lowered myself back into the chair.

"What if I don't want to be here?" I said. "What if I just grab a jacket and walk away?"

"You can't do that."

"Why not? Look at me. I'm as normal as you or anyone out there," I said gesturing at the window. "Why do I need to be here?"

Forsythe stared at me, his eyes harsh. After what felt like an eternity, he said, "You know why."

"No I don't," I snapped.

"You're a legally committed ward of the state." His voice now carried a tone of annoyance. "By law, for your safety and the public's welfare, you cannot leave until you're medically discharged."

"When will that be?"

"I don't know. Maybe never."

I took a calming breath and eased back into the chair's softness. Forsythe folded his arms and pushed back into his seat. A heavy stillness filled the room, each of us waiting for the other to speak. Finally, I swallowed hard and said, "I'm sorry. You're right. I know I can't leave. Where the hell would I go? You're the only person I know—you and Liz and Debbie."

Forsythe smiled sympathetically. "You have a few more acquaintances than that. Remember, you've been here a while. In fact, you've become the buzz of the campus. News about you has spread fast."

I issued a humorless chuckle. "You mean I'm now a celebrity?"

"Becoming one."

"Humph. Imagine that."

Forsythe flipped open my chart and dug through it for a few seconds. He pulled out what appeared to be some printed notes. "You want to talk about Leo Tracy—the person you say shot you?"

"Yeah," I muttered. "I do."

In a numb trance, I walked myself back to the ward and stopped at the nurses' station. Dr. Moss, Liz, and a nurse I hadn't met sat behind the three-sided counter.

"I'm back," I said, placing my arms on the station's half wall to support my weakening legs.

Liz and the other nurse looked up and smiled. Moss's eyes never left the computer screen she was planted in front of.

"Hi, Matt," Liz said. "No worse for the wear?"

I shrugged.

The other nurse stood and offered her hand. "Hi, Matt. I'm Miranda Collins."

I shook her hand. "Hi."

"Miranda has been taking care of you for some time now," Liz offered. "Mostly evenings."

Miranda looked hopefully at me as I studied her face, looking for features I'd given the fictional characters in my little world of delusion. Finding none, I said, "I'm going to lie down a bit before lunch." I spun around and walked to my room.

I collapsed on the bed, landing on my stomach, burying my face in the pillow. Wanting to block out everything from the room, I wrapped a second pillow around the back of my head, covering my ears. I ran through my session with Forsythe again. He suspected I was dealing with a form of repressed memory I had unwittingly altered, inventing the Leo of my delusional world in an effort to protect my mother from my abusive father.

I had learned the real Leo Tracy was a nasty drunk who drifted from job to job, girlfriend to girlfriend, and regularly beat my mother. It sounded too familiar.

After Mom's death, the state Department of Social Services placed me in a series of foster homes. Forsythe expected I had been the victim of abuse in at least some of them.

According to Forsythe, schizophrenia tended to run in families, often showing up during the victim's twenties, as had mine. However, he knew of no history of the disease in my family. He said the abuse of my early years, coupled with witnessing the brutal death of my mother, might have triggered my illness.

As the minutes passed, the account of my real mother and father began to sicken me. I heard the food cart rattle in the distance, but had no appetite. I lay numb with grief; a black shroud of depression slowly encased me, and I began to weep.

19

Early the next morning, I received a complete physical exam from a young internist named Nathan Cross.

Dr. Cross never asked about or even mentioned my schizophrenia. His sole concern was my physical health.

Short with an athletic build, Cross was an affable, talkative fellow. Come to find out, he had a serious penchant for sailboat racing.

"You race sailboats?" I asked, wondering just how fast a sailboat moved.

"Anything from twenty-seven foot Solings to forty-six foot J-Boats."

I had never considered sailboats racing machines, but as graceful objects that dotted the horizon on warm summer afternoons, drifting lithely wherever the breeze beckoned. But not Cross. He said his club raced them hard year round.

"Even in the winter?" I asked.

"The Frostbite Tournament," he called it. "As long as the harbor is free of ice and the wind is below thirty-five knots, we're out there."

This sounded more like punishment than a pastime. "You guys must be a hearty cut," I said. The very thought of an icy mist breaking over the bow in late January made the stethoscope he slid across my back feel twenty degrees cooler.

"It's not as bad as it sounds—as long as you dress for it and stay out of the water."

"You've wound up in the water?"

"A couple of times."

"That's got to hurt," I said.

Cross chuckled. "Definitely tends to wake you up."

"I don't know, Dr. Cross," I said after a moment, shaking my head.

Cross leaned back and gave me a goofy look. "Think I should see one of the shrinks on my way out?"

I liked Cross. He spent another ten minutes just gabbing—more about boats and a little about Slater State. Elevating my mood, he made me feel more like an acquaintance than a patient. I was still laughing at his final story when he left the room.

After a late breakfast of waffles (by request), I showered and got ready for my ten o'clock session with Forsythe. While changing into street clothes the state had so generously provided, I wondered what exposé Eric had racked up for me this time. I was still reeling from the day before.

I took my time treading a path to his office. In the elevator, I let the doors slide shut and waited a good minute before punching the button for the fourth floor. I didn't know if I wanted to do this today.

On the quick ride up, I thought it ironic I held more fear for the real world than for my delusional one. It was hard to explain the feeling—more like an anxious trepidation than an outright terror. I guess it was sort of what a prison lifer must go through when he's finally paroled. That was me—paroled after a nearly two-decade sentence.

Forsythe's door was open. He sat at his desk, chewing Nicorette and cradling the phone with his shoulder while he shuffled through a stack of papers. A large cup of coffee from some place called Starbucks sat front-and-center on his cluttered desk. Caffeine and nicotine—the good doctor, brilliant and urbane, had his vices.

I entered the office and collapsed into the chair.

"Matt," he said hanging up the phone, "Good morning."

I responded with a quick nod.

"That was a colleague of mine, Dr. Mark Bingly, at Fairmont Hospital in Philadelphia. His AU-811 patient, an artist who spent thirty months in a stupor," he said, the excitement building in his voice, "is painting again."

"That's great."

"It's remarkable. I'm telling you, Matt, there's nothing but good news coming in from the field. This drug is going to change the mental health world."

Forsythe took a hit of his coffee, smacked his lips, and, coming down a peg, said, "So, how you feeling today?"

"I feel okay."

He spent a few moments lifting papers and charts, apparently looking for something. "I mean, emotionally," he said.

I shrugged.

He gave up his search and sucked in a long breath. "I know this isn't easy, Matt. I know you're struggling with what I dropped in your lap yesterday, but I believe the best way to deal with these truths is to face them head on. I considered withholding the facts about your parents for a while, at least until you were more used to dealing with the adjustments you're being forced to make, but when I learned of the Leo Tracy of your delusional world, I felt it best to tell you right off."

"It did suck the wind out of me."

"I'm sure it did. But you've heard the worst of it now."

"No more blockbusters?" I said.

"None that I'm aware of."

A sense of relief flowed through me. I'd come prepared for another shocker, and was comforted by the news there'd be none—at least not today.

Forsythe took another swig of his expensive Joe and flipped open my chart. Without looking up, he shot off a series of questions. "In the last twenty-four hours, have you heard any voices you can't explain?"

"No," I answered.

"Had any visions, hallucinations?"

"None."

"Any irrational fears, phobias?"

"No."

"Have you had the feeling someone may be after you, watching you, out to get you?"

I smiled. "You mean paranoia? No."

"How about dreams. Anything strange, untoward?"

I shook my head. "No. Nothing."

Forsythe raised his chin. "Are you depressed?"

I hesitated. "A little."

He nodded. "Appetite?"

"Not that great," I said.

"I don't consider mild depression unusual. I'll prescribe something. We'll nip it in the bud."

He glanced back at the chart. "What's your outlook like?"

"What do you mean?"

"Are you optimistic, or do you have a sense of doom, waiting for the other shoe to fall?"

"I don't know. I guess I'd like to get out of here someday," I said, looking beyond him and through the window.

"And do what?"

The question staggered me. *What* would *I do if I got out of here?*

"Get on with life, I guess. Get a job, a place to live."

Forsythe folded his hands and smiled broadly. "You know, *that* is a distinct possibility."

I couldn't help but think things were moving a little too fast. Less than a week before, I was consumed with a life that didn't exist. But still, it had boundaries, limitations I knew and respected. As strange as it sounded, I was comfortable in that place. Although the thought of being forever paralyzed by a gunshot to the head still horrified me, I had accepted that life.

However, we were talking now about the real world, where all stops are pulled and limitations rolled way back. *What did this world now expect of me? What did I expect of myself? Could I possibly live on my own again—support myself, contribute something?* Everything had to slow down for a while; I needed time to think.

For the remainder of the session, Forsythe asked me about the people of my delusional world. I talked about Roger. I found myself smiling when I explained Roger's obsession with fishing. My eyes filled when I talked of how sick he got and of the hollow sense I felt on learning of his death. I told Eric I felt embarrassed and foolish for holding such strong emotions for a character who existed only in my mind.

I spoke of the anger I experienced when I discovered Tina pilfering Roger's pain medication, and how the rage enabled me to cry out for the first time. I talked of Nancy's kindness, told him of the fear I experienced when crazy Robbie wheeled me into the blizzard, and explained the boundless frustration I felt in realizing Monica would never divulge her knowledge of Leo.

"These people were all so real to me," I said. "They weren't like characters in a dream. They had personalities strengths and weaknesses, too. They felt pain . . . joy. If you told me they were in the next room, I'd believe you." I hesitated a few beats. "I actually miss them."

Forsythe listened without comment. He took an occasional note and studied me carefully, often biting on the inside of his cheek. If he had explanations or theories, he was keeping them to himself.

During a pause, he glanced at his watch, opened the top drawer of his desk, and plucked out another piece of Nicorette. "Why don't we stop here?" He unwrapped the gum and popped it in his mouth.

"Sure," I said, more than ready to quit. Bearing my make-believe soul was wearing.

Forsythe turned open an appointment calendar on the corner of his desk. "Tomorrow morning, I've scheduled you for some tests with Dr. Jordan from ten to noon. Peggy is one of our staff psychologists."

"What kind of tests?"

"It's a series of assessment tests—cognitive, motor skill, intellectual function . . . that sort of thing."

"No needles?" I asked, joking.

"Nah. Pretty painless stuff."

"What about tomorrow's session?"

"How 'bout tomorrow afternoon at two?"

"Okay," I said.

Eric flipped his calendar shut, and then flipped it back open. "Oh yeah." He pointed near the bottom of the page. "Tomorrow at five-thirty, I'm being interviewed by Dr. Rosenthal; she's the TV health reporter for Channel Three. She wants to talk about you."

"Me?"

"Yeah. You're big news now. The hospital's PR person shot out a press release about you yesterday. The suits think good press is good for the hospital—something positive they can bring up during annual budget requests."

I wasn't sure what to think. I saw headlines: "Freak awakens from two decades of sleep."

20

Peggy Jordan, an attractive brunette with a curvaceous figure and a splash of freckles across her high cheeks, was all business.

Dressed in a cranberry oxford blouse and form-fitting khaki slacks, she moved across the room with the fluid refinement of a ballet dancer, making her way to the other side of a large conference table.

Sitting opposite me, she smiled tersely, opened a black nylon attaché case, pulled out a clump of folders, and plopped them unceremoniously onto the table.

Dr. Jordan introduced herself and then, with all the finesse of a drill sergeant, launched into her ten-minute explanation of the testing process. The pretty psychologist lacked a matching disposition. I quickly realized this was going to be a long morning.

For the next two-and-a-half hours, I struggled through a series of written, verbal and dexterity tests. At times, Dr. Jordan grew annoyed with me, especially when, an hour into the session, I grew tired of her pissiness and began acting like a smart-ass.

I'm not sure which of us was more relieved when we finished, but Peggy wasted no time packing up, flashing me a phony smile, and bolting from the room.

"Thank you," I said as the door slammed. "Hope I passed."

After lunch, I killed an hour in the dayroom watching an old episode of *The Rockford Files* with two other patients, neither very garrulous. All patients, it seemed, were wary of one another, each considering the other a greater nutcase. I couldn't imagine becoming drinking buddies with too many residents here at Slater State, but hey, who was I to talk? I was the hospital's schizophrenic poster boy.

At five minutes of two, I got up and began moving in the direction of Forsythe's office. I now walked with little discomfort, my legs having regained most of their lost strength. On the way to the elevator, I passed through a section of hallway with large, floor-to-ceiling windows on both sides. The sun shone through brilliantly, warming the area with radiant heat. I paused and stared out onto the grounds.

It was a beautiful day. I was antsy for freedom, tired of being cooped up in the confines of an insipid, red brick prison. AU-811 was promising me a new lease on life. I promised myself I'd make up for half a lifetime wasted. All I needed was the chance.

Forsythe's door stood wide open, but the office was empty. The lights were on and the computer fan hummed away. With our appointment time approaching, he couldn't have gone too far, so I decided to take my seat and wait.

My eyes swept the now all too familiar room. The bookcase still overflowed with journals and books, and the desk remained heaped with papers and patient charts. One thick chart lay open, adjacent to a pile of others. I leaned forward to get a better look. It was one of my charts. Forsythe had apparently been going through it.

Without thinking, I rose from the chair, walked to the door, and snuck a look up and down the hall. Not a soul in sight. I gazed back at the desk. *Did I want to do this? Sneak a look at my chart—maybe discover something about myself, a secret Forsythe was keeping from me?* I thought about it for a long moment, finally reasoning I had the right to look at my own medical chart—the right to know everything.

Taking one more peek up and down the hallway, I hurried to Forsythe's side of the desk. A twinge of guilt tumbled through me. *Screw it. This is America. I have the right.* The chart was opened to the *Treatment Plan* section. Next to dates of our visits were Forsythe's scribbled notes, which I had trouble deciphering. His handwriting was doctor typical—unreadable. *He couldn't have gone to a Catholic school. Then again, maybe I hadn't either.*

I leaned forward and flipped through the chart, holding the original page with my index finger. After a few seconds, I found a section titled *History*. I quickly scanned the page. It was filled with medical mumbo-jumbo describing the history of my illness, but that wasn't what I wanted. I rapidly fingered through a half-dozen pages before I found it: "Family History."

It's not that I didn't believe Forsythe's story of my mother and father, I just had to see it for myself. If I saw it in black-and-white, I'd have to accept it. Otherwise, I held out hope the story wasn't true, perhaps instead, a psychobabble ruse to prepare me for a truth more benign. I know it sounded foolish, but it was all I had.

"If we expect to make progress, we're going to have to start trusting each other."

Forsythe's words startled me, forcing a surprised grunt from my throat as I reflexively pushed myself erect. He stood at the door frowning, a covered Styrofoam cup of cafeteria coffee in his right hand.

"I . . . my parents," I stuttered, flushed with embarrassment and regret. "I . . . I just wanted to see for myself. It's—it's hard to accept. I'm sorry." I started to move away from the desk.

"No," Forsythe said calmly, holding out the palm of his free hand. "Go ahead. Read it."

"What?"

He moved to the upholstered chair and dropped into it. "Have a seat. Read all you want." He removed the cup's plastic lid and took a noisy sip.

"Umm," I said, feeling foolish, "that's okay. I don't think I need to." I was nervously rubbing my thumbnails with the index finger of each hand. Forsythe snapped his head toward the chart, indicating for me to continue.

I settled slowly into the chair and slid the chart closer, reading. It was all there; Forsythe had left out nothing. The gnawing returned to my gut. When I finished, I pushed the chart away. Forsythe gave me a look, arching his brows.

"I'm sorry, Eric. I'll have to learn to accept it."

"It's okay, Matt. Given the chance, I'd have done the same thing."

"Honestly?"

"Honestly." He took another swig of coffee.

We started talking. I remained seated behind the desk and he in the chair. Within minutes, Forsythe's soothing discourse and amiable approach had dispelled any remaining sense of guilt.

He asked more questions about my fictitious world. He had an insatiable interest in my imagined day-to-day life. Come to find out, he was seeking similarities between what I perceived as real and reality itself. A lot in the two worlds overlapped.

Take Robbie, for example. He did exist, Eric told me. And he did push me out into that howling blizzard. Much of what I recalled as real from the incident had occurred. An orderly named Tyrell rescued me. Robbie, the paranoid schizophrenic who left me to perish, now resided in Building Two, which housed the more difficult patients in locked wards.

I also found out where my perception of locked-in syndrome—a term that, to the best of my knowledge, I had been unfamiliar with—came from. Up until six years ago, due to an austere healthcare budget, some state rehab patients *were* treated and cared for at Slater State. For almost a year of my stupor, I roomed with a patient suffering the malady. I had subconsciously absorbed facts of my roommate's symptoms and applied them to myself.

Near the end of the session, I told Forsythe about my pause in the glass hallway and my desire to walk around outside. He explained the rules of freedom at Slater. Here, independence was an earned privilege, not a right.

"The rules specify five different levels," he explained. "Level One is confinement to the ward, and Level Five allows a patient autonomous off-campus authority. Right now, you're a Level Two, which means you may move throughout the building independently."

"What level do I need to get outside?"

"Level Three."

"Who grants that?"

"I do."

I nodded and decided I wouldn't push, figuring he wanted a little more time with me before he'd consider cutting any strings.

Forsythe rose from the chair and dropped his empty cup into the wastebasket. I got up and moved out from behind the desk. It was just past three—session over.

"By the way, that reporter from channel three will be here later. Would you mind being present during our interview?"

"I guess not," I said, not terribly keen on the idea. I still had this "freak" thing in the back of my mind.

He could tell. "Are you sure?"

"Why not? Maybe I'll be on TV."

Forsythe shot back a quick grin. "Great. I'll meet you in the conference room at five-thirty."

"I'll see you then."

21

Rounding the corner, I eyed a flurry of activity in and around the conference room. A collection of curious staff mingled about in small groups, murmuring in quiet tones. Two technicians working with purpose ran thick, black cables from the conference room out to hallway outlets.

Outside the doorway, bathed in artificial light from camera lamps, stood Eric Forsythe, accompanied by two hospital officials—all dressed in dark gray suits. They were speaking to a tall, slim, olive-complected woman. Her wavy black hair came to rest atop the shoulders of a perfectly tailored blue jacket. Although her knee-length skirt was rather conservative, I guessed she was only around thirty.

Slowing my approach and uncertain where to go or what to do, I moved in their direction until I caught Forsythe's eye. He made a comment to the woman and waved me over. She spun around and smiled. Strikingly beautiful with large dark eyes, full lips, and perfect white teeth, she held out her hand.

"Dr. Rosenthal," Forsythe said, "I'd like you to meet Matt Tracy."

Rosenthal beamed. "Mr. Tracy, what a pleasure." She took my hand in a firm handshake.

"Call me Matt."

"Dana," she said, pumping my arm.

Forsythe introduced Martin Ewing, the hospital administrator, and his assistant, Lou Fisher. Both men nodded my way but never offered their hands, as if touching me would soil them or, even worse, inflict them with some hideous mental disease.

Rosenthal's producer, a stout, middle-aged gentleman with a cleanly shaven scalp and sparkling beads of forehead perspiration, ushered us all into the brightly lit room, directing Ewing, Fisher, and me to the conference table. He moved Eric and Dr. Rosenthal to the front of the room, positioning them in front of a wall with the backdrop of a large, framed panoramic photo of downtown Boston.

With the technicians conducting final sound and light checks, Rosenthal briefly reviewed the interview plan with Eric and her producer. I watched quietly from the conference table, separated by two seats from Ewing and Fisher.

We learned the interview would take about ten minutes but, when edited down, the entire piece would consume less than ninety seconds of air time when it appeared later that week. That included a shot of me walking through the hall, and perhaps another of me standing in front of the nurses' station, talking with Forsythe.

The producer handed Rosenthal a wireless microphone, checked once more with the two technicians, called for quiet and snapped two fingers in the direction of his health reporter.

By six-thirty, the ward had returned to a dull normality, and the television crew was in a van on their way back to the station.

Shortly after dinner, Liz came into my room, drew some blood, and hung a bag of AU-811. I asked her about my latest kidney function report, knowing that Forsythe would have informed me if the previous batch of blood work had proved ominous. She told me the test had come back normal and to stop worrying. I took her advice, settled into a chair, and clicked on the TV.

Later in the evening, Forsythe surprised me with a brief visit. He strolled in while I watched what had become the latest craze of prime-time television—a reality show.

"You're still here," I said.

"Just trying to get caught up. Had to write a couple of orders." He glanced up at the TV. "What are you watching?"

"A reality show. They've dropped two competing teams into the desert, each with a gallon of water, a knife, and a plastic tarp. What kind of people would want to do that?"

Forsythe shook his head and watched the screen for a while. "So what did you think?" he asked turning to me.

"You mean the interview?"

"Yeah. How do you think it went?"

"Good. You did all the work. I just walked down the hall."

"But you were the main attraction."

"Oh yeah? Then how come no one asked for my autograph?"

"Let's wait until the piece airs Thursday night."

"I'll have my pen ready."

Forsythe smiled briefly. "Well, at least Ewing was happy; he'll get his mug on TV. Doesn't hurt to stay in the boss's good graces."

He took another look at the reality show. The first team was already fighting over the water. "I've got to get home, Matt." He patted me on the shoulder. "See you in the morning."

"Goodnight," I said, and watched him leave.

In the morning, I wandered up to the fourth floor a half-hour early for my session. Exiting the elevator, I glanced down the poorly lit hallway of offices. The door to Forsythe's office was closed. A third of the way down was a small alcove that served as a waiting area. Three wooden, double-seat sofas with well-worn, orange cushions formed a "U" around a small table.

I strolled into the area and sat on what looked to be the least stained seat cushion, leaning forward to peruse the pile of magazines strewn across the table. None looked familiar. As I picked up a copy of *People* and began thumbing through it, it occurred to me that some of the names and faces were familiar. Like the Red Sox players I recognized, I had apparently registered these people into my catatonic memory at some time, perhaps while sitting in front of a television.

I skimmed through a story about a five-year-old in Texas who had spent fourteen hours trapped in an eighteen-inch well shaft. A photo showed a grateful young mother holding the rescued little boy, who appeared unfazed by his new celebrity.

On the corner of the table lay a paperback with the bottom third of the cover torn away. I reached over and picked it up. It was a well-worn copy of *The Catcher in the Rye*. I held the book in my lap and stared at it for a while. *I know this book.*

All of a sudden, the story of Holden Caulfield filled my mind. I remember we had to read the book for a high school English Literature class. Sister Jean Marie, my eleventh grade English teacher. *Yes, I remember it.* I recalled discussing characters from the book; it was all coming back. We spent two weeks reading and discussing the story, and another two days trying to determine if Holden ever achieved his goal of finding people who understood him, even after being placed into a psychiatric institution and then sent off to another school by his parents.

I couldn't believe how clear it all seemed; it was as if it had happened yesterday. In my mind's eye, I saw Sister Jean Marie pacing back and forth in front of the class, holding her copy high and saying, "There's a little of Holden Caulfield in each of us." I could see the classroom, and where I sat—third row, third seat. *Jesus, my memory was returning.*

I never heard him approach or knew how long he had been standing there, but when I looked up, Forsythe was poised in the hallway watching me, a cup of coffee in one hand, his tan, leather briefcase hanging from the other. I stood and held up the paperback.

"My memory. I think it's returning."

Forsythe tilted his head and arched his brows, clearly intrigued.

"*The Catcher in the Rye.* I read it in high school."

A grin cracked his face. "Why don't we go into the office and talk about it?"

I tucked the book into my back pocket and fell in behind Eric.

For the next two days, my mind flowed like a faucet. It was as if a huge valve somewhere deep in my brain had been cranked wide open, gushing forth an unimpeded steam of memories. I spent hours sitting in the dayroom, gazing into the courtyard, recounting my past. At times, the memories—the good with the bad—came faster than I could process them. Sometimes I'd recall an incident, but was unable to comprehend or place it. Even when I slept, my past emerged in dreams. I saw faces I recognized from childhood, school, and college.

There were many parallels of my real life and my made-up, schizophrenic life. Often the imaginary memories were distorted to be more palatable, like the one of my father, for example. I now remembered what a brutal bastard he actually was, but I had made him Leo's father in my fictitious world, and invented a perfect dad to take his place.

I no longer confused real memories with the phony ones. Memories from my real past were clear and succinct. Those from my delusional existence were different; they resided on the far side of a tunnel. That was the only way I could explain it to Forsythe, and as time passed, the tunnel grew longer and the opening smaller. The real world was chasing away the demons.

Every three days, Forsythe participated in a one-hour conference call with scientists at Portland Pharmaceuticals and the other investigators with AU-811 patients. "Patient memory blasts," as they called them, were being reported from all areas.

Word of the AU-811's unprecedented success in the first phase trials were leaked by Portland, and overnight the tiny pharmaceutical company's stock shot from less than eleven dollars a share to nearly twenty-one bucks. Stuart Moody, Portland's President and CEO, was suddenly the sweetheart of the business world, and inundated with calls from the likes of *Forbes*, *Businessweek*, *The Wall Street Journal*, and *CNBC*.

Thursday afternoon, I watched Moody being interviewed on one of CNBC's financial shows. Portland's sixty-three-year-old chairman oozed with enthusiasm as he spoke of Atrazipine's first-phase clinical trials. Moody hinted Portland Pharmaceuticals had other psychotropic agents in the research pipeline, and promised investors his company was fast becoming a frontrunner in the mental health drug arena. By market close, Portland stock had gone up another two bucks.

That evening, Debbie and Miranda were working the night shift and joined me in my room to watch Channel Three run its piece on Forsythe and me.

Dana Rosenthal sat in the studio. "There may possibly be a remarkable breakthrough in treating the devastating disease of schizophrenia," she began. "For years this disease has destroyed lives and families, but now, a small Seattle pharmaceutical company has launched worldwide clinical trials of a drug called Atrazipine, or AU-811, as it's known to its investigators. The drug has shown remarkable success in treating a rare form of schizophrenia in which patients lapse into a catatonic stupor, leaving them unresponsive to their surroundings, sometimes for years. Earlier this week, I visited Slater State Psychiatric Hospital, one of the state's largest mental health facilities, where Atrazipine is in the early stages of clinical trials."

The screen switched to a front view of Slater from the highway.

"Here, a patient we'll call Patrick, after receiving the investigational drug, emerged from a nearly two-decade catatonic stupor, one of the longest on record. At Slater, I spoke with Dr. Eric Forsythe, Patrick's psychiatrist and one of AU-811's principal investigators."

The shot showed Rosenthal and Forsythe in the conference room. The edited version included a few short questions and answers, and then a five second video of me walking the hall toward the camera.

"Today, thanks to the experimental drug, Patrick and nearly two dozen like him have their lives back."

The shot flashed back to Forsythe. "There is no reason to believe these patients can't eventually lead fully productive lives and again become contributing members of society."

The shot went back to Rosenthal in the studio. "Like most drugs used in the treatment of chronic illnesses, Atrazipine will have to be taken for life, or until a cure for schizophrenia is found." Dr. Rosenthal smiled in the direction of her female co-host. "Carol?"

Carol thanked Rosenthal and moved on to the market closings. Debbie and Miranda turned in my direction and applauded.

"Nice job, *Patrick*," Debbie said, giving a thumbs up.

I shook my head in mock, humble disgust. "Don't you two have something to do?"

They left, making silly comments about being star-struck. I grabbed the copy of *The Catcher in the Rye*, opened it to my dog-eared page, and started to read.

22

Neil Jones despised his first name.

A solid kid in his early twenties, with a head of thick, curly-black hair and a wide gap between his front teeth, Neil insisted on being called *Jonesy*.

I met Jonesy, a bipolar patient being treated for depression, in the dayroom on Saturday afternoon. He lay sprawled out on the sofa, wearing cargo shorts and an oversized Grateful Dead T-shirt, watching a golf tournament. I hated golf. I wanted to watch the Sox-Tigers game. I almost turned to go back to my room when he started talking. To my delight, Jonesy came across as relatively normal.

"You're the guy they had on television the other night."

Oh shit, I thought. *Here we go.* "You saw it?"

"All the staff's been talking about you. You and Dr. Forsythe have put Slater on the map."

A bit uneasy and embarrassed, I shrugged. "Our ninety seconds of fame."

Jonesy studied me for a while. "You like golf?"

"Hate it," I said.

"Me, too. Change it if you want."

"How about the Red Sox game?"

"Go for it," he said, sitting up. "Have a seat." He held out the TV remote.

I took the clicker, sat at the far end of the sofa and flicked through a dozen channels before finding the game. It was the bottom of the second inning and Detroit had a two run lead. We sat quiet for a few minutes before Jonesy spoke.

"So, what's it like?"

I turned and, though pretty sure I knew what was coming, gave him a puzzled look.

We locked eyes. "I know a little about your story."

"How would you know anything about me?" I asked.

"The staff talks. Most of the patients haven't got a clue what they're yapping about, or even give a fat rat's ass, but I listen. It interests me."

"Why would anything about me interest you?" I said defensively.

"Because my mother's schizophrenic and her mother was schizophrenic. I'm wondering if it's going to happen to me."

"Seems to be a lot of it going around."

He eyed me without expression for a moment. "Hey. It's a mental institution."

His words caught me off-guard and I started laughing. A second later, Jonesy broke into a rip-roaring belly laugh. He had a piercing pitch to his howl, and the sound made me laugh all the more. The harder I laughed, the shriller Jonesy's became. Before I knew it, both of us were doubled over on the sofa, hee-hawing to beat the band.

When it all finally trailed off to sporadic chortle, we both wiped the tears away with the backs of our hands.

"So, what?" I said, still convulsing slightly. "We the only two normal fruitcakes in here?"

That drove Jonesy into another howling fit. I couldn't help myself, and broke down again, snorting through my nose.

When at last we had nothing left, we collapsed in exhaustion on opposite ends of the sofa, exhaling long sighs.

"You're one funny son-of-a-bitch," Jonesy said through a half-giggle.

"*Me?* You're the funny bastard."

It took a full minute to catch my breath. When it was over, the whole event felt surprisingly refreshing, filling me with a sense of renewal. I hadn't laughed like that in twenty years.

By the time I returned my attention to the game, a grand slam had put Detroit on top by six runs, and the Red Sox were into their bullpen.

"Looks like our boys are in trouble," Jonesy noted.

"It would appear so."

We watched in agony while the Tigers piled on another four runs, making it an eight-run third inning for Detroit, with only one out. Boston was signaling for its third pitcher and, sensing all was lost, we flipped the channel back to golf.

Jonesy and I sat and talked for more than an hour. The more we talked, the more I liked him. He reminded me a bit of myself before I became ill. He was twenty-two and attended a small community college, where he studied computer technology. He'd been struggling with a bipolar disorder since he was fifteen. Medication kept the disease in check most of the time, but this was his third admission for depression. This stint was scheduled for three weeks. He was on day eight and claimed to be feeling fine.

He asked questions about me. Unfortunately, I had few answers, because I'd spent most of my illness in an impenetrable fantasy world.

Jonesy was a true veteran of Slater State Hospital. He knew the place inside and out, all its important policies and most of the staff. He promised to fill me in on the patients and staff members to steer clear of. Number one on the list was Ewing's assistant, Lou Fischer.

"He can get you tossed into a lock-ward in a New York heartbeat," he warned.

"Are you speaking through experience?" I asked.

"Not me. But I've seen it happen, even over a doctor's protests. Fisher claims it's his job to protect patients, staff and the public. He can overrule the docs. I heard he put a guy into Building Two for calling him a faggot."

"You kidding?"

"No. And I think he *is* a fag, to boot. I won't even make eye contact with him."

"Thanks for the warning," I said.

Jonesy had a Level Four pass, allowing him access to the public areas of all buildings and the hospital grounds, and could take off-campus trips under the supervision of staff or family. I explained that my pass restricted me to the building. Aside from my own ward and the path to Forsythe's office on the fourth floor, I told him, I'd not really seen the place.

"Do you know there's a recreation room on the second floor?" he said.

"There is?" I said, surprised. At first this struck me as odd; it sounded more like a college dorm than a hospital building. But then I realized entertainment was considered a form of therapy.

"A nice one. It's got a ping-pong table, regulation pool table, card tables, a couple of arcade games, and a big screen TV. There's also a small library and an Internet computer room on two."

"Internet computers?" I said, having heard the phrase but not understanding it.

"Oh, that's right. You slept through the computer age. I'll show you later. You're not going to believe it."

Once again, I was only vaguely familiar with something that had its inception, as Jonesy so aptly put it, while I slept. As before, I must have sponged in what little I knew about the subject from my daily environment while in fantasyland.

Jonesy offered a tour of the second floor. We walked back to the ward, checked in with Liz, and set off, hitting the stairwell and climbing two flights.

"So, how do you like Forsythe?" he asked.

"I like him. He's easy to talk to. Seems like a regular guy."

"He's my shrink, too."

"Really?" I said, surprised by the coincidence.

"Yeah. He's one of the good guys."

There were no wards on two. The second floor was reserved for administrative offices on the north end and the cafeteria, commissary, rec room, library, and computer room on the south end. A large lobby area furnished with a pair of leather sofas, four matching leather chairs, and some end tables separated the two areas.

Jonesy led me into the commissary and introduced me to Gina, the woman who ran the place. Gina, a middle-aged woman with a decent figure for her age, big hair, and a face that had caught too much sun in its earlier years, lit up when she realized who I was.

"My boyfriend and I watched you on TV the other night." She eyed me up and down. "You look completely . . ."

"Normal?"

"I'm sorry," she said, her face quickly reddening.

"It's okay," I said. "I'm still trying to get used to it myself."

She looked puzzled by the comment, but then changed her expression to a wide-eyed smile. "Let me show you around our little store." Gina dashed out from behind the register and began forging a path toward the back, pointing things out as she moved.

The small store was packed with merchandise—canned goods, bags of chips, pretzels, popcorn, and pork rinds filled shelves against a portion of one wall. The other part contained toiletries of every type. In the center area sat racks of clothing, underwear, jackets, hats, gloves, socks, shoes, and sneakers. There was a small area with stereos and TVs, another with a display of watches and other basic jewelry. Against the back wall stood two large, glass door refrigerators—one stocked with soda, juice, and water, the other with sandwiches, milk, yogurt, cheese, and other snacks.

Gina worked the nickel tour of her little empire back to the register. Jonesy thanked her, bought us both a Hershey bar, and led the way out.

Moving down the hall and past the cafeteria, my guide greeted several people—by name—passing in the opposite direction. Some returned the compliment while others, mostly patients by their looks, ignored him. Regardless, Neil Jones had the stuff to easily make friends. He was a breath of fresh air in an otherwise bleak environment, and I was glad to have met him.

We spent the afternoon shooting pool. He beat me in every game, but never gloated. Instead, he talked a little about himself and his schizophrenic mother. Jonesy was smart; he understood that schizophrenia followed family lines. As the broad reach of the disease registered with me, I feared for my new friend. He was too good a guy to be burdened with this monster of a disability.

23

Liz glided into my room just after breakfast, her face beet-red with sunburn.

"Looks like someone snatched a few rays over the weekend," I said.

She pursed her lips and shook her head in disgust. "I can't believe I did this. I only wanted fifteen or twenty minutes on the back deck, but I fell asleep in the chaise lounge for over an hour. I'm so *mad* at myself."

I gave her a concerned half-smile. "Hurt?"

Gritting her teeth she said, "My legs are killing me."

She wore green scrubs, but I pictured her legs matching the raw tone of her face, burning with each step she took. "Ouch," I muttered.

"Got that right."

Liz began clearing the bed table I had managed to clutter up with paper cups and Kleenex. "Dr. Forsythe telephoned a while ago. He rescheduled your ten o'clock appointment to two this afternoon."

"How come?"

She shrugged. "He didn't say."

"Thanks," I said when she cleared the last cup.

"Never mind thanks. Clean up after yourself." She shot me a chiding, motherly glare.

"Sorry."

"Yeah," she said. Hands laden with table trash, she spun and hurried from the room.

I reached over, grabbed *The Catcher in the Rye*, found my mark, and dove back in.

"Aren't you supposed to be with Forsythe on four?"

I glanced up and caught Jonesy peeking around the door's threshold. According to the hallway clock, an hour had flown by.

"Hey, Jonesy," I said. "Naw, he rescheduled for this afternoon. C'mon in."

Jonesy brought the rest of his frame around the threshold and into the room. "Whatcha reading?"

I held up the paperback with its torn cover. Approaching, he strained to see the title.

"Ah. Holden Caulfield."

"You know it."

"They wouldn't let me graduate until I did."

"Same here. Those nuns were ruthless," I said, saving my page and placing the book on the bed table. "So what's up?"

"I'm heading outside."

I glanced out the open window. Sheets of sunlight bounced from the mattress cover of the empty bed next to mine. Another perfect spring day. "Wish I could go with you."

"Listen, when you meet with Forsythe this afternoon, ask him to write orders for a Level Three. I bet he'll do it."

"You think so?"

"Look at you, man," he said, framing me with his hands. "You look like you should be in a shirt and tie commuting to the office in your BMW."

I chuckled. "I don't think you'd want to be on the road if I were driving. It's been a while."

"Hey, a year from now, Slater State will be nothing but a nasty memory, tucked away in the 'to be forgotten' file of your gray matter. You're as good as out of here."

I regarded Jonesy's words for a short while. *Did he really believe that?* I hadn't given much thought to the future; the past consumed all my time. I was too busy working my way to the present to concern myself with the future, but there it sat, as if saying, "what do you intend to do about me?" Like it or not, I had a future, and sooner or later, I'd have to deal with it.

"So, you gonna do it?"

"Huh?"

"The pass. Are you going to ask Forsythe?"

"Yeah. This afternoon," I said.

"Good. We'll get you outside and shoot some hoops. You play?"

A smile cracked my face as a memory of playing high school varsity came streaming back. "At one time."

Jonesy clapped his hands. "Excellent. You don't know what it's like trying to get some of our fellow residents to play a little one-on-one."

"I can imagine."

Jonesy spent a few more minutes planning our great outdoor adventure before making tracks for the cafeteria, where they sold gourmet coffee pumped from insulated Thermos bottles. He was headed for a cup of hazelnut vanilla.

At ten minutes of two, I set off for Forsythe's office. I took the elevator to the fourth floor, passing the small waiting area where I'd found *The Catcher in the Rye*. There, two middle-aged female patients occupied opposite sofas, each lost in an open magazine, waiting to be called for her appointment.

Glancing down the run of hallway, I noticed a flow of activity. A half-dozen bodies moved across the shinny floor tile, some scurrying about with a sense of urgency, others standing and chatting. Several office doors—including Eric Forsythe's—stood wide open. Monday was a busy office day for the headshrinkers.

"Good morning," I said at Forsythe's door.

Eric raised his head from an opened journal. "Matt. Come in. Have a seat. How was the weekend?" He closed the publication and pushed it aside.

I worked my way to the upholstered chair. "Pretty good," I said, falling into the plump cushions.

"Good. Why don't you tell me about it?"

"Okay," I said, and dove into the story of meeting Neil Jones and our time together. When I finished, Eric sat silent, fingering a pencil, his face expressionless.

"So, you like this Jonesy guy?" he asked finally. The tone of his voice suggested he was less than pleased I had befriended Neil.

"I enjoy his company." And then, knowing the answer, I asked, "Do you know him?"

"He's under my care."

I wasn't sure what that meant. "So, you're all right with this."

Forsythe snapped his head back and forth as if shaking off a bad thought. "No. Fine. I'm glad for you. Just don't let Mr. Jones go making decisions for you."

I smiled cautiously. "Don't worry."

Forsythe slid open the top drawer of his desk, picked out a piece of Nicorette, and unwrapped it. "Anything else?" He pushed the gum into his mouth.

"As a matter of fact, there is something."

Chewing earnestly, Eric hiked his brows.

I took a breath. "I want to go outside unattended. I'd like a Level Three pass."

Holding my breath, I watched for his reaction, but Forsythe had the uncanny ability to telegraph nothing. Instead, he chewed his gum intensely as he considered my request.

"I don't see why not." He leaned forward, opened my chart, and made a quick note.

Yes! I tingled with joy like a kid who had just gotten the BB gun he'd always wanted.

"Anything else?" he asked.

It took me a second to get it out. Shaking my head, I said, "I'm happy."

"Good," he said, and started looking through my chart. "I've got the results of the tests you took with Dr. Jordan last week. I'd like us to go over them."

He pulled out a wad of papers held together by a large paperclip, the first page a summary of Peggy Jordan's professional assessment. He took a minute to reread it, and then we discussed the findings.

The test results panned out fairly normal for a guy my age. I wasn't a rocket scientist, but I'd arranged the odd-shaped blocks Dr. Jordan had placed in front of me well within the allotted time. My IQ came in at 112. My intellectual function, cognitive abilities, and motor skills were all within normal limits. Pretty mundane results, considering the likely outcome of the same tests if administered a month earlier.

Forsythe was pleased. "Pretty average results for a normal forty-seven-year-old." He looked up from the reports and the corners of his mouth spread in a proud grin.

"You really feel that way? You know . . . that I'm normal?"

Forsythe seemed to measure his words before speaking. "I think we're getting there."

"But it's the drug," I said. "It's the AU-811. That's the normalcy factor. Without it, there's no normal. Right?"

He leaned back in his chair and folded his hands in his lap. His Nicorette chomping eased markedly.

"Right now, there are millions of people in this country leading normal lives because of drugs—AIDS patients on protease inhibitors, cardiac patients on anti-arrhythmics, cancer patients saved by chemotherapy. Without the drugs, their lives would be anything but normal. You're just one of those patients, Matt. One of millions."

Forsythe's lecture continued. He spoke of his once- clinically depressed patients now holding down skilled jobs as cops, schoolteachers, and engineers, all thanks to modern anti-depressants. I sat and listened, feeling a bit foolish I had dared whine about being tethered to a drug the rest of my life, especially when the drug's effects were as profound as AU-811's. *Consider the alternative and quit belly aching*, I told myself.

The subject changed. Forsythe began discussing some of the previous evening's conference call. As expected, the AU-811 investigators were flushed with excitement, exchanging anecdotal information of their particular patient's progress while symbolically patting each other on the back. The news was good. No new cases of renal insufficiency, and Portland Pharmaceuticals announced it was shipping an oral form of the drug to all sites. The capsule dose-form was slightly less expensive to produce than the IV. Soon, I'd be popping two capsules a day rather than getting an IV every other. Eric said we'd no longer have a need for the catheter in my arm. *Fine with me.*

When he flipped my chart shut—the signal my session was over—I stood to leave. Forsythe immediately held up his palm.

"One more thing."

I waited.

"Sit," he ordered.

I eased back into the chair and waited.

He scratched the corner of his eye and drew a long breath. Something was coming—something bad. He stared at me for what felt like minutes. My heart was off on a gallop.

"There's a reason I changed our session from this morning to this afternoon."

He removed the gum from his mouth, wrapped it in a scrap of paper, and dropped it into the wastebasket next to the desk. My palms began to sweat.

"Yesterday afternoon, I received a call from someone who saw the news piece on you last Thursday night. That person insisted on coming in and speaking with me." He shifted in his seat. "We met this morning at ten. And though I was restrained in what I could say about you, the news piece pretty much laid out your case. She would like to see you."

I felt my face twist in perplexed curiosity. "She?"

"It's Trisha," he said.

"Trisha?" My voice creaked two octaves higher.

Forsythe nodded. "She's sitting in the next office."

24

I shook my head in anxious bewilderment. *Trisha in the next room?* All thoughts instantly flashed back to my last memory of her: the tearful, "I've got to move on" visit in the hospital room of that other world. I recalled the emptiness that filled me when I watched her leave. *Did it really happen?* There was no tunnel in the memory, but I couldn't be sure. My lips parted, but offered only silence.

Forsythe sat statue still, eyeing my response. "What do you think? Would you like to see her, or should I ask her to leave?"

"Trisha," I managed to whisper before my mouth transformed into a face-splitting smile. "No," I barked. "I mean, yes." My voice softened. "*Yes*, I'd like to see her."

"Are you sure?" he asked. "It wasn't my intention to spring this on you. I could have her come back another time."

My eyes shifted to the photo of Forsythe's wife and daughters. "It's okay. I'd like to see her."

Eric got up and left the room. I sat in silence, trying to prepare myself. *What would I say? Who would speak first?* Numb with apprehension, I gazed down at my trembling hands and shoved them into my armpits. *Maybe I shouldn't do this today. Why not wait a couple of days, as Forsythe suggested? Give myself some time to prepare?*

Without warning, the door swung open. Forsythe entered the office, walked to his desk and sat. He nodded. "She's waiting." He opened the Nicorette drawer, fished around a moment, and closed it. He motioned with his head in the direction of the next office. "Go ahead."

I rose from the sanctuary of my chair, took a deep, calming breath, and said, "Wish me luck."

Forsythe went back to his keyboard without responding.

My chest felt like a clamp had been placed around it and tightened, one turn at a time. Each of my feet weighed fifty pounds. My heart hammered like a diesel engine, and my mouth turned arid as the Sahara. *Was she half as nervous?*

I managed to get out of Forsythe's office on rubber legs and shuffle the ten feet of hallway to the next door.

A small Formica sign said the office belonged to Dr. David Gold. I sucked in a shallow breath, tapped twice and pushed open the door.

She sat, with the composed posture of a magazine model, in the closer of two chairs facing Gold's desk. Turning her head, she struggled to her feet. I stepped in, closing the door behind me.

She smiled faintly. "Hello, Matt."

My God, Trisha had aged well. She was a year younger than me, making her forty-six, but she looked to be in her late thirties. Her red hair was now a deep auburn. Crow's feet had formed in the corners of her eyes and tiny, fledgling wrinkles encroached her upper lip. Regardless, she remained a gorgeous woman.

"Trisha," I managed to sputter.

"You look wonderful," she said.

"Thanks. I wasn't expecting a visitor." I mussed my hair with my fingers. "I would have cleaned up a little better." I laughed nervously.

Her smile broadened. "You look fine. Really."

An awkward moment passed and a weighted stillness filled the room until her soft voice broke the quiet.

"Why don't we sit for a minute?" she said, motioning to the other seat.

"Sure." Stepping behind her, I quickly surveyed my old lover. Her silk, floral print dress prominently displayed her womanly curves. If she'd gained a pound over the past twenty years, it failed to register.

I sat and tried to adjust myself comfortably, first crossing and then uncrossing my legs. I must have looked foolish.

She cleared her throat quietly. "Umm, I'm a bit nervous."

"Me too."

"So why are we so nervous?" A quiet chuckle.

I shrugged.

Trisha looked down at her feet. "I saw the piece about you on the news last week. It took the wind right out of me seeing you walking down that hall. I just . . ." She looked up. "I just had to see you."

"I'm glad you came."

"It's just that. I don't know. I walked out on you when you needed me most. It was selfish, and I've carried that guilt ever since." Her eyes were welling up. She looked at me and the corners of her mouth fell. "Matt. I'm so sorry."

"That was a long time ago." I touched her hand. "It's all right, Trish. You did nothing wrong. What could you have done for me? Please. Don't beat yourself up any more over this. Most of the time, I didn't even know if you were real or imagined."

She stared at me and shook her head, mascara-colored tears streaking her cheeks. I reached for a box of Kleenex on the desk, pulled out three tissues and handed them to her. She patted the tears.

"It must have been horrible having no one all that time."

"I lived in a delusional world, Trish. I had plenty of company there."

She looked at me. "Honestly?"

I snorted an awkward laugh thinking about Roger and Tina. "I'll tell you about them some time."

The tears ceased and her smile returned. "I had a talk with your doctor this morning."

"Eric."

"Yeah. What a nice man."

"He's pretty cool."

"He said the drug, AU-something—"

"811."

"Yes. It's unlike anything he's ever seen. He said it's transformed you pretty much back to the way you used to be."

"It's an experimental drug with no history, but . . . so far, so good. I'm sort of playing guinea pig."

"He told me about the results coming in from the other sites. It sounds fantastic, Matt."

"The shrinks are all giddy about it. They think it might put places like this out of business."

This time she patted my hand. "I'm so happy for you."

The room fell silent again, and we both studied our feet.

"Well, I had better go," she said, getting up and lifting her jacket from the back of the chair. "Dr Forsythe said I should only stay ten minutes."

I got up slowly. "He calls the shots." I shuffled my feet, finding it difficult to maintain eye contact. I forced myself. "Thanks for coming, Trish. It means a lot."

"I almost didn't do it. I'm glad I did."

"Me too." I bit my bottom lip.

"I'd better get going. Bye." She kissed me lightly on the cheek, turned, and hurried from the office.

"Trisha," I called after her.

She stopped and turned.

"Come back anytime. I don't get many visitors."

She smiled softly and disappeared into the hallway.

I eased back into the chair and stared off into space. A hint of her perfume lingered. I closed my eyes and inhaled deeply.

Trisha's words remained in my head. *Why had she come? Did she really want to see me, or was she merely trying to ease the guilt she'd been carrying all these years?* Not that it mattered; it was all ancient history from another lifetime. I'm sure she now had a full, active life outside these walls.

On the way out, I poked my nose in Forsythe's door. The office was empty, which surprised me. I thought he'd be anxious to analyze me, post-Trisha. I glanced up and down the hall. No sign of him.

"Humph," I uttered, and set off for the cafeteria. I needed a cup of coffee.

Jonesy stood at the serving line, holding two plates of chocolate cake with chocolate icing. He looked to be weighing each, bouncing one hand and then the other.

"Take them both," I said, sliding my tray up to his.

"Matt-man," he said, his eyes trained on the plates. "This one's bigger." With a smirk of smug satisfaction, he held up the dish in his left hand and placed it on the tray. Pushing everything to the coffee dispensers, he asked, "Did you get your pass?"

"I got my pass." I threw him a haughty grin and placed a plate of cake on my tray.

Jonesy lit up. "Way to go, Matt-man." He pumped his fist.

"He still has to write the order, though."

Jonesy cranked a cup of French roast from one of the Thermoses. "A mere technicality, my friend," he said, pointing a finger at me. "Better start honing those b-ball skills, old-timer."

"I'm afraid this sorry excuse for a body ain't quite ready for that. I'd be happy to make it one walking lap around the property, for starters."

"We'll get you into shape, Matty. Don't you go worrying about that."

I drew out a cup of Columbian from one of the metal Thermoses and trailed Jonesy to the cashier. We paid with chits, a ration of coupons resident-patients were given by the hospital to buy incidentals in the canteen and cafeteria. We found a table well away from a group of dependent patients ushered in from one of the wards and under the watchful eye of a lone nurse assistant.

We ate our cake in silence. Jonesy went at his with both hands, eating noisily, chocolate crumbs dropping to his tray. I preferred my fork.

While I chomped and sipped, I couldn't help but notice a table of patients belonging to the group we had distanced ourselves from—fellow comrades of the Slater loony bin.

They were three men, all rumpled in appearance. One guy looked to be somewhere in his sixties. He wore an old, knitted Buffalo Bills cap, and the front of his gray sweatshirt was soaked with drool. The other two were in their mid-forties, wearing printed t-shirts, baggy jeans, and untied sneakers. They sat there totally detached, their glazed stares focused to infinity, impassively moving their forks between plate and mouth. I wondered if any knew the others existed.

Jonesy caught me gazing and glanced over his shoulder. He swallowed his mouthful, licked his lips, and said, "Thorazine zombies."

I nodded and stuck my nose back in my tray.

When we finished, Jonesy wanted to go across the hall and shoot a little eight-ball in the rec room. Not in the mood, I tried to worm out of it, but he insisted on one quick game. Reluctantly, I acquiesced. We played three games. Mercifully, the young hustler allowed me to win once—barely.

The room grew increasingly noisy, filling with residents allowed a few hours of afternoon recreation. Jonesy didn't like crowds, so we gave up the table and headed back to the ward.

I couldn't get Trisha out of my mind. The picture of her sitting in Gold's office kept streaming back to me—her eyes welling, the tears streaking her cheeks. I had to talk about it, get another opinion. *Why didn't Forsythe wait to speak with me after I met with her? Wasn't this an important milestone in my therapy? Was he testing me, pushing the therapeutic limits of AU-811 in order to discuss it on the next conference call?*

I glanced over at the only friend I had in the world.

Jonesy waved at a passing brunette wearing a short, floral dress. "Hey, Robin."

She flashed back a business-like smile. "Hello, Neil."

"One of the social workers," he whispered to me.

"Pretty," I said, amazed at how many people this guy knew.

"She's married, one kid."

Working our way across the leather-furnished lounge, I spilled it. "I had a visitor today—an old friend."

Jonesy shot me a surprised look. "Really?"

"An old girlfriend. She saw me on the news last week."

He smiled and raised his brow. "No kidding?"

"The thing is," I said, "I'm not sure if she was there to—"

Without warning, Jonesy spun on his heel and yanked me by the bicep in the opposite direction. His expression instantly changed from glib to worried concern. I glanced over my shoulder in time to observe Lou Fischer step from the elevator and head our way. Eyes glued to the floor, Jonesy shoved me toward the stairwell door.

"We'll take the stairs," he said.

"Jonesy, what the hell—"

"Don't let him see you, Matt."

We hurried through the door and into the stairwell. Jonesy took off ahead of me and bolted down the stairs.

"Wait a second, will you?" I protested.

He increased his stride, leaping two steps at a time, turning, and disappearing down the next flight. I heard the ground floor door open and close. I continued down at a more reasonable pace, my footsteps echoing through five floors of stairwell.

When I walked through the door and onto the floor, Jonesy was waiting, leaning against the opposite wall with his arms folded, his countenance back to normal.

"What the hell was that all about?"

"It was Fischer. I told you, stay out of his way."

I stared at him, open-mouthed.

"I'm telling you, Matty, he's evil."

I waited a few seconds. "You know, you're starting to sound a lot like some of the other fruitcakes penned up in here."

He turned his stare down the hallway toward the nurses' station. "Trust me. I know what I'm talking about. Stay out of his way."

"Has he ever threatened you? Because if he has, we can talk to Forsythe and—"

"No!" he snapped. Then he calmed. "No. He's never threatened me. If I just stay out of his way, I won't give him the chance to throw me into Building Two, with the rest of the walking dead he has rotting up there." He locked eyes with me. "If you're smart, you'll do the same." He pushed off from the wall with his left foot. "I'm gonna go watch some TV."

25

Forsythe raised the still-steaming coffee to his lips. His eyes gleamed with delight when the hot liquid found its mark. He swallowed audibly, placed the cup in front of him, pushed his six-foot bundle back in the chair, and formed a pyramid with his fingers, rubbing the tips in tiny circles.

"Tell me about your meeting with Trisha."

I sat up in my seat. "Not much to tell. It only lasted a few minutes."

"Do you wish it lasted longer?"

"We barely had a chance to say hello."

Forsythe stopped the finger circles and folded his hands in his lap.

"What went through your mind when you first saw her?"

"How beautiful she still was. And how bad I must have looked."

He gave a weak, smiling nod. "Any regrets about going into that room yesterday?"

I thought a moment about yesterday's first impressions—and wondered again about her real reason for showing. "I'm not sure."

"What aren't you sure about?"

"I don't know. Why she came, I guess."

"Didn't she say?"

"I'm not sure."

Forsythe leaned forward, placing his forearms on the desk. "What did she talk about?"

"Her guilt over running away when I got sick. I'm just wondering if it was all some sort of . . ."

"Absolution?"

"Yeah. Absolution."

Forsythe thought for a moment. "Perhaps." He took another slug of coffee and licked his lips. "Or maybe she just wanted to see you."

I twisted my mouth into a scoffing snarl. "Why?"

"Maybe she still has feelings for you."

"Come on, Eric," I said, shaking my head. "That was twenty years ago. We were friggin' kids."

"The feelings I'm talking about can last forever."

I snorted a bitter laugh. "Look at me." I slapped my hands on my chest. "I'm a goddamn schizoid. Who in their right mind would have feelings for me? Did you see her? She could have any man she wanted." I felt a pang of anger. "You were right on the money. It was just a catharsis. Women do that shit—twenty years of pent-up guilt all puked out in Gold's office. I'm a fucking whack-job whose fragile sanity is being held together by the glue of some experimental drug. Without it, I'd still be in La-La land, chasing ghosts." I collapsed back into my chair and exhaled a long breath.

Not surprisingly, Forsythe remained composed. He absently tapped the fingers of one hand on the desk while taking my measure.

"I'm sure you noticed I wasn't here when you finished yesterday. That was by design. If we met moments after you finished with Trisha, still insensate with the shock of it, I doubt it would have proved very productive. I wanted to give you a day to let it brew, if you will."

"So I could make an ass of myself in front of you?" My voice was contemptuous.

"That's what you call it. I saw something I was hoping I'd see: a heretofore-absent range of deep-reaching emotions—anger, passion, apprehension, delight, affection. You've demonstrated them all quite well."

I rubbed my bearded chin, soaking it in. I think he was telling me my little hissy-fit was what he wanted to see. I surrendered an open-mouthed smile, shaking my head. "Why the hell would anyone want to be a shrink?"

He raised his coffee to his mouth. "Never met one who couldn't use one."

I laughed just as the phone rang. Forsythe excused himself, picked up the receiver, and pressed it to his ear. He doodled on a pad while he took his call. I relaxed, shifting my gaze to the window. It was cracked open six inches, and the curtains, once white, but now beige with age—gave way to an occasional puff of gentle breeze. The sound of vehicles passing four stories below came and went. In the distance, a motorcycle ran through its five gears.

After a few questions edged with irritation, a closed-eye nod, and a deliberate shake of the head, Forsythe glanced at his watch and said, "I'll be there. Thanks." He hung up.

"I'm afraid I'm going to have to cut this short, Matt. Our chief of staff just called a mandatory ten-thirty staff meeting."

"Nothing like short notice," I said.

"Budget panic. We're all about to be treated to another belt-tightening lecture. This time, he's dragging along the CFO." He reached for his coffee.

"Uh, just one more thing."

"Sure," he said and took two short swallows, his prominent Adam's apple bobbing in cadence.

"Can an administrative person like Lou Fisher pull rank on one of the docs here?"

Pausing, Forsythe seemed caught off-guard by the question. "What do mean?"

Chewing my lip a second, I thought how to best word my question without raising suspicion or sounding as paranoid as Jonesy. "Could he move a patient from one area of the hospital to another over your objections?"

"Of course not." He squinted. "Why."

"I just want to dispel a rumor I heard."

"Fischer is administration. Neither he nor anyone else on the second floor has sway over any clinician when it comes to patient care. Sure, they twist our thumbs from time to time, especially when it involves resources, but when it comes to the patient, the clinician has the final say. Always."

I'd hit a nerve. His words were passionate. Obviously, he'd had previous run-ins with the paper shufflers dictating how best to practice his profession; no doubt an unceasing challenge in the bureaucratic environment of a state-run hospital.

Eric closed my chart and got to his feet, glancing again at his watch. "Tomorrow at ten?"

"Yup," I said, rising. "Oh, did you happen to write that order for my pass yet?" I almost didn't ask, afraid I'd stir some irrational ire and suffer a summary denial of the request.

"This morning."

"Thanks." A rush of relief washed over me. *Freedom to roam the estate. An emancipation.*

Forsythe glanced toward the window. "Go take a walk. It looks like a nice day."

"I'll do that."

He snatched his brown herringbone sports coat from the wall hook. "See you tomorrow. Close the door when you leave." He winked and dashed from the office.

I reported back to the ward with the intention of informing Debbie and Miranda I was leaving the building to try out my new Level Three pass. When I approached the nurses' station, Debbie looked up from her chair. "Just the person I'm looking for."

"Now what did I do?"

"Dr. Forsythe has written you some new orders."

I bellied up to the counter. "My pass," I said.

"Yes, you've been sprung from the building and," she pointed to the short, plastic catheter protruding from my right arm, "that little number's coming out. As of today, you're on oral AU-811 twice a day. I'm going to give you your first dose right now." She jumped to her feet, rounded the corner of the station, and made her way to the med closet. "Wait for me in the treatment room. I'll be right in."

I crossed the hall to a small treatment room and sat on the end of the examination table, studying the heparin-lock—a short, yellow-tinted tube protruding from my arm. A minute later, Debbie breezed in, expending a bit of what seemed to be limitless stores of frantic energy. She held out a small medication cup.

"Here you go."

I took the cup and she dashed to the sink to draw a glass of water. I stared down at my salvation in oral form, a small red capsule with tiny white markings. Squinting, I strained to read the inscription—PORTLAND 811.

"Down the hatch." She was back at my side, holding out the glass.

"Here's looking at you, beautiful." I tipped back the med cup, swallowing the cherry-colored gelatin capsule and chasing it with a gulp of water.

Before I could brace myself, Debbie pulled the heparin lock from my arm and replaced it with an ordinary bandage.

"There you go," she said, holding up the tube. "We still friends?"

I gently rubbed the bandage with the palm of my hand. I was free of the last visible vestige of my mental illness.

We spent a couple minutes chatting while she cleaned up. I caught up on the twins' latest bedevilments and heard her plans for a family vacation to Nova Scotia. When she had placed the last errant supply item into one of the stainless steel cabinets mounted on the opposite wall, she came to me, crossed her arms, and smiled cleverly.

"You know, Matt, I still marvel when I look at you. For too long, that hollow body imprisoned too nice a person. If it wasn't for AU-811, we would have never known. It's wonderful having you here the way God intended." Her tone softened. "Sometimes you forget about the souls lurking in the bodies of the patients out there, and then you realize that if it wasn't for some organic error that took place long ago in the womb, those poor souls might instead today be doctors, lawyers, businessmen or college professors." She heaved a heavy sigh. "It just seems so unfair, so cruel." She stood motionless for a while, her wounded green eyes staring off into space.

Finally, she twitched, snapping from her trance of self-imposed pity. "Anyway, you're good to go." Her face flashed a two-second smile.

I slid off the table, saying gleefully, "*I'm* going out for a walk."

"Wish I could go with you."

"Maybe next time."

"Catch a few rays for me," she said, and scurried back in the direction of her workstation.

I had been here before. During my stint at Slater State Hospital, I'd undoubtedly been taken out to the south grounds many times. It all appeared as it had in my fantasy world—luscious green lawns, shaded by huge maples, and bordered by red brick walkways that ran from the building to the road. I wondered if sometime in the past, a nursing student named Monica had actually wheeled me here, sat with me at a bench under one of the maples, and told me her sad story.

It was past noon and I observed a scattering of employees, most of them maintenance people, strewn among the benches and seated at three picnic tables in a shaded area, eating from bagged lunches. The sky, coated a deep blue, was dotted with puffy cumulus clouds like white brush blotches on a painter's palette. I squinted in the bright sunshine, remembering Monica's amber sunglasses. I'd buy a pair from Gina later this afternoon, I decided.

Still giddy with my newfound freedom, I crossed the asphalt drive and strolled along the north-facing brick walkway. I felt exhilarated, taking in deep breaths of fresh spring air while a gusty breeze patted my face.

Halfway down the walk, I came upon a bench embraced by a trio of tall maples and dropped onto it. Gazing out onto the lawns, I noticed the intermittent showers of the previous three days had rendered the grass a rich, moist green, and it was in need of mowing. About thirty feet in front of me, two Hispanic women in housekeeping garb sat on the ground, arms surrounding knees tucked tight to their bosoms, taking in the mid-day warmth. I looked off to the distant woods and thought of Trisha.

Wandering into the rec room an hour later, I found Jonesy in a game of eight-ball with one of the male ward clerks.

"Matt-man," he called out, chalking the cue tip, studying his next move.

I wandered to the table, stepped behind him, and watched him sink the shot. Taunting the clerk with his cue stick, he hurried to the opposite end of the table.

"So where you been, man?" he asked.

"Outside."

"Ah, touring the palace grounds?"

"Something like that."

With a loud crack, Jonesy sunk the eight ball over the disgruntled groans of his defeated challenger. "You owe me another Pepsi, Greg. Double or nothing?"

Greg tossed his stick onto the table. "I gotta get back. Find someone else to hustle."

"You owe me four sodas, big guy," Jonesy said, pointing his cue at Greg's departing back.

Greg waved him off without looking back.

"Sore loser." Jonesy placed his stick next to Greg's. "Want to grab a bite? I haven't had lunch."

"I could force something down."

"After you," he said, pointing the way.

I ordered a grilled cheese while Jonesy scrutinized the posted menu as if it offered a fine bill of fare. After a good two minutes of deliberation, he opted for the tuna salad plate—a dreadful looking combination of watery tuna fish, wilted lettuce, tomato, French fries, and a rubbery dill pickle.

We poured two large Cokes from the self-serve fountain. Working our way through the line, Jonesy mumbled something about his preference for Pepsi, bemoaning the fact they didn't offer a choice of colas. At the cash register, he repeated his complaint to the cashier, a large black woman who, with rolling eyes, reminded him that she just ran the register and to take all complaints to George, the cafeteria manager. Jonesy shrugged her off.

The place hummed with a late lunch crowd. We chose an empty table near the windows that offered a view of the west parking lot—two acres of warm asphalt heaving with vehicles of all colors and shapes.

Jonesy went to work on his meal, lathering a quarter bottle of catsup onto a pile of under-cooked fries. He clamped onto half his sandwich with one hand and tore off a huge portion with a single bite. He spoke as he chewed, spitting shards of mayonnaise and tuna.

"So, how'd it feel to get out there?" He nodded toward the window, chewing with the ferocity of a starving animal.

I dug for the right word. "Liberating," I said.

"Liberating," he repeated, making a face of agreeing contemplation. "Good description. Like when the allied forces marched into Paris."

"Stop making fun of me, Jonesy." I bit off a piece of my grilled cheese.

He snickered through another chomping mouthful and turned his attention to the window.

For a while, we ate in silence, listening to the din of chatter and the clatter of eating utensils bouncing from plates and trays.

"Forsythe cut me short today. Had to attend a meeting called by his boss."

Jonesy looked at me indifferently.

"I asked him about Fischer."

He stopped chewing, froze for a moment, then swallowed with effort. "Why would you do that?" he said.

"Fischer has no say over patient care."

"Bullshit."

"It's true, Jonesy. Forsythe confirmed it for me. Fischer is administration. They're paper pushers down the hall, concerned with budget, building maintenance, running the day-to-day operations of a hospital—not telling the docs how to practice."

Jonesy glared at me, steely-eyed.

"Neither Fischer nor anyone else from the front office can put you, me . . . *anyone* into Building Two. Your fear of that man is unfounded."

He shifted his gaze to the tuna plate and pushed it away. "How 'bout a game of pool?"

"Are you listening to me?" My frustration steamed to the surface. "Fischer is harmless. He can't touch you. Whoever told you he has the power to put you away is full of it."

Jonesy stared at me for a long moment, and then stood slowly. With an ugly smile and in a quiet voice, he said, "I'm going back to my room to take a nap."

"Jonesy," I said as he turned to leave. "For Christ's sake, Jonesy."

He walked off. I heaved a sigh and tossed the remains of my grilled cheese at the plate.

26

A cold, wind-whipped rain rattled the windowpanes, rousting me from a dreamless sleep at ten minutes of seven.

I had slept fitfully through the night, and lay motionless for several minutes, staring at the ceiling, listening to the tuneful wind, eddying about the building's exterior contours.

When I finally forced my aching bones from the bed, I shuffled barefoot to the window, pressed my forehead against the cool glass and gazed with chagrin at the scene outside.

The sky was a moody slate gray, casting the world into perpetual dusk, its features contrasted by the white headlights of passing traffic. A gusty wind tossed sheets of rain across the drive below, flooding every imperfection of pavement.

"Shit," I muttered. My plan to sit in the morning shade of the picnic area and read the legal thriller I'd borrowed from the library was ruined.

"My cat does that."

I spun around. Miranda had entered with the breakfast menu and my morning dose of medication.

"What?"

"When it rains, Goldie sits on the back of the living room sofa and stares out the window for hours."

"Then I know how she feels. I had outside plans for today."

"It didn't happen to include chasing mice, did it?"

"Funny," I said.

"Because if it did, I'll bring her over here to keep you company. You two can mope together." She held up the paper medication cup. "Here're your meds." She placed the cup on the bedside table and raised the menu sheet. "Want to order?"

"Just coffee and a plain bagel with a little cream cheese."

"Okay." She wrote it down and turned to leave.

"Hey, Miranda."

Halting, she looked back.

"Is Jonesy up yet?"

"He's in the shower. I just gave him his meds."

"Did he seem okay?"

She shrugged. "Classic Jonesy. Why?"

I shook my head. "Nothing."

She looked at me curiously. "Take your meds," she said and left the room.

After my session with Forsythe, I found Jonesy in the rec room playing video pinball. Chomping his bottom lip, he spoke to the ricocheting silver ball as if it were alive. The machine replied in electronically generated bings and bongs and an escalating digital scorecard.

"Hey, Matt-man," he said, acknowledging my presence but never removing his eyes from the game.

"Jonesy. What's up?"

"Three free games so far." He gestured with his head at the scoreboard. Red numbers indicated 23,925 points and the number 3 under *free games*.

With a jolting twist of his entire frame, the game went dark, the word *Tilt* flashing in large red letters.

"Damn," he spat, slapping the side of the machine. "What do you say, want to play a game?" He stepped aside.

"Nah, I don't think so."

He shrugged and moved back in front of the machine, pushed the large red start button, and the game again came to life. For the next ten minutes, I watched him run off his three freebies without winning a single additional game. Jonesy acted like his normal self, the scene from the day before apparently forgotten. I decided not to bring it up.

We grabbed a quick lunch in the cafeteria, where we sat at a window table and watched the howling torrents bathe the outside world. Afterward, we retreated to the computer room and, as promised, Jonesy navigated me through a crash course on the worldwide web.

Two hours later, my head spun with fascination. The words *Internet, e-mail, Google,* and *website* now populated my vocabulary. Ebay especially intrigued me: an electronic shopping center where I could purchase or sell anything imaginable. Jonesy proved it. He told me to name the first thing that came to mind. I replied, "Pink giraffes." Within seconds, the screen displayed a choice of fourteen pink giraffes, with bids ranging from thirty-five cents to two-hundred-twenty dollars.

"Want to bid on one?" he asked grinning.

Jonesy had a three o'clock session with Forsythe, so I headed back to my room to do a little reading. I was beginning to collect books—I had accumulated a small pile of paperbacks on my bed stand, some from the library, others left behind by outpatients in various waiting areas. For me, reading had replaced television. I believed it better exercised my mind.

When I later wandered into the ward, I nearly knocked Liz to the ground. Without warning, she had rushed from the linen closet with an arm full of bedclothes and directly into my path. She cried out in surprise and I instinctively reached for her arm to keep her from falling. We apologized in unison before breaking into laughter. I retrieved the sheets knocked to the floor and placed them back into her outstretched arms.

"Thanks, Matt. I've got to get my mind and feet on the same planet."

"Can I help you with anything?" I felt sorry for the nurses—two were constantly doing the work of five.

Liz started for one of the rooms. "How are you at making beds? Oh," she stopped and turned. "You got some mail today. On the counter." She pointed to the nurses' station. "I was going to bring it to you."

"Thanks," I replied.

I walked to the station, snatched the envelope from the counter, and headed for my room. I'd received a handful of cards since the TV piece had aired, mostly kind words from families of other schizophrenic patients. I didn't particularly enjoy receiving them; I didn't feel I was a kindred spirit to those people. To me, my schizophrenia was more a label than a disease. After all, I had no symptoms. I felt and functioned as any normal, forty-seven-year-old man would. And though I knew without the miracle of AU-811, I'd regress to the worst of the worst, I chose to ignore that fact and push it to the back of my mind.

The envelope was small, handwritten, and bore no return address. I sat in the chair, opened the envelope, and pulled out a small card with a single red rose printed on the cover.

> *Dear Matt,*
> *It was wonderful seeing you last week.*
> *I'm sorry it was all so short. I'd very much like to see you again. Please call me anytime after seven p.m. 617-555-0989.*
> *—Trish*

My eyes remained fixed on the card for a long time. I read and reread the four lines until they registered. *Trisha was asking to see me again.* Perhaps Forsythe was right; maybe some feelings *could* last forever.

I leaned forward in my chair in order to see the hallway clock. Three-fifteen. I had nearly four hours of waiting to endure.

I picked at my supper, but a gnawing trepidation had displaced my hunger. Time crawled by. Seconds were like minutes, minutes like hours. I tried reading a book, but after three pages, I'd comprehended nothing. Trisha consumed my thoughts. I put the book down, wandered to the bathroom, flicked on the light and looked into the mirror. I ran my hand over the half-inch of trimmed beard that covered my face. Before I could talk myself out of it, I picked up the electric razor, popped out the beard trimmer, and began shaving. In five minutes, it was over; someone different stared back at me. Maybe I looked younger, maybe I didn't. I'd ask the nurses, but it's what Trisha thought that mattered.

I waited until seven-fifteen before heading out to the second floor lobby to grab a pay phone. It killed me to hold off that extra fifteen minutes, but I figured calling her at seven sharp on the day I received the card would be too—I don't know—presumptuous.

The lobby teemed with people coming and going. Six-to-eight were prime visiting hours for family members who held day jobs.

Crossing the lobby, I noticed a girl in her late teens, dressed in hospital-issued apparel, surrounded by what I judged to be her family. The group occupied the mid-lobby leather furniture and sat quietly, staring at their feet, looking grim and helpless.

Through despondent eyes, the girl gazed down at a small white teddy bear she held in her lap—no doubt a gift from the mother seated next to her. The mother was stroking the sick daughter's arm while whispering words of loving reassurance.

A quiet groan escaped me when I turned into the lobby's main entranceway and noticed both pay phones in use, both by women chatting up a storm, oblivious to the outside world. A third person, a tightly built black kid in baggy jeans and an oversized black sweatshirt, seemed to be waiting for one of the phones to free up. His actions showed he was growing more and more impatient by the second.

I pressed myself against a spot on the opposite wall and waited. In what felt like twenty minutes—but in reality was only five—one of the women finished her call and, as expected, floppy-drawers took her place. I shifted from one foot to the other, clutching the card with Trisha's number.

The black kid spoke for less than a minute. I stood close enough to hear he had called for a cab. When he hung up, I stood there a moment, paralyzed with fear, feeling like a junior high, zit-faced adolescent about to ask the homecoming queen for a date.

My hand shook as it dialed the number. After hearing an interminable series of clicks and pops in the earpiece, the phone rang at the other end. My heart hammered. On the third ring, she picked up.

"Hi, this is Trisha. I can't come to the phone right now but . . ."

Damn. Her answering machine. I checked the lobby clock—half past seven. *Damn, Damn . . .*

"Hello? Hello?"

My throat tightened. She had picked up and I couldn't speak.

"Hello?"

"Trish?" I managed.

A pause. "Matt?"

"Yeah. It's me. Hi."

"You called," she said. I detected a sense of relief in her voice. "How are you?"

"I'm doing well. Umm, I got your card."

"I'm glad you did."

A quiet moment passed.

"I don't know," she said. "It's just that, you know . . . that meeting was so awkward and rushed. I felt it would be nice if we could sit down a little longer and, you know . . . talk over a cup of coffee or something."

"I'd like that, Trish."

"I'm glad you feel that way."

"Umm, what about Saturday?"

"This Saturday? Sure. Ah, what time?"

"Can you meet me in the second floor lobby—same building as last week—at, say, two?"

"Saturday at two."

"Great, I'll see you then, I guess." A nervous laugh got by me.

"Is there anything I can bring you? Anything you need?" she asked.

"Nothing I can think of."

"Well, then you take care of yourself. I'll see you Saturday. Bye."

I held the receiver to my ear for what seemed like an eternity, listening to the dial tone and staring at the booth's perforated soundboard, trying to figure out the fluttering in my stomach.

27

Wearing the disconcerted expression of a lost little girl, Trisha exited the elevator. Her head darted left and then right as she acclimated herself to the large second floor lobby. With bearings gained a moment later, she pointed herself across the large expanse and started in the direction of the information desk.

Seated in one of the lobby's leather chairs, I rose to my feet. She immediately noticed me, smiled brightly, and headed in my direction. I took a few steps toward her, stopped, and waited.

Casually dressed, she wore jeans, a light green sweater, and brown flats. A long-strapped leather handbag—too small to hold much of anything—hung from her right shoulder. She held a white paper bag in her left hand. Her eyes widened as she closed within a few feet. I unfurled a broad smile.

"Hello," she said, wrapping her free arm around my neck and gently hugging me.

Her sweet scent invaded my nostrils. I awkwardly placed one arm around her diminutive waist, returning the gesture.

"Trish, I'm so glad you came."

She leaned back and studied my face.

"You shaved," she said, running her hand along my cheek.

"I figured it was time. A little too much gray."

"This is the way I remember you. I like it better. Stepping back, she held up the paper bag. "Coffee—black, with three sugars."

"You remembered."

"Some things aren't that easy to forget. You did drink six cups a day. We went through two pounds a week."

I smiled, recalling my obscene caffeine addiction. "Then you'll be pleased to know I'm down to one—sometimes two—cups a day."

A moment of silence passed.

"You look great, Trish."

She blushed and looked away. "Thanks."

"No, I really mean it. You've hardly changed."

"You look good too, Matt."

Another quiet beat.

"Uh... how about we take a walk outside?" I suggested. "There's a little grove out back where we can sit."

"That sounds nice."

I took the paper bag and led her through the lobby. Working our way down the stairs to the southern entrance, I broke into a nervous ribbon of small talk, describing the recreation and computer rooms, Jonesy, and a few other things that I'm sure sounded daft, but Trish listened politely.

Outside, the sun bore down from a cloudless sky. Trisha pulled a pair of oversized sunglasses from her bag and slid them on. I cursed inwardly, having left mine back in my room. I squinted and shaded my brow until my eyes adjusted.

"What a day," I said.

"Isn't it beautiful? But it's supposed to rain later."

I shot a glance skyward. "You could fool me."

With a nod, I motioned toward the picnic grove. "There're a few tables over in that shaded area."

We crossed the paved drive to the brick walkway and moved in the direction of the grove.

"Just how much freedom do they give you here?" she asked, peering at me through her black-framed Christian Diors.

"Enough. I can go wherever I want, so long as I stay on the grounds."

"Does that bother you? I mean, being confined to the hospital grounds?"

I shrugged. "I haven't run out of room yet."

"It's beautiful," she said, taking in the spread of lush green lawn.

We cut across a portion of grass, forging a direct path to the grove.

"So, what are you doing these days?" I asked.

"Well, I have a place in the city, and I work for Lehmann Financial. It's a large group that manages mutual fund investments. Pretty boring stuff, but it keeps me busy almost sixty hours a week."

"Can't leave time for much else."

She looked at me and snorted an uneasy laugh. "That's what my ex said."

"You're divorced?"

"Four years in July. Paul was in sales. Traveled a lot. We hardly saw one another."

"How long were you married?" I immediately regretted the question. "I'm sorry. I don't mean to pry."

"That's okay. I don't mind talking about it. We were married twelve years."

"Kids?" I asked.

"Who had time?" She looked over at me, her auburn hair glowing like embers in the bright sunlight. "My second biggest regret."

We reached the picnic grove and settled together at the first table. I drew the two coffees from the bag, crumbled it to a ball, and tossed it into a nearby trash receptacle.

The coffee was still hot. We each managed a couple of long sips, one waiting for the other to speak. Trisha placed her cup on the table, whirled on the bench seat, and faced the lawns.

"You're probably wondering why I'm here."

I looked at her but said nothing.

She nodded once, affirming her suspicion. "It isn't what you think. I'm not here to liberate myself from some store of pent-up guilt; I've learned to live with my guilt. I'm here because I care about you—I always have. In all these years, a day hasn't passed that I haven't thought of you and the time we had together."

I turned to face her, straddling the bench.

"I married Paul for the wrong reasons," she said. "He reminded me of you—some of his mannerisms, his demeanor, how he sat there and took it when I let go with one of my tirades. I constantly compared him to you, but in the end, it didn't work. The surrogate just didn't work out."

She took a shallow sip of coffee, glanced over at me and smiled sadly. "When I saw you on TV last week, I bawled my eyes out for an hour. It was like you had died and then been reborn. I know that sounds corny, but that's the only way I can describe it."

A tear formed in the corner of her eye, then rolled down her cheek.

"I don't blame you if you hate me or question my motives for being here." She angrily wiped the errant tear away and gave me a helpless look. "Sometimes I can't stand myself."

"Trish. Stop it." I placed my hand on her arm and squeezed it. "What the hell do you think you're doing? Look. I'll admit I questioned why you came last week, but now I'm the one on a guilt trip. I don't know what I can say to make you feel better but—"

"Tell me you forgive me. That's all."

"Trish," I said softly, "I forgive you. You did nothing wrong. I would have done the same damn thing. I was hopelessly sick. You were twenty-seven-years-old. You did the only thing you could. You got on with your life, and I'm glad you did. You've nothing to be ashamed of. Now please, stop it."

I slid over and put my arms around her. She turned, held me tightly, and whimpered into my chest. We embraced until her whimpers stopped.

When we separated, I patted a tear from the corner of each of her green eyes. She sniffled and swallowed hard, an embarrassed smile then spread across her face.

"Thanks." She turned her gaze to her feet. "I feel so foolish now."

"Don't." After a short pause, I added, "Besides, we've got some catching up to do."

Smiling at me, she nodded.

We sipped coffee and filled the next thirty minutes carrying on about the old days. In no time, I had her laughing as I recounted our first meeting and the all-nighter at the Albany bus station—a couple of stranded chumps. I inquired about old friends whom she kept in touch with and how they were doing. I was surprised by the success of some and the failure of others. It appeared none of the early marriages had worked out. Many of our friends were on their second or third. Back then, we were all so cocky, full of piss and vinegar. We never imagined any of us were capable of making a wrong decision.

Clouds started rolling in from the west and a breeze picked up, cooling us off. We decided to stroll the grounds and set off along the pathway that hugged the main drive.

As we walked, all of what Trisha had spoken of conjured up memories. The memories rushed back until the point in life at which my mental illness rendered its ugliness; that's where my recollection of the past became fuzzy. I asked her about that particular time span. She hesitated at first, but then opened up.

"It started about a year after we moved in together. You were having these terrible dreams. You'd wake up in the middle of the night and start talking nonsense. You'd talk about things that weren't there. It frightened me, but then a week or more would pass where you'd be fine.

"One night, I woke up and you were gone. I heard your voice coming from the kitchen, so I grabbed by bathrobe and snuck down to see who you were with."

A quiver tainted her voice.

"You were sitting at the kitchen table. There were two coffee mugs, one in front of you, the other across the table. You sat there stirring an empty mug, carrying on a conversation with a nonexistent person. Actually, it was more an argument than a conversation. I stood and listened, and when I realized who you thought you were speaking with, my legs gave out and I sank to the floor, shaking."

I stopped walking and looked at her. "Who was it?"

She hesitated. "Your dad."

Neither of us moved for a moment.

"I heard you say if he ever touched your mother again, you'd kill him. I was so scared, so freaked out, I couldn't move. A short while later, you got up, walked right past me, and went back to bed. I spent the rest of the night on the living room sofa, terrified."

"I don't remember even a bit of that."

"You started getting worse. I'd come home and find you talking to ghosts. You spent hours writing to people who didn't exist. You'd write long, rambling, nonsensical letters, even address and mail the envelopes. Every one of them came back. When I showed them to you, you claimed it was a conspiracy, and ATF agents were behind it. You stopped going to class. You were fired from your job at Chen's—"

"Chen's Liquors?"

"Yes," she said, "Chen's Liquors. I repeatedly tried to get you to a doctor, but you insisted there was nothing wrong. In fact, you accused *me* of being the mental case. And then one night, things got really bad. You were screaming at someone named Costello—who you claimed was a government agent—telling him to get out of the apartment, but no one was there. When I tried to calm you," she held back a second, looking down, "you hit me."

"No," I moaned. "Oh, Trish. Oh, God."

She stopped and faced me.

"Maybe I shouldn't go on."

I saw fear in her eyes—trepidation that my reliving the beginnings of the illness might bring it on again.

"Did I hurt you?" I asked.

"Not as much as it broke my heart when I understood what I had to do. I ran across the hall, hysterical, to Judy and Mike's. We called the police. They came with paramedics and took you away." She paused. "I'll never forget that look you had— never in a million years."

The rapidly approaching cold front began to spread a milky veil overhead, and the breeze sharpened its edge. I noticed Trisha rubbing the back of her upper arm.

"Are you getting cold?"

"It's turning chilly," she replied.

"You're right. Why don't we head back?"

We spent another hour sitting in the second floor lobby. Trisha answered my questions, though I'm sure I asked too many. Yes, she was dating guys from the firm, but nothing serious. She did, however, spend a good portion of the workday fighting off the pathetic advances of married men hoping for a lapse in her moral character. Looking at her, I couldn't blame them. She'd definitely qualify as my fantasy office affair.

Trisha had done quite well at Lehmann Financial, I learned. She was a senior sales executive, earning a salary that afforded her the luxury of an eighteen-hundred-square-foot townhouse on the downtown waterfront. She apparently had it all going for her— killer looks, job status, financial security, enviable real estate—yet here she was, sitting next to me on a worn leather sofa in the lobby of a state psychiatric hospital, smiling and touching my knee as she spoke.

When I walked her to her car sometime after four, the skies had darkened and it had begun to sprinkle. She had parked at the near end of the lot, not too far from the main entrance. We stopped behind a new, dark-blue sedan. She fished through her tiny handbag for keys.

"Nice car," I said. "New?"

"Four months old."

I read the rear nameplate. "Lexus?"

"Ever heard of it?"

I shook my head slowly, looking the handsome vehicle up and down. "Don't think so."

"It's just another car." She pushed a button on her key ring and the machine came to life, belching strangely, blinking its rear lights, popping the door locks.

My brows arched. "Not like any car I've ever owned."

"They're all like this now."

"Really?" Wow."

Trisha fidgeted with her keys a moment and drew a breath. "I truly enjoyed myself today, Matt." A weak smile spread across her face and we locked gazes. "I can't tell you what it does for me to see you so well. It's as if this enormous weight I've carried all these years has been lifted." Her eyes moved to the ground and then back. "If you don't mind, I'd like to come back and see you again."

"Nothing would make me happier, Trish."

She opened her handbag, plucked out a business card, and handed it to me.

"You mentioned your friend was teaching you the computer. Do you know about e-mail?"

"A bit."

"My e-mail address is on the card. It's probably the best way for us to stay in touch. You'll have to set up an e-mail account, if you haven't already, and send me a message so I'll have your address."

I looked at her as if she was speaking Greek.

She laughed. "I can't imagine what it must be like to be cast into the jaws of the computer age all at once."

"Jonesy will help me." I glanced at her card. "I'll send you an e-mail as soon as I can."

"I'll look forward to getting it."

A moment passed.

"Well, I'd better scoot." She stepped forward and gave me a peck on the cheek. "Take care of yourself."

I pecked her back. "You too, Trish."

She opened the door, slid behind the wheel, and gave me one last quick, fleeting smile.

We exchanged waves before she pulled away and disappeared down the long drive to the highway. The sprinkles had changed to a soft, light rain. I stood staring down the empty drive for a lengthy minute before heading to shelter.

28

Sunday's weather couldn't have been more miserable. The temperature had plummeted, and an easterly wind carried in a cold, steady mist from the ocean. From the window, I watched a couple dash across the parking lot, each trailing a slipstream of white breath. Another day stuck indoors.

I had spent most of the morning sitting by a cafeteria window table, sipping French roast, and trying to read Stephen King, but my mind kept drifting back to the day before. I still had the scent of Trish's perfume in my head.

The cafeteria was slow. The aroma of bacon, sausage and onion drifted from the grill, where the short-order cook and a line-server argued in Spanish. I, a few housekeeping staff members on a coffee break, and two nurses' aides made up the smattering of customers.

Earlier, I had gone looking for Jonesy, anxious to set up my e-mail address, but a sister visiting from Connecticut had taken him off campus for the day. Jonesy never spoke much of his family or about any other personal issues. He rarely spoke of his illness or treatment. For such a glib, outgoing individual, he remained aloof when it came to private matters.

I turned my attention to the novel for another ten minutes before glancing up to see Lou Fischer, pumping coffee from one of the Thermos canisters. Dressed in jeans, a white Polo shirt and boat shoes, he looked more like a graduate student than a hospital executive. I wondered what brought him to the salt mine on a Sunday morning.

Fischer paid for his coffee and spent a minute chatting with the cashier. He displayed a pleasant demeanor and appeared genuinely interested in what the woman had to say. I heard him bellow a laugh before he pushed off, nodding. *Maybe he wasn't the stiff I'd pegged him for.*

Fischer hurried across the floor, and halfway to the exit, veered in my direction.

"Good morning, Mathew. How are you?"

"Pretty good, Mr. Fischer. How about you?"

"Terrific." He cocked his head to read the book cover. "Stephen King. Love that guy. *Bag of Bones*. That one's definitely on my list."

I held up the paperback. "You're welcome to it when I'm finished."

"Thanks, Matt, I appreciate that."

"My pleasure," I said.

"Everything going all right?" he asked.

"No complaints."

"Great. How's Dr. Forsythe treating you?"

"Good."

"Wonderful guy. Great doctor." He said it like he meant it.

"The best," I said.

"Well, I'm glad all's well. Let me know if there's anything you need."

"I will. Thanks."

"Got to run. Wife and kids are in the car. I had to stop and pick up a report. We're on our way to a Disney flick." He rolled his eyes, as if to say he'd rather be shooting nine holes. "Take care, Matt."

"You too," I said.

He nodded and was off.

I watched him leave. *Not a bad guy after all*, I thought, and then thanked God Jonesy wasn't here.

Between slugs of coffee, Forsythe absent-mindedly twisted a paperclip and listened intently to my account of Trisha's visit. When I finished, his face split into a wide grin, as if to say, "I told you so."

"You were right," I said, conceding the point.

"This woman has some rare qualities."

"She does. So what do you think? Am I doing the right thing?"

"What do you mean?"

Forsythe was forever answering my questions with questions of his own, usually in some form of "what do you mean?"

164

"I want to see her again, but sometimes I feel we might be leading each other on. I know the relationship can never go back to what it was."

"Why not?"

"Come on. It's been twenty years. She's lived another lifetime since then. She's been married and divorced. She's successful, beautiful. I can't help wondering why she'd want to waste even a second of her time on someone like me. Maybe I shouldn't encourage it."

"It doesn't have to go back to the way it was, Matt. Perhaps she'd like to establish a platonic relationship. From what you tell me, I can see she truly cares about you, and you obviously care about her."

"I don't know if I should get into something we both may wind up regretting."

Forsythe rubbed the back of his neck with both hands. "My advice is to let things take their own course for now. You two are intelligent enough to figure this out. Just let it happen."

Forsythe jotted a few notes in my chart, giving me a moment to digest it all. I decided to follow Trisha's lead. I'd take the passive role and wait to see what developed. I tried to ignore it, but a tiny flame was flickering deep within me, and it left me uneasy.

As he wrote, Forsythe talked. "I've scheduled an appointment for you with Barbara West. You'll see her instead of me at ten tomorrow morning. She's a social worker. I think its time you start meeting with someone from her department."

"Why?"

"Because I don't expect you'll be spending the rest of your life here."

Suddenly, the prospect of being released from the protective bounds of Slater seemed a true reality. *Where would I go? How would I support myself?* The thought of actually walking out of here, leaving my nurses, Forsythe, and the care and security of Slater State Hospital frightened me. My expression must have conveyed the angst.

"Don't worry," Forsythe said in a soft, amused laugh, "you won't be booted out of here until we both feel you're ready to fend for yourself."

What a conflict, I mused. I was *desperate to leave but afraid to go.*

Before we finished, I raised the subject of off-campus privileges. I didn't like the idea of confining Trisha to the walls of a mental institution if she were to continue her visits. Besides, I hungered to taste the outside world after twenty years in a bubble. Normally, patient off-campus supervision was restricted to family and staff, but Forsythe agreed to make an exception and allow Trisha the responsibility. He promised to write the order later that day.

I caught up with Jonesy after lunch, finding him right where I wanted him—in the computer room. I snuck up behind him and watched over his shoulder for a while. He was playing a computerized football game. The quality of animation appearing on the screen astounded me. The characters appeared three-dimensional, grunting and taunting each other, while real stadium sounds filled the background. The Miami Dolphins were leading the Washington Redskins by a touchdown.

"Which team are you?" I asked.

Jonesy flinched and looked up from the monitor.

"Matt-man. What's up? I'm the fish."

"Dolphins aren't fish; they're mammals."

"Whatever," he said, banging the keyboard a little too hard.

"Don't break it," I said.

With a few deft key taps, the game disappeared, and the words *Spot Action Sports* flashed across the screen. Jonesy whirled in his chair, facing me.

"What'd you quit for?"

"I didn't quit," he said. "I saved it to the drive. I can pick up where I left off anytime. So, what's up?"

"How was parole?"

"My sister took me home. I spent all day eating pot roast and playing driveway basketball with my two nephews."

"Sounds like fun."

"I had a good time. How'd it go with you? She show?"

"Of course she showed." I gave him a rap on the shoulder.

"You scare her off, or is she coming back?"

I presented the condensed and sanitized version of Saturday's event, and mentioned the e-mail deal.

"I need to set up an e-mail account. How do I do that?"

"Very easy. This place has its own e-mail server."

"A what?"

"Never mind. Pull over a chair." He turned back to the computer and began hacking at the keyboard.

Within minutes, Jonesy had me set up with my own account. After I fished out Trisha's card, with her e-mail address, I shot off my first Internet message:

> *Hi, Trish,*
> *E-mail all set up. Let me know if you get this.*
> *—Matt*

Jonesy slapped my back. "See? Nothing to it."
"How long will it take to get there?"
"It's there now."
"Now?" I asked, amazed.
"Speed of light, baby. Best part is, it's free. Mail without the stamp, anywhere in the world."
I gave him a you're-pulling-my-leg look.
"Welcome to cyber world, Matt-man."
Seconds later, the machine chimed.
"Whoa," Jonesy said. "She just replied."
"Already?" I was dumbfounded.
He showed me how to retrieve the message. An instant later, the screen lit up with Trisha's reply.

> *Good afternoon. Got your message and*
> *address. On my way to a meeting. I'll*
> *e-mail you later——Me*

"This is wild," I said.
"This is nothing. Instant messaging makes e-mail look ancient."
"Instant *what*?"
Jonesy pushed back from the computer and gave me a good, long look. "Wait 'til you get a load of what's out there."
That same scary feeling ran through me one more time.

29

A wall of dense plastic sheeting, stapled to a frame of two-by-fours, cordoned off the busy work area. Large men wearing hardhats and steel-toed boots worked their way in and out of the heavy curtain, carrying supplies to and from a freight elevator. The area roared with the ceaseless racket of power tools, and a fine white dust thickened the air. Half finished, half still under construction, the fifth floor was undergoing a total renovation.

I found Barbara West's newly refurbished office at the finished end of the hallway.

Barbara, middle-aged, rapidly graying, and carrying an extra thirty pounds, stepped from behind her desk, shook my hand, and offered me a seat.

The state had spent a few dollars on her side of the renovation project. Her office was tastefully done in a blue theme. The dark blue rug, pale blue walls, and blue and brown chair-rail strip provided the room a cozy appeal. The office was neat and organized, the furniture new, my chair comfortable.

Barbara shut the door and started off with small talk, apologizing for the noise and complaining the entire construction project was six weeks behind schedule. She said the racket gave her headaches, and pointed to a bottle of Tylenol on her desk.

We spent an hour discussing my functioning outside the hospital's confinements. She spoke of vocational training, government subsidies, and halfway homes. Any release for a chronic patient required a several-step process, gradually easing the individual back into society. She was especially concerned with my case; a person oblivious to the world's progress for the better part of two decades required special planning.

She decided the transition would begin with a job. Barbara had arranged a twenty-hour-per-week position in the hospital's pharmacy, and set up an interview with the pharmacist for later in the afternoon. The job paid five dollars an hour and involved running medication carts around the facility, and stocking ward medication closets. I liked the idea—it beat washing pots and pans in a kitchen—but dealing with drugs sounded a bit intimidating.

Barbara assured me I met all the requirements and that all necessary training would be provided. If I had once stacked shelves with bottles of booze, I figured substituting bottles of pills should prove a cinch.

The pharmacy was situated on the other side of a large, bank-teller type window on the basement level of the building. For security, the window offered a wall adorned with certificates, licenses, and diplomas that obscured view of the department's large drug inventory. An empty stool and computer terminal occupied the space between the window and wall.

I pushed a white button under the instructions: "Push for Service." The muted ring of a bell sounded somewhere inside. Thirty seconds later, a little round man in a stained white shirt and knitted mustard tie sauntered up to the window.

"Help you?" the man said.

"I've got an appointment with Henry Laird for an interview."

The little man opened his mouth and pointed at me.

"You're Matt."

I nodded, giving him a tight smile, and he gestured toward the door. I heard a buzzer sound and the lock released.

The little man stood at the door and offered his hand. "I'm Jack Connelly, one of the techs."

I pumped his hand. "Pleased to meet you, Jack. Matt Tracy."

"Yeah, I know. Saw you on the tube." He eyeballed me head to toe. "What an amazing story. Me and Hank have been following you since the AU-811 arrived; Hank knew about the drug from one of the journals. Couldn't believe it when we were picked as one of the investigational sites." Jack eyed me like a young kid ogling a rock star.

"Is Mr. Laird in?" I asked.

"Oh, sure. In his office out back. I'll show you."

I followed Jack, watching him waddle his way around work-benches and machinery to the back of the pharmacy and Laird's office. He led me in.

"Hank. Matt Tracy's here."

Henry Laird stood behind his desk, unfolding his full, six-foot-four-inch length. He was well into his sixties, with a lean build and a thick plug of white hair. He held out a hand of remarkably long fingers and we managed a firm handshake.

"Have a seat, Matt."

I sat on a brown plastic chair and watched Jack vanish into the pharmacy.

Laird had already decided to hire me—Barbara had sent him a pseudo-resumé. He was especially pleased with my college background.

He talked a little about AU-811 and other similar drugs due for release in the next twenty-four months, but none, in his opinion, held the potential of AU-811. This didn't interest me as much as Henry might have thought. AU-811 worked for me, and that's all I cared about.

He gave me a tour of his basement kingdom, explaining the packaging and dispensing machinery, the ordering and inventory methods and the security system. He presented a brief overview of the job and told me that, starting Monday, I'd be working afternoons with Jack. I must have looked a bit overwhelmed, because Henry told me not to worry—Jack had been here forever and stood ready to teach me everything I needed to know. His words eased my doubts.

Ten minutes later, I was back in my room with my nose buried in *Bag of Bones*.

After an hour of reading, my head was ready to explode. My vision hadn't been tested yet, and prolonged reading brought on dull headaches. I figured a pair of reading glasses was in order and made a mental note to mention it to Forsythe.

I wandered out to the nurses' station, said hello to Liz, and inquired about Forsythe's order for supervised leave.

"Yeah, he wrote it a few hours ago." She shuffled through a stack of printed orders. "Here it is." After studying it a moment, she asked, "Who's Patricia Kelly?"

"Trisha. A friend."

"I'll bet you're excited about getting out of here for a few hours."

"Petrified is more like it."

Liz gave me a sympathetic look. "Yeah, I can imagine. But don't worry. It's still the same crazy, screwed-up world you remember."

"I'm sure it is."

I thanked her and walked down the hallway to the dayroom. I found Jonesy immersed in a game of five-card draw with two of

Slater's more perceptive tenants. A pile of chits sat in front of Jonesy. I doubted pure luck fully explained his lopsided success.

"Looks like you're buying dinner," I said.

"Hey, Matt-man. Open spot across the table," he said, gesturing. "Grab a chair."

"No, thanks. I'll hold on to my money."

"Oh, don't let this pile of winnings intimidate you." He squeezed open the cards of his newly dealt hand.

"Lucky bastard," said one of the participants, a bony man with a full beard and long ponytail. His hapless expression conveyed another lousy hand.

"Luck has nothing to do with it, Foster." Jonesy said, arranging his cards. "*Nada*. It's all skill, my hairy friend. S-k-i-l-l. I'll take two." He slapped down his cards and smiled.

Five minutes was all I could take watching my hustler friend dupe his opponents out of their week's ration of coupons. I slapped him on the back. "I'm taking a walk outside. Catch up with you later." Jonesy acknowledged me with a nod, sliding his bet to center table.

Outside, I headed in an unexplored direction—the north end of the campus. Above, the late afternoon sun struggled through an obstinate film of cloud cover, brightening the world for a moment or two before ducking back behind the gloom.

I followed the walkway between buildings One and Two and wound up detouring my way around a work area, set up by contractors working the fifth-floor renovation.

A temporary chain link fence encircled a large McMullen Construction crane, engaged in hoisting building materials. Five floors up, a window had been knocked out and enlarged to accept the supplies. Fascinated, I stood and watched as several large, unwieldy sections of prefabricated wall were moved from the ground to three men, unfazed by heights, waiting at the make-shift opening fifty feet above me.

After a while, I pressed on.

Beyond a large parking lot, I came to the basketball court. Standing beneath the hoop, I thought of Jonesy's challenge and wished for a ball. It had been a long time since I last took a shot.

The sun finally punched through the clouds, revealing a patch of blue sky, warming my face and brightening the quiet grounds. Growing hungry and realizing I hadn't eaten since breakfast, I decided to head back, grab a bite in the cafeteria, and then compose an e-mail to Trisha.

30

Early that evening, Trisha and I exchanged a series of e-mails. She was stuck in the office working on a project due out in the morning.

The messages started out short and grew a little silly, but it was fun. I found myself laughing out loud reading her responses, many of them referring to incidents twenty years earlier that held meaning only to the two of us.

When I told her of my new job and off-campus privileges, she wrote it was wonderful news and wanted to celebrate by taking me to dinner. Before she indicated her need to get back to work, we agreed on Thursday evening. I signed off, promising to meet her in the lobby at six sharp on Thursday evening.

I left the computer area, ran down a flight of stairs and started back to my room. Crossing the first floor lobby, I was drawn to the front windows by a flashing of light. A spring thunderstorm was cascading its way through the area, dropping torrents of water that ran in rivulets along the sloping front drive. The evening sky flickered with brilliant, blue-white veins of lightening, followed by sharp rattles of thunder that shook the glass in its frames.

Thunderstorms had always fascinated me. The power of nature unleashed in one mighty show of wind, rain, and lightning—Mother Nature reminding us of her less-maternal side. I stood behind the protective plate glass and watched the storm bloom in intensity. Hail began to fall, white marbles fiercely bouncing off the paved drive. One particularly close lightning strike dimmed the lobby lights a moment before a booming clap detonated a second later, forcing me back a step.

The storm had drawn a handful of people to the windows, all captivated by its unbridled fury. After another five minutes, and with no sign of the violent weather letting up, I retreated to the security of the inner building and back to my ward.

Passing Jonesy's room, I noticed the lights were out and wondered where he was.

Through his window, a bright strobe of light scarred the outside sky. In the quick glitter, I thought I caught someone in a corner of the room. I walked reluctantly to the doorway.

"Jonesy?"

Another flicker of white light revealed my friend, cowering in a heap against the wall. I gave my eyes a few seconds to adjust to the room's dimness.

"Hey, you okay, man?" I stepped in and approached him.

A flash and an immediate crash of thunder caused him to shudder uncontrollably and moan like a frightened child.

Good Lord. Jonesy was terrified of thunderstorms. I stood there for a moment, unsure what to do. Here was this outwardly confident, always-in-control kid, now a mound of trembling terror, paralyzed with fear by an electrical storm.

"It's nothing to be scared of. You're safe in here," I said.

He buried his face into his hands, drew his knees up, rotated sideways, and fell into the fetal position.

I tried again. "Jonesy. You want me to get the nurse?"

He managed nothing but a trembling moan.

I hurried from the room, finding Miranda and Debbie in the medication closet, conducting an inventory.

"Something's wrong with Jonesy," I said.

"What do you mean?" Debbie asked.

"I think it's the storm. He's all balled up and whimpering in the corner of his room."

They glanced at each other with disconcerting looks, and then stepped from the closet.

I'll call the POD," Debbie said, referring to the on-duty psychiatry resident.

Miranda gave me a gentle shove. "You go back to your room, Matt. We'll take care of this."

Retreating to my room and glancing over my shoulder, I saw Debbie grab the phone and Miranda hurry in the direction of Jonesy's room.

I flopped onto the bed and opened my book. I tried reading, but with each lightning flash, I envisioned my friend wrapped in a knot of fear. I got up and drew the blinds.

An hour later, Debbie came in with my evening dose of medication.

"How's Jonesy doing?" I asked.

"He's sleeping."

"Is he going to be all right?"

"He's fine."

She handed me the medication cup. "I've got to pass out meds," she said and left.

I tried reading but, again, my mind refused to cooperate. I was too hyper. It had been one hell of a day, and its images looped through my head. I decided to take a hot shower, watch the news, and turn in.

In the morning, I met with Forsythe. He began the session with a proposal that we start meeting three times a week instead of daily. He felt my adjustment had thus far been nothing short of remarkable, and explained that my new treatment plan called for seeing less of him and more of Barbara West, with the ultimate goal of being discharged. But he assured me I'd have input at every step of the process. He promised nothing would move faster than what I could handle.

After the session, I wandered down to the second floor and found Jonesy in the computer room, playing another video game. I dragged over a chair from the next table.

"Matt-man," he said. "What's up?"

"Hey, man. How you feeling?"

He looked at me like I had two heads. "I feel fine. Why?"

I shook my head. "Nothing."

He turned back to his game. "I heard you're now among the employed."

"How'd you know that?"

"I've got my sources. Nothing gets by Jonesy."

I snorted. "I guess not."

I watched him play the computer keyboard like a musical instrument. On the screen, a machine gun fired, killing gross-looking aliens, splattering scaly body parts and green blood in all directions.

"This is pretty sick stuff, don't you think?"

"What do mean, 'sick'?" He never looked up. "This is fun, man."

I watched for another queasy minute. "What do you say to taking a break from saving the world and grab a cup in the café?"

"Sure." With a quick dozen keystrokes, he saved the game to memory and jumped to his feet. "Let's go."

We started for the door.

"So you get to work with Jack Connelly." He chuckled.

"What?" I asked, turning into the hallway.

"The guy's a space shot. He's out there where the buses don't run."

"He seemed like a decent enough—"

"Shit," Jones hissed, ducking back into the computer room.

I looked up and saw Lou Fischer leaving the cafeteria, moving away from us and in the direction of the administrative offices.

I took a breath, uttered an expletive, and walked back into the computer room. Jonesy was inside, next to the door and backed against the wall.

"Which way'd he go?" he asked.

"Back toward his office. Look, Jonesy—"

"The bastard's been following me all morning. See if he's gone."

The fear in his face was genuine. I hooked my head around the doorframe. "He's gone."

Jonesy heaved a sigh and, like nothing had happened, he smiled. "Let's go."

When he moved, I grabbed his arm. He looked me in the eye, then shifted his gaze to his arm.

"Look," I said. "Fischer isn't after you. He's a regular guy. I talked to him the other day. He's not the threat you think he is."

He yanked his arm from my grasp and clenched his teeth. "He's evil. A monster. If you know what's good for you, you'll steer clear of him. I know what I'm talking about."

With that, he spun away, stormed back to the computer, and resumed his game. After a long minute, I walked to the cafeteria and had my coffee alone.

Trisha eased her Lexus onto the main drag in front of the hospital, and I watched the red brick features of Slater State Hospital vanish behind a row of glass-front buildings that lined the street. My gut managed a restless stir when the mothership disappeared. Trisha's little car was catapulting me twenty years into the future.

My eyes darted around, expecting to discover some futuristic way of life depicted in the old comic books I read as a kid. A lot could happen in twenty years. But what I saw was just more of the same—more buildings, more traffic, more impatient people hurrying to get nowhere. Nothing had changed, only multiplied and quickened.

Trisha offered no hint of where we were headed. Her one clue came in her last e-mail, in which she told me to dress casually—a relief, since I owned no nice clothes. The jeans, clean shirt, sneakers, and light jacket I wore seemed appropriate. She wore a pair of faded jeans, a lavender V-neck sweater, and blue Nubuck shoes.

Within minutes, we were speeding along a back road, listening to some old Jethro Tull on a stereo system that sounded like no car stereo I'd ever heard—two hundred watts driving sixteen speakers.

Trisha reached over and lowered the volume. "So, how are you doing?"

"Okay, I guess. Feels a little strange."

"This is going to be fun." She glanced over and gave me her trademark smile.

"Fun, huh? Where are we going, Chuck E. Cheese?"

She laughed. "They have hot dogs at Chuck E. Cheese?"

"Hot dogs?" I gave her a look.

"Yeah, hot dogs. And that's the only hint you're getting."

"Hot dogs," I mumbled, thinking.

A moment later, a small device set on the center console lit up with a ring. Trisha snatched the gadget from its holder and glanced at its miniature, green-glowing screen.

"I'm not taking this," she said firmly, setting the device back onto the console. "It's work, and I'm off the clock."

Curious, I asked, "What is it?"

"Oh, Matt," she said, pity lacing her tone, "you've missed so much. It's a cell phone. The whole world is now connected by wireless telephone."

"Yeah, that's right," I said. "I've seen the TV commercials with that 'can you hear me now' guy walking around." I stared at the tiny contrivance. "Looks too small to be a real telephone."

"Oh, it's a phone all right, and it's become nothing less than an electronic ball and chain. Once you land in the wireless world, there's no escape."

We merged onto the Mass Turnpike and headed east for a half an hour before the Boston skyline poked above the horizon.

"Boston," I said. "We're going to Boston."

"Maybe."

Tossing my head back, I grunted in frustration.

"Okay, okay," she said, laughing. "In the glove box."

I reached over and pulled opened the glove box.

"The envelope on top," she said.

With one brow arched in intrigue, I lifted out the envelope, held it up, and gave her another look.

"Go ahead. Open it."

My mouth fell slack-jawed when I slid out the two Red Sox tickets. "Fenway Franks," I said turning to her.

A huge smile had claimed her face. "Bingo."

The ballgame turned out to be the first of two surprises Trisha had planned for the evening. After we watched the Sox trounce the Angels, she drove from Fenway Park to Huntington Avenue and one of our favorite old haunts—Ricco's Pizza.

The place hadn't changed much. Inside, the booths were still the same, only twenty years older. Ricco, however, was long gone. The two Greek brothers who now owned the place offered additional menu choices, like salad with lima beans, feta cheese, and Baklava.

The usual raucous college crowd had seized more than half the ancient, beat-up wooden booths. Through shrill howling laughter and the blare of clamorous conversation, they chomped on pizza and guzzled beer poured from plastic pitchers. Trisha motioned to the front, and as though it was meant to be, our favorite booth by the window sat empty.

We quickly weaved our way to the front, a couple of out-of-place oldsters, catching wary glimpses from the puerile group of barely twenty-one-year-olds drenched in beer and raging hormones. Sliding into the bench seats, we found our spots as if we'd been there yesterday.

"This feels kind of weird," I admitted.

"Last time we sat here, this group was still in diapers."

I peeked over my shoulder and caught a couple sets of eyes staring. I shook my head. "Too bad youth is so wasted on the young."

Trisha smiled weakly, then shifted her gaze out the window to the busy flow of street traffic.

"After I got married," she said, "we bought a house down the road in Newton. I commuted in and out of the city every day, driving right by here. Every evening on the way home, I'd try to catch a glimpse of this booth and see if it was occupied. Many times it was, and every once in a while, I'd think I'd see you sitting here, sometimes alone, other times with someone else."

She moved her gaze back to me and folded her hands on the table.

"Once, I actually stopped, parked, and walked over here to check. I think the poor kid and the girl with him thought I was nuts. I was beginning to think so, too. After that, I changed my commute to avoid the place. In a week or so, I'd convinced myself the new route was too circuitous, but in reality, I missed driving by here. It was my one remaining connection to you."

Finished, she gave a slight shrug. I placed my hands on hers.

"I'm sorry I've put you through this all these years," I said.

"Don't be, Matt."

"For you," I continued, "it's been almost twenty years. For me, it seems like only a few months since we were together."

She tightened her grip. "All I care is that you're well now. That makes it all worthwhile. Don't feel bad for me. I've lived a petty good life all this time. You're the one who's been cheated out of a quarter of yours."

"I don't feel cheated. You don't miss what you never had."

"Then I guess we should both stop feeling sorry for each other," she said.

"I agree."

Trisha ran her eyes around the pizza parlor.

"You know what?"

I shook my head. "What?"

"We've got to find a new place."

I stole a quick glance behind me.

"I think you're right."

"Want to leave?" she asked.

"I wasn't that hungry anyway."

Walking back to the car, I felt that, in her own way, Trisha had broken whatever spell Ricco's had over her. From now on, perhaps she could drive by without searching the window.

31

Awash in the orange hue of sodium lights, the Lexus came to rest in front of Building One. I didn't want the evening to end. My taste of freedom and the company of the only woman I ever cared for were as addicting as any opiate.

I glanced at the green readout of the dashboard clock—ten forty-six. My eleven o'clock curfew loomed.

"I still have another fourteen minutes."

Trisha turned to me with a devilish look. "A lot can happen in fourteen minutes."

"I wouldn't know."

"Yeah, right," she said with a poke at my arm.

I grabbed her wrist and pulled her toward me. She didn't resist. We embraced in a long, seductive kiss, our eager tongues probing, our breathing deep and forceful. She buried her face in my neck, her steamy breath inciting me. Memories of her bare, gentle curves, her way of touching, her smell, her taste, flooded forth. I drew a hard breath and eased her back.

She looked away like an embarrassed teen after a first kiss. "You'd better get in. I don't want you late your first time out."

I checked the clock. Another five minutes had ticked off. As it had the entire evening, time flew.

"Oh, I have one more thing for you." She opened her handbag, pulled out a plastic card, and handed it to me. "It's a prepaid phone card. You can call me from the payphones free of charge by first dialing the number on the back. It's good for a hundred and twenty minutes of calls."

I flipped the card over, attempting to read the small print in the low light. "Thanks. I'll pay you back with my first check."

"It cost five bucks. I'll try not to lose any sleep over it."

A quiet moment passed.

"You'd better go," she warned.

"Yeah, I better." I caught her eyes. "Thanks, Trish. This was . . . wonderful."

"It was." She leaned over and kissed my cheek. "Go."

"Goodnight." I opened the door and slid out.

"Goodnight, Matt. And call me."

"I will."

I closed the door and waved. She smiled one last time and drove off. When her taillights disappeared, I rushed into the building.

I flashed my pass to the security person at the front desk. After glancing at the clock on the wall above him, I hurried in the direction of my ward. I had five minutes—plenty of time.

Images of Trish played in my head. I smelled her shampooed hair, felt her warm, petite body pressed against mine, tasted her mouth, saw her sparkling green eyes.

The far end of the first floor corridor was dark, the lights turned off to conserve energy. Through the black passage, enough light escaped the central ward area to illuminate my way. I had walked this path often enough to do it with my eyes closed.

Rushing past the darkened dayroom, an odd noise slowed my pace. Listening hard, I heard it again—an unfamiliar, low growling sound coming from inside. I turned back and stuck my head into the room. My eyes quickly adjusted to the dim glow of outside light that passed through the room's large windows, presenting the familiar outline of its features.

I heard the sound once more—now more like a gurgling noise—coming from the area of the television set. Another gurgling, and then a weak moan. I reached my hand inside the doorframe, felt for the light switch, and flipped it on.

The overhead fluorescents flashed to life, filling the room with white light. It took a second to comprehend the scene, and when I did, a wave of nausea ripped through me. Jonesy, his hands covered with blood, stood over a collapsed Lou Fischer, blood gushing in pulses from a large neck wound, a crimson puddle rapidly forming around his head. A sickening gurgle came from the ugly gash, spraying a mist of dark red onto the white tiled floor.

Jonesy dropped the knife and gave me a blank, haunted stare. "Matt-man."

"What did you do?" My voice crackled with panic.

"It's over," he said thinly and started toward me.

I backed out the door and screamed down the hall, "Help! We need help down here. Now!"

Seconds later, two figures bolted toward us, tearing down the hallway.

"Hurry!" I sounded like a madman.

Jonesy pushed his way past me.

"It's all over Matt-man. He can't touch us now," he said backing in the direction of the stairwell door. A second later, he was gone.

"Holy shit!" said David, the night aide, when he bounded into the room.

Miranda screamed when she saw the carnage. "Oh my God." A second later, she was on her knees, applying pressure to the wound with both palms. "Get help, David." She was crying.

"It was Jonesy," I said. "He's in the stairwell."

I ran for the stairwell door, plunged into the landing, and stopped. Footsteps high above me—followed by the crash of a door—echoed through the vertical concrete chamber. I yelled Jonesy's name and started up after him.

My lungs were burning and a sour taste had filled my mouth by the time I reached the fifth floor landing. I stopped to catch my breath before pushing through the door. *What if he was waiting for me? Would Jonesy harm me? He had dropped the knife. Did he have another?*

"Jonesy? It's Matt." I cocked my head and listened. "I'm coming in."

When my breathing slowed, I eased the door open and prepared for the full force of Jonesy's attack.

32

The hallway lay dark and silent. A single set of overhead lights, mid-corridor, cast the entire hallway into a dingy luminance. I stepped through the open door, shooting my gaze left and right, expecting Jonesy to charge from the shadows. Ten feet to my right, I saw the hasp and attached padlock that once secured the plywood door that led to the construction area. Next to it lay a short-handled sledgehammer.

I stepped to the opening and peered inside. A few caged bulbs, dangling from an electrical cable strung across the ceiling, lighted the area. I moved inside and carefully wove my way around tools and materials strewn across the floor. Plaster bits cracked beneath my feet.

"Jonesy. It's me, Matt. I've got to talk to you."

I stopped and looked in the first room. It was dark and empty.

"Come on, man. Where are you?"

I listened again, trying to hear movement.

"Down here."

His voice sounded weak and distant.

"Where?" I said.

"Here."

I stepped over a pile of sheetrock, moving in the direction of his voice.

"Can I talk to you?"

"Talk all you want," he responded calmly.

I had it pegged. He had ducked into the last room on the left, where the final light bulb of the string hung.

"Jonesy, I'm coming in."

I stopped just before the doorway and poked my head in. Enough light from the overhead bulb spilled into the room for me to see Jonesy standing before the large, black hole. He had pulled a large plywood covering away from the opening—the opening through which, a day earlier, I had witnessed supplies being hoisted.

I stepped into the room and to one side, trying not to block the light.

"Jonesy. It's me, Matt."

"I did it for you, too," he said, moving in an agitated manner. "He was going to put us both into Building Two. Lock us away forever with all the fucking freak cases we never see. He was plotting against us. The son-of-a-bitch had been following me for days. Every time I looked over my shoulder, he was there. I knew he'd be coming for me one of these nights. Him and his goons ready to drag me away to Two under the cover of darkness. Me and then you, Matt. Do you have any idea what they do to patients in Building Two? Do you?"

I shook my head, not knowing what to say or do. He stood less than two feet from a fifty-foot drop to the ground.

"Jonesy, why don't you move away from that opening? You're making me nervous." I took a step in his direction. He held up his hand and wagged his finger and chuckled.

"You don't believe me, do you?"

"Of course I believe you." I took another step. "Look. Let's talk in the hallway where there's a little more light."

Jonesy's mouth fell opened and his brows hiked high as if a revelation had just dawned.

"You're with them," he said softly, pointing.

"What? I'm not—"

He cut me off. "Yes, you are. You're a plant. One of Fischer's stooges. You were sent here with this elaborate bullshit story of being in a stupor for years in order to gain my trust. To befriend me and then hand me over."

I held out my palm. "Jonesy, please, it's not true. It's your illness, man. You're imagining all this. It's in your mind."

I took another step forward, putting myself within ten feet of him. His head snapped back and forth until he eyed a three-foot rod of iron rebar next to his foot. He scooped it up and swung it at me. Fear filled his hardened eyes.

"You stay the fuck away from me." He waved the bar wildly.

"Jonesy, listen to me. This is getting bad. I'm your friend. I'm not with Fischer's people or anyone else. I'm a patient here, just like you."

"Bullshit." He swung again.

I had to do something, quick. I didn't know this Jonesy, a sick, terrified man. I thought of charging and tackling him to the ground, but then what? He was younger and stronger than me. I had to gain his trust. A number of scenarios buzzed through my head.

"I can get us out of here." I was desperate. "You and me, Jonesy. I can have us forty miles from here in a few hours."

The words gave him pause. He slowly lowered the rebar.

"Listen, I'm your friend. I've never done a thing to betray your trust. We've got to move fast. We'll take the stairs, bolt out the south entrance."

His expression eased. He was listening.

"Trisha just dropped me off. We'll go to a gas station and call her cell phone. She can turn around, pick us up, and take us to her place. We'll figure something out from there."

Jonesy's shoulders slumped, his arms hung by his side, the rebar dangling from his right hand.

"You can do that?" he asked, his voice broken and weak.

"Trust me."

A feeble smile cracked his face. "Thanks, Matt-man."

I was about to step forward and take the bar from him when a sharp *bang* startled us both. The outside hallway erupted into a confusing mix of loud, shouting voices. Jonesy's eyes, glaring in disbelief, met mine. He raised the rebar.

"You lied to me."

The sound of rushing voices closed to within several feet of the room.

I raised my palms and shook them. "No. No I didn't. I have nothing to do with them."

"Liar," he shouted.

I stood frozen, out of options.

"In here," a deep voice called over my shoulder. I heard footsteps pour into the room.

A terrifying rage transformed Jonesy's face. He raised the rebar rod over his head and flung it at me. "Jackal Bastards!"

I spun away, arms up. The iron whipped past, clanging off the wall and floor behind me. When I turned back an instant later, Jonesy was gone.

33

Neil Jones's demons perished along with their host on the gray, concrete loading dock slab five stories below the makeshift opening—a building code violation for which McMullen Construction was, in due course, cited and heavily fined.

Two days after the incident, I learned the truth about my friend, Jonesy. He wasn't the manic-depressive he claimed, but a paranoid schizophrenic being treated with a traditional medication regimen and hospitalized for a dose adjustment. Jonesy *had* fallen heir to his family's mental illness legacy, a fate he verbally dreaded. It left me wondering if he ever actually knew.

Lou Fisher became the tragic victim of Jonesy's irrational and growing paranoia. Why? I'll never know. Fischer died in Miranda's arms within minutes of the attack, the knife to his throat penetrating deep enough to exit the side of his neck, severing his carotid artery along the way. He left a wife and two young kids. He was thirty-one.

For two long weeks, the shit hit the fan around Slater. I was confined to the ward while an endless parade of officials—from the police, the DA's office, the department of health, and a half-dozen other agencies—conducted interviews, all drilling me with the same questions, over and over.

The first twenty-four hours proved the most chilling. As a suspected accomplice in Fischer's murder, I was confined to my room, an armed police officer at the door. During that time, the cop had to accompany any person entering the room, Forsythe included.

During my confinement, Trisha, fortunately, had been allowed to visit. She sat with me every evening, held my hand, and soothed my worries until visiting hours ended. The fires of a two-decade-old romance were slowly rekindling.

The official inquiries ended on a Saturday. I was cleared of all wrongdoing. In fact, some investigators hailed me as a hero for risking life and limb in trying to reason down a "madman." I exhaled a sigh of relief when the assistant DA—a short, plump, curly haired woman dressed in an ill-fitting two-piece pantsuit—informed me I was no longer considered a suspect.

After a short, late-morning meeting with Dr. Forsythe and Barbara, I was graciously granted the privilege of an overnight pass. I had to get away from this place—far away.

That evening, Trisha drove me into Boston's Little Italy—the Italian North End. We waited an hour for a seat at Richaroni's, a cramped, eight-seat, hard-to-find restaurant on a well-hidden side street. Our wait was rewarded with the most delicious veal parmigiana, roasted vegetables, and cannoli I'd ever tasted.

Afterward, stuffed to the gills, we strolled the North End's busy, narrow streets, attempting to walk off a portion of our gluttony. Two hours later, we were at her place sipping coffee, then twice made love on her Camelot, wood post bed.

In the morning, Trisha prepared Spanish omelets and fried up a good half-pound of bacon. I managed to figure out the coffeemaker and brewed us a strong pot. We took our breakfast out onto the balcony and watched the waterfront slowly come to life.

Sipping coffee and gazing out onto the harbor, I thought of Jonesy. It bothered me that I had witnessed his blooming paranoia without realizing it. *Could I have prevented what had happened? Saved two lives?* I saw Fischer's baby face flicker in my head, his brown eyes bulging at me in shocked disbelief, while life drained from the gash in his neck. I fought to fend off the wave of guilt.

"What are you thinking about?" Trisha's eyes narrowed, studying me.

I snapped from my reverie with a guarded smile. "Nothing . . . and everything."

She placed her warm hand over mine as if to say she understood. I grabbed her wrist and pulled her to me. She kissed my neck and rested her head on my shoulder.

"I'm growing very fond of you, Mathew Tracy—again."

I placed my arm around her shoulder and squeezed her. "I can't describe what it's like to have you back again, Trish. A nightmare transformed to a dream."

We spent an hour laggardly warming ourselves in the sun's mid-morning glow, working on the pot of coffee, planning the day. We settled on taking the Lexus on an easy drive up the coast to the north shore and wandering the tourist traps of Marblehead, Rockport, and Gloucester.

By seven in the evening, we were chasing the sun as it dipped into the western horizon, the Lexus speeding us westbound on the turnpike, pointed in the direction of Slater Hospital.

I sat slumped in the leather passenger seat listening to a jazz station, thoroughly exhausted from Trisha's whirlwind tour through the old, historic fishing towns.

A cloth bag stuffed with T-shirts, sweatshirts, jerseys, cargo pants, and a pair of tan topsiders, all my size, lay on the backseat—her payment for dragging me through no fewer than thirty different downtown shops.

When our exit popped into view, I was suddenly reminded of something.

"Tomorrow's my first day in the pharmacy." I had forgotten all about it. My start date had been delayed two weeks because of the Neil Jones investigation.

"That's right," Trish said. "Back to the working world."

"Yeah. How about that? Bankers' hours and no commute."

She shot me a fake sneer. "Lucky stiff."

After a breakfast of cold cereal, I showered, shaved and dressed for a scheduled nine-thirty appointment with Barbara West. She wanted to see me before I started the job.

My gut knotted in the elevator on its way to the fifth floor, my first time back to five since the incident. I tried to ignore the thoughts streaming through my mind.

"Jackal Bastards"—Jonesy's last words rang in my head like a white-hot thunderclap, searing my skull. My friend had died desperate and terrified, convinced I'd betrayed him. I never should have chased him up those stairs and tried to reason with him; he was a sick kid, and I had no idea what I was doing. I should have left it to someone who knew how to deal with the situation. I had screwed up, and I felt responsible for his death.

The elevator doors opened onto a noisy construction site—men speaking in raised voices over the clamor of machinery. Everyone moved as if nothing had happened there two weeks earlier. I could almost hear their thoughts. *One of the fruit-loops took a header out our window the other night. The Russian judge gave him a nine-point-eight.*

I turned down the hall, avoiding even a glance at the area, and quickly cut my way into Barbara's office.

After a thirty-five minute meeting during which Barbara lectured me on "employment responsibility" as a paramount step toward discharge into the community, I ducked down the stairs closest at her end of the hallway and hustled to Forsythe's office for my ten o'clock.

During the preceding two weeks, I had talked to Eric *ad nauseam* about Jonesy and Fisher, spilling my guts until nothing remained. During my brief confinement, Eric had come to my room each morning and rung me dry.

Today, back in his office, I wanted it all behind me. I was finished talking about Jonesy and Fischer. This time, I wanted to talk about Trisha and Matt. I plopped into the chair wearing a Cheshire grin.

Forsythe furrowed his brow. "Pleasant weekend?"

"You might say that."

He smirked faintly and looked away. Opening his Nicorette drawer, he pulled out a stick of gum and held it up. "Dentine. I'm off the Nicorette." He unwrapped the stick and flicked it into his mouth. "So, want to talk about it?"

I did. So I reshuffled my bones in the chair and opened up, detailing my twenty-four hour visit to the city with Trisha. Forsythe scratched notes, pausing occasionally to ask a question.

When I finished, he lay down his pen and stared at me for a while. His impossible-to-read expression caused me to squirm in my seat.

"Well?" I asked.

"Well, what?"

"I don't know. Do you think we're moving too fast? Am I pushing things a little too hard?"

He did it again. "What do you think?"

"Why do you do that?" I asked, frustrated.

"Because my opinion is unimportant here."

"Your approval is."

"I'm not your priest or Boy Scout leader. Unless you're breaking the law or causing harm to yourself or someone else, my opinion or approval remains irrelevant."

"But you're my Goddamn shrink. Give me some direction here."

"I did. I told you to let things take their own course. Sounds like you have. Quit fighting the outcome."

I took a deep breath. "I just want to do the right thing. I don't want to lose her again."

"Do you love her?"

I nodded. "Madly."

"Have you told her?"

"I'm afraid I'll scare her off."

"Is she pretty independent? Settled in her ways?"

"It's not so much that, although that is a factor."

"It's your history, isn't it?"

Forsythe hit it square on the head. *Who, in their right mind, would consider a future with a twenty-year schizoid?* My eyes fell in defeat. "You've got it," I whispered.

I spent day one of the new job shadowing Jack Connelly. Using one of the computers and a large printer, we rendered drug orders ward-by-ward, and then spent two hours filling requisitions from an intimidating landscape of bottles and boxes stacked on an array of large metal shelves.

With the ward orders filled and packed onto the "Blue Magoo", a battered, ugly, turquoise cart the size and shape of a large refrigerator, we wheeled our pharmaceutical booty through a tunnel system to Building Two and the locked wards that had so terrified Neil Jones. I felt my heart thumping as we pushed the Blue Magoo into the basement-level elevator. Jack and I squeezed in next to the large cart. With a stubby index finger, he punched the number five button.

"I always start on the top floor and work my way down," he said.

"Why's that?"

The doors closed, squeaking out for oil. With a sudden shudder, the cab ascended.

"I don't know. Always made sense to work top to bottom." Connelly looked at me and shrugged as if everybody did it that way. "You can do it bottom to top if you want, I guess."

The elevator cab moved arduously slow, emitting an unnerving *thump* when each floor passed. We shuddered to a halt on five, and the doors slid open with a metal-on-metal grind.

"Sounds like this baby needs a little maintenance," I said, stepping out.

Jack followed, pulling on the Blue Magoo. "These elevators have to be forty, forty-five years old. Been stuck in 'em a dozen times. Once, for three hours with two nurses. One of 'em, Denise Berry, wigged out the whole time. She always took the stairs after that. Finally quit and went to Mass General."

We stood in a small lobby flanked on either side by large metal doors. Each door framed a single, square-foot glass window.

Jack motioned to his left and then right. "Five East, Five West." He pulled the cart in the direction of Five East.

"A couple of things before we go inside," he said. "These doors are locked for a reason."

His words chilled me. Jonesy's greatest fear was what lay beyond those doors. My pulse quickened.

"To keep these patients confined," he continued, stopping in front of the heavy, gray metal door and fishing a set of keys from the pocket of his lab coat.

I pictured a ward full of the hopelessly deranged, bouncing off the walls of rubber rooms, and howling like mad animals.

"Do I need to be concerned?" I asked.

Jack shot me a bewildered look.

"I mean, are the residents . . . dangerous?"

Jack chuckled annoyingly. "You mean in here? Hell no, Matt. The place is full of patients with chronic dementia, too far gone for a nursing home. Doors are kept locked to keep them from wandering away. Second floor has the acute patients—mostly suicide risks. Got to keep those guys locked in, too. The only wards where patients might pose a risk are those housed on one. Those are the troublemakers, but they're so zonked on medication, nobody there's going to bother you."

What I witnessed beyond the metal doors of Building Two confirmed Jack's description. The demented patients, most of them old and fragile, called us "Mother," "Father," and other family names. Some referred to us as "Doctor," while others cursed at us. All suffered severe dementia, but none posed a danger. Patients on the other wards considered us little more than a curiosity when we passed through. There were no snake pits, rubber rooms, or lobotomized monsters wandering glassy-eyed. Jonesy's image of a chamber of horrors was a figment of his illness. I only wished I had him here to prove it.

I received a hard time from Debbie and Liz when we stocked my own ward. They just couldn't keep themselves from ribbing me. Jack got a hoot out of it. By four-thirty, we had finished our rounds and were back in the pharmacy.

At the end of my shift, Hank Laird called me into his office to complete a daily progress evaluation for Barbara West. With little enthusiasm, he ran through the range of questions in less than three minutes and then sprung me loose.

I bolted to the computer room and shot Trisha an e-mail.

34

The old, beat-up *Physician's Desk Reference* Henry gave me had taken precedence over my stack of unread paperbacks. I spent hours combing through the PDR's thirty-four hundred pages, learning what I could about many of the drugs I worked with every day.

The pharmacy fascinated me. The enormous number of medications employed to treat the ill was intriguing; the computer controlled packaging and dispensing machines were dazzling.

Jack Connelly was a good mentor. Unfazed by my endless questions and eagerness to learn, he was keen to teach. He even brought in information on a six-month pharmacy technician program at a local community college and encouraged me to apply.

"I think you can get the state to pay for it," he suggested. "Talk to Barbara West. She'd know."

The pharmacy's other tech, Hillary Tate, worked part-time, Mondays, Tuesdays, and Thursdays. Twenty-three years old, she was seven-and-a-half months pregnant with her first child whom she was carrying high—in fact, she looked ready to drop a set of twins at any moment. Short, with long, black hair, a teen-ager's face, and shy brown eyes, Hillary looked too young to be a mother. She was smart, quiet and a hard worker, but appeared uncomfortable in her state. I tried to help her whenever possible.

"Her husband wants her to quit when she delivers," Jack confided. "That would leave a permanent opening here."

His suggestion amused me. If I ever did choose pharmacy as a career, it would be somewhere far from the grounds of Slater State Hospital. But I kept that thought to myself.

Things were rolling without a hitch. My AU-811 therapy was unremarkable, and my blood work, mercifully had been reduced from twice a week to once every ten days.

Forsythe, freshly back from a New York City conference where the AU-811 investigators had gathered to offer findings and present cases, returned heartened by what he had learned. The first AU-811 patient had been discharged—a thirty-two-year-old San Diego woman whose stupor ended at five months. She was now home with her family.

The investigational agent had exceeded all expectations and Eric, a prominent principal investigator, was summoned by the editors of the *Journal of Psychiatric Medicine* to author a paper on the drug.

Trisha and I became, once again, the genuine article. We spent weekends at her place and spoke of eventually moving in together. We planned a future—often from between the bed sheets while we held each other. She swore she'd have waited another twenty years to feel the warm glow now beating deep within her.

Barbara West continued paving the way for my release. She enrolled me as a temporary beneficiary in the state's Medicaid health program and secured Social Security benefits to tide me over until I became self-supporting. The hospital discharge committee was considering a three-week release date. She told me to start thinking about job interviews.

Life was looking good—too good. When the other shoe finally fell, it crashed to earth like a ton of stone.

35

The cup of Starbuck's coffee remained unopened on the desk. Leaning forward, Eric Forsythe studied the paper he held in both hands, while, with the slightest sketching of a grin, I spent the same quiet minute recounting my weekend.

Forsythe placed the paper on the desk, removed his reading glasses, and massaged the bridge of his nose.

"We've got a problem, Matt."

"Now what?" I asked in a smart-assed tone, figuring some bureaucratic blunder was about to delay my upcoming release. *Nothing Barbara can't handle.*

He bit his lip. "This is serious."

"What?" The smirk fell from my face.

"It's your blood work." He lifted the paper. "Your creatinine is up to three, and your BUN's at forty-nine."

I shook my head. "I don't understand."

He fixed his eyes on me. "You're going into renal failure."

His words knifed through me, pushing my weight deep into the chair's cushions. A sickening stillness seized the room.

My throat cramped into a knot, reducing my voice to a raspy quiver. "Renal failure?"

Forsythe let out a long breath. Worried concern marked his face. "I've left a voicemail with Karen Moulton at Portland Pharmaceuticals; she's the physician in charge of the AU-811 project. I want to discuss this with her before we do anything." He glanced at his watch. "It's only seven on the west coast."

My disbelief switched to sudden anger. "I can't stop taking this drug, Eric. You've got to do something." I slammed my fist hard into the armrest.

He raised his hands. "I'm not going to do anything right now. I'm going to speak with Karen, and then we'll come up with a plan."

I glowered at Forsythe, wanting to blame him. I felt my new life ebbing away.

"We're in this together, Matt. We'll figure it out."

I rubbed my forehead. "Please. You can't stop the drug," my voice cracked. "Everything in my life is starting to fall into place. Please, Eric," I pleaded, "don't send me back."

Forsythe drew in a breath and held it a moment. He glanced at the phone.

"I'll talk with you as soon as I speak with Dr. Moulton."

I don't remember my walk back to the ward; in a daze, I don't recall whether I took the elevator or stairs. It was like traveling through a collapsing cavern while the steel clutches of panic squeezed the breath from me.

When I reached my room, I stumbled into the bathroom, fell to my knees, and threw up until nothing remained. Afterward, I crumbled to the cool tiled floor, my head buried in my arm, too weak to move.

I thought about Trisha. *How would I tell her?*

Two hours later, Forsythe found me in the dayroom, pale and lethargic, staring blankly at a TV game show. He walked in and sat next to me on the sofa. I turned and looked at him. His calm gray eyes foretold nothing.

"Hey," I muttered.

"Diane told me you were sick."

"Puked my guts out."

"You all right now?"

I looked away and nodded.

"You didn't go to work."

"Diane called Laird for me.

Eric stared at the TV show for a short while. "I spoke with Dr. Moulton."

"And?" I turned back, meeting his eyes, and not seeing good news. My gut tightened.

"You're not the only one, Matt. In fact, you're the fourth long-term 811 recipient to show signs of acute renal failure in the past five days. The problem is infiltrating the study."

My stomach sank. *The drug was failing us, one patient at a time. We were all going back. Slowly, surely, we were all going back.*

"I'm sending you over to Mercy tomorrow morning for some tests; I've arranged a consult with one of their best nephrologists. Meanwhile, I'm going to have to reduce your dose."

"No," I whimpered, my eyes begging.

"I have to before it destroys your kidneys."

"I'd rather die."

"I'm sorry, Matt. I've no choice." Forsythe sighed and rubbed his bottom lip. "AU-811 has a relatively long half-life. Any effects of a lower dose won't be felt for a few days. That gives us time to come up with something. Portland has scheduled a conference call for this afternoon. I'll know more after that."

He moved to his feet. "We haven't given up yet—not by a long shot."

I looked up at him helplessly. He returned a mirthless smile, then left the room.

For the next hour, I stared at the wall across the room, listening to the sounds of the building, trying to deny the inevitable.

Jonesy's death had created a large void in my life. He was my one, true friend at Slater State. I needed him; I needed someone to talk to besides Forsythe. I needed to hear Jonesy's quick wit, to get his friendly counsel on how to explain all this to Trisha, and when. I was paralyzed with fear at the prospect of telling her. This time, I knew I'd lose her forever.

I found I couldn't eat. A solid knot sat heavily in the pit of my stomach. The thought of food nauseated me. Hoping to ease the queasiness, I stopped by the canteen and bought a can of warm Coke. After that, I removed the phone card from the drawer of my bedside table, dropped it into my shirt pocket, and went for a walk. My mind needed clearing.

Wandering out onto the south grounds, I found a bench next to a large garden of sweet-smelling Trumpet Lilies in full-bloom. I sat and fished the phone card from my shirt pocket, placed my warm Coke next to me, and began spinning scenarios of breaking the news to Trisha.

I wondered if I was being premature. With so little understood about AU-811, who knew what would happen? Reducing the dose might have little or no impact on the drug's therapeutic effect. Perhaps I should wait and see what happened.

But what if the dose reduction had a profound effect, a threshold point where the drug suddenly stopped working its magic, and I wound up unable to tell Trisha myself? *No. That can't happen. Not again.*

I tumbled the plastic card between my fingers, weighing options.

"Hi there, beautiful."

"Matt." The delight in Trisha's tone instantly lifted my spirits. "I'm so glad you called. Did you get my e-mail?"

"No. I haven't had the chance to get to the computer room today."

"I've got to go to Chicago tomorrow morning."

"Chicago?"

"Yes," she said, a hint of dread in her voice. "I've got to go out and save an account. One of our biggest clients is threatening to pull stakes and go with a competitor. I'm packing now. Want to get to bed early. I've got a six-fifteen flight tomorrow morning. I've got to be ready for this one."

Her unexpected news threw everything off kilter. I wanted to see her tonight. *Damn. Now what?* I couldn't let her leave for such an important trip dragging along the foreboding baggage of my situation. She had enough to deal with.

"How long will you be there?"

"As long as it takes. Hopefully, no more than two days." A pause. "I'll miss you, Matt. Terribly."

"I'll miss you, too, babe."

"We'll make up for it when I get back."

"I can't wait."

"Neither can I." She gave me a girlish giggle.

A silent moment passed. Before saying anything, I'd see how the tests turned out.

"I'd better get going," she said. "I want to finish reviewing the contract and load some stuff into my laptop so I can work on the plane."

"Good luck out there, Trish. I'll see you when you get back."

"Try my cell phone tomorrow night if you get a chance."

"I will."

"I love you, Matt."

"Love *you*, Trish."

And she was gone.

36

I felt foolish riding in the back of the ambulance, reading a magazine I'd lifted from the lobby, but that's how the hospital insisted all patients be transported. Thankfully, we drove within the speed limit and without lights or sirens.

Mercy Hospital, the place I'd fantasized spending weeks recovering from a bullet to the head, sat on a hill in a suburb outside of Boston. Its modern, cement-faced walls rose majestically twelve stories above the asphalt-paved grounds. Its prominence was evident by the hundreds of vehicles parked in white lined lots surrounding the sprawling complex and the ceaseless flow of people passing through the main doors.

From the ambulance dock, aides hustled me by wheelchair—another requirement—to the sixth floor and the nephrology clinic, where I met with Dr. Walter Tompkins.

Tompkins, a nephrologist, interviewed me, gave me a cursory examination, and explained the battery of tests he'd ordered. It didn't sound like I was headed for a day at the park.

By five that afternoon, I was exhausted. I'd been poked, prodded, pricked, x-rayed, undergone two ultrasounds, and injected with a dye that burned like acid. They took at least a gallon of blood from my veins, made me drink nasty-tasting liquids, and then required me to pee everything into a measuring beaker. I just wanted to get back to my room at Slater and crash onto my bed.

Knowing I'd return too late for dinner, Miranda had ordered me a meatloaf sandwich from the kitchen and stuck it in the nurses' refrigerator. She brought the food in shortly after I got back and placed it on the bedside table.

"Hungry, Matt?"

"A little."

It was a lie, but I knew I had to eat something besides the bowl of chicken noodle soup I'd been served hours earlier at Mercy.

Miranda removed the plastic wrap from the sandwich dish, popped the top of a soda, and set everything in front of me.

Miranda was a shy woman who rarely looked anyone straight in the eye. With the exception of the rainy day cat story, she and I never had a conversation of more than a few words. As a rule, she did what she had to do and then left. This time she stood there, her hazel eyes gazing squarely into mine.

"You know, don't you?" I said quietly.

She closed her eyes and nodded. "It's in your chart."

I picked up my sandwich and took a bite.

"I'm going to be fine." I winked.

A ripple of a smile came to her face. "I know."

I continued chewing through a happy face, swallowed, and took a swig of soda.

"Thanks for saving me some dinner."

"You're welcome." She remained silent for a moment, then said, "I'll be out at the station if you need anything."

I nodded my thanks and watched her walk out of the room. I forced down half the soda and most of the sandwich and then sprawled out on my bed, closing my eyes. I was beat, but far too wired to doze off. I tried anyway.

At seven o'clock, I gave up, grabbed the phone card, and started my way to the lobby pay phones. I passed Jonesy's old room at the far end of the hallway. It was empty—bed covers removed, a bare mattress and pillow collecting dust. I slowed and glanced into the corner where he had cowered like a frightened child during the thunderstorm.

The dayroom where Lou Fischer drew his last breath was also quiet, all evidence of his senseless death long ago removed with disinfectant and bleach, the entire incident glossed over with a fresh coat of buffed wax. I didn't bother slowing.

I reached Trisha in a cab on her way back from a dinner engagement with clients. She sounded beat, but it was therapeutic to hear her voice. She was excited I called, and that lifted my spirit.

"What'd you do today, handsome?"

"Oh, you know, the usual."

"How was work?"

I hated lying to her. It made me squirm with shame. "Great. A good day in the pill factory." I kept it upbeat.

"'The pill factory.'" She laughed. "That's cute."

"When you coming home, Trish?"

"Tomorrow, I hope. I've got a ton of work to do when I get back to my room. The office has already faxed a mountain of stuff to the hotel, and I've got an eight-thirty call scheduled with our consultants. It looks like I'll be up most the night, but it's the only way to get out of here tomorrow."

"Wish I was there with you."

"Then nothing would get done."

"You little vamp," I said playfully. "It's a good thing you're nine hundred miles away."

"Whatcha say we meet halfway?"

I laughed. "Deal."

We talked until she arrived at her hotel. I turned in a fine acting job, putting up a convincing front that all was well back home. When I hung up I felt like a rat for lying to her. Trisha deserved the truth, but first, I had to be sure. I wasn't going to drag her through any more than I already had.

The following day, I met with Forsythe at the usual time.

Forty-eight hours had elapsed since he had halved my dose of AU-811. I felt fine. No hint of the disease—not yet. It was like waiting for the guillotine to strike, listening to the fall of its finely honed blade before all went black.

Forsythe absently tapped his pen on my chart, thumbing through some papers.

He looked up. "How are you feeling?"

"So far, so good," I said.

After a pause, he nodded slightly. "Good."

"So what's next?" I asked.

He rapped the papers with his pen. "Your renal clearance tests from Mercy are not good."

I expelled a defeated sigh.

He continued. "AU-811 affects a part of the kidney known as the glomeruli. Those are little tube-like structures filled with tiny capillaries that filter the blood. The drug seems to inflame these structures and destroy capillary permeability. In simple terms, the ability of your kidneys to filter blood is being compromised, allowing dangerous toxins to accumulate. If it's allowed to continue, your kidneys will shut down, and you'll have to be placed on dialysis."

Forsythe flipped to the next page.

"The good news is your creatinine clearance and BUN have stabilized for now. They're still too high, but at least the numbers aren't worsening. Sometimes we can control the numbers with drugs known as corticosteroids; that's something we might have to consider."

A wisp of hope shot through me. "You mean you can stop it?"

"I don't know. Corticosteroids are not without their own catalog of nasty side effects. I'd like to avoid them if possible. I'm hoping that by reducing the amount of AU-811 and spreading the dosing interval to every other day, we'll slow the progression of the kidney disease. It's a waiting game, Matt. We'll wait and act appropriately."

I walked out of Forsythe's office mildly encouraged. Making my way to the elevator, I summed things up: My renal numbers were high but stable; we had a backup plan to use drugs if the numbers started sneaking up, and most important, no untoward effects after forty-eight hours on a half-dose of AU-811. I was walking a tightrope, but there remained a sliver of hope. I was grateful I hadn't yet told Trisha.

Work at the pharmacy helped take my mind off my troubles. I had to concentrate when picking medications from stock. The job provided much needed therapy.

It turned into a busy day. Jack Connelly had called in sick and Hillary, tired and distressed from what was turning out to be a difficult pregnancy, was moving slowly and deliberately. I spent the afternoon chasing the clock.

By the time I returned to my room, my feet were throbbing. I collapsed on the bed and grabbed a forty-minute nap before Debbie gently woke me. She had my medication.

"Are you drinking all the fluids you can manage?" she asked, handing me a large tumbler of water.

"Enough to make me pee like a race horse."

"Good. You've got to stay hydrated. What did Eric say about coffee?"

"One cup a day."

She faked a shudder. "That'd kill me right there. You're looking at a girl who pumps the stuff through her veins."

Debbie remained in front of me in a mother's pose, hands on hips, until I downed the entire tumbler of water. She awarded me with an "attaboy," took the tumbler, and dashed from the room.

I tried Trisha's cell at seven-thirty and held my breath waiting for her to pick up, hoping she was on her way home. I wanted to hold her, feel her softness against me, bury my face in her shoulder, and breathe her sweet redolence. The disappointment arrived all too quickly.

"I'm going to be stuck here until Friday noon."

Her words sucked the life out of me.

"I'm so sorry, Matt. My boss and one of our CPAs are flying out here tonight. The whole deal is going down the toilet. They've forced out our big guns. There's no way I'm getting out of here before then. It's a big account; we can't afford to lose it."

"I understand. You stay there as long as you need to. We'll have the whole weekend, I hope."

"Oh, don't you worry. I'm out of here Friday by noon. This girl isn't spending the weekend in Chicago, no matter what. If necessary, I'll fly back here on Monday."

We talked for twenty more minutes before she reluctantly hinted work was waiting. I had to let her go. Trying to hold on to her for as long as possible, I listened to the sound of her clicking off and the eventual dial tone before gently cradling the handset and heading to my room.

37

Though thoroughly exhausted, I had trouble sleeping Thursday night.

The day had been a blur. It started with Barbara West at nine, then an hour with Forsythe, an examination by an internist, blood work, and a five-hour stint in the pharmacy. By all rights, I should have slept like the dead, but I remained restless, tossing and turning.

I had had a strange feeling all day—an exhausted, fuzzy feeling—hard to explain, but present nonetheless. It bothered me, but, hell, I was forty-seven and pushing my body and mind harder than I had in twenty years. I wasn't used to it. All that—and the fact that I'd be with Trisha in twenty-four hours—had my nerves dancing a jig. The last time I glanced at the wall clock, it read three-fifteen.

I woke from the dream startled, confused, and soaked in sweat, my heart pounding like a piston. I had lost Trisha.

She was standing on an ice pack being swept away by a raging river. I ran along the river's bank screaming for her to hold on, trying to figure out what to do. She stood there unconcerned, smiling and waving as the current continued to pull away. I dove into the icy water and started swimming.

The river emptied us into a warm, calm, green ocean. I put my head into the water and swam until my arms and legs seized into cramps. When I looked up, Trisha was a tiny speck on the horizon miles away. I called to her. Unable to swim another stroke, I looked back to shore, but found myself surrounded by ocean. When I stated sinking and breathing in water, I woke up.

My knees wanted to buckle when I stood and shuffled to the bathroom. On the way, I caught a glimpse of the clock—five minutes after seven. I turned on the water, crawled out of my pajamas, and stepped into the shower.

After an English muffin and a glass of orange juice, I grabbed my Grisham paperback and headed to the cafeteria for the day's solitary cup of coffee.

I had the morning to myself. Forsythe had taken the day off, which meant waiting until Monday for the results of my blood work.

My body felt strong, considering I carried only four hours of sleep under my belt. In fact, I felt better than I had in two days. I'm sure knowing Trisha was headed home had a lot to do with it. I couldn't wait to see her.

Reading a good book passes the time quickly. For three hours and two cups of coffee—I figured I deserved an extra cup after the week I'd had—I remained lost in the pages of *The Chamber*. I had to put it down when one of those annoying headaches bloomed behind my right eye. I still hadn't done a thing about having my eyes checked.

Just after noon, I called Trisha's cell. She was back in her room packing, delighted the team had managed to save the account and thrilled she was heading home. As always, her voice brightened my mood. She was scheduled into Boston just after four, and promised to be in the lobby downstairs no later than seven-thirty.

"Have I got plans for us," she said with a tease.

"Do you now?"

"Yes, I do. You and I, Mr. Tracy, are going to spend a romantic weekend in Newport, Rhode Island. I've rented a sailboat for Saturday. We're going to spend the day leisurely sailing Narragansett Bay. Not only that, we are staying at the elegant Victoria Hotel, right in the heart of the historic mansion district. I'm so psyched."

"You're remarkable, Trish. When did you do all this?"

"Last night. Online," she added proudly.

I laughed out loud.

"What?" she said.

"I just love you so much. You're an absolutely amazing woman. How could I be so lucky?"

"No," she said softly. "I'm the lucky one, Matt. There's no one on this earth more amazing than you."

An hour-and-a-half after the grounds of Slater State Hospital faded in the rear window, the lights of the Claiborne Pell Bridge, spanning from Jamestown to Newport, rose like a carnival spectacle from the horizon.

The damp tang of salt air tweaked my nostrils as Trisha navigated the Lexus over the hills and curves of Route 138, Van Morrison pumping from all sixteen speakers, the moon roof half-cracked.

My skin tingled with anticipation when I caught her sparkling green orbs sneaking a glance my way. She must have felt it too, because her face broke into a wide, mischievous smile.

The roads of downtown Newport were clogged with Friday night traffic, no doubt thickened by the unseasonably warm May evening. The sidewalks teemed with young people, many from the campus of URI located across the bay in South Kingston. Everyone looked spirited, which only served to raise our already-towering level of excitement.

Taking it all in, we crawled the entire length of the main drag at a snail's pace, until reaching a side road that led us up into the Historic Hill section of the city. My driver knew her way around. A quick turn onto Quincy Street, another onto Bellevue, and we were there.

Trisha threw the car into park and turned to me. "Wait until you see the suite."

"Suite? You got us a suite?"

The valet, a college-aged kid tucked into a white shirt, red tie, and black slacks, opened Trisha's door while a bellhop in a red vest and hat wheeled a brass cart to the rear of the car.

I got out, stretched my back until it cracked and took in the hotel's four-story, red brick expanse. With a gray slate roof, copper flashing, and impressive gabled-end towers, its architecture was more ivy-league college than hotel. But we were in the center of Newport's famed historic district, where century-old opulence was the norm.

Our second floor suite, two spacious rooms awash in colonial elegance reminiscent of an early English inn, faced west, its giant windows offering a grand view of Newport Harbor.

The bedroom, its walls adorned with an impressive tapestry and several ornately framed works of art, contained a Queen Ann style four-poster bed, with matching dressers and nightstands. Pink marble covered the large adjoining bathroom.

I stood between the two rooms, awe-struck.

"Like it?" Trisha asked, slipping her hands around my waist and pressing her head to my chest.

"Are you kidding? This is unbelievable." I eased her back. "This had to have cost a small fortune."

She cocked her head and gave me that naughty look of hers.

"You let me worry about that." She started unbuttoning my shirt. "Besides, we're celebrating tonight."

My innermost urge for her ignited deep inside and flashed to the surface.

"So I guess a late dinner is out of the question?" I asked, arching a brow.

She unfastened the last button, ripped my shirt open and ran her warm, wet tongue across my right nipple. "Not before I gobble you up, first."

She kissed my chest and my neck, and then pressed her mouth to mine. Our warm tongues entwined, dancing about in a fling of hungry desire. I scooped her in my arms and carried her to bed.

An hour later, we ordered room service: marinated New York sirloin, baked potatoes, and a large bottle of Pinot Noir.

Settled in front of the gas–fueled, stone fireplace and dressed in thick, white terry-cloth robes, we devoured our meals like starving castaways, laughing at each other's sudden banishment of civil table manners.

"I'm sorry, but I'm so hungry," Trisha said with a mouthful, raising her glass of wine.

Still chewing, I raised my glass in a toasting gesture. "I managed to work up a pretty decent appetite myself."

Trisha finished first. Placing her quarter-filled wine glass on the coffee table, she leaned back into the sofa, closed her eyes, and squeezed out a sensuous groan of absolute contentment.

"This is so perfect," she said.

I set my plate down and pulled her to me, resting my chin on her head. I could feel her heartbeat. She wiggled herself closer. I relished the feel of her warm body tucked against me, the softness of her hair in my face, her moist breath on my neck.

"I love you so much, Trish," I said.

She kissed my throat and moaned. A moment later she broke from my arms, rose to her feet, took a quick, deep breath and smiled. With her thumb, she pulled at the loop of the terrycloth belt. The robe slipped from her shoulders and fell to the floor. She picked up her wine glass, winked, and walked to the bedroom.

I grabbed my glass, the bottle of wine, and fell in behind her.

38

In the morning, we woke to the sound of wind whipping in howls past the grand windows. I rolled out of bed, pulled back the heavy velvet drapes, and looked out onto the bay. It was covered in foaming whitecaps.

"Kind of windy out there," I said.

Trisha joined me and peered over my shoulder. "Wow. Looks more like a gale. I'll have to call the boat rental place and see if it's supposed to calm down. We certainly can't go sailing in this."

"Guess not," I mumbled. Disappointed, I released the curtain and flicked on the TV to catch a forecast.

After we showered and dressed, Trisha called the boat yard. A cold front had zipped in from Canada during the night, bringing with it strong easterly winds and small-craft warnings from Eastport to Block Island. All rentals were canceled for the day, forcing Trisha into Plan B—mansions, museums, and shopping. I wouldn't have minded a trip to the dentist, so long as we were together.

After breakfast, we took the late morning tour of Newport's famed mansions—The Breakers, The Elms, Rosecliff, Marblehouse. The enormous old homes, casually referred to as *summer cottages* by their original aristocratic owners, graced eighty acres of prime Rhode Island real estate.

After the tour, we descended the hill to downtown and ate lunch at a small outdoor café on the waterfront.

I watched Trisha pick at her meal, similar to the way she had her breakfast. She was quieter than usual and seemed troubled. I hoped it wasn't me. I thought back to everything I'd said and did that morning but came up with nothing.

"Something bothering you, Trish?"

She looked up, surprised. "Huh? Oh, no. Just zoning."

"Is it work?"

"No. It's nothing. Really." She broke into a wide smile, and her green-eyed glow rose to its normal brightness. "Hey," she said grabbing my hand, "let's buy a kite and take it out to Brenton Park."

"Where?"

"Brenton Park. It's a beautiful spot right on the ocean just outside of town."

"You're a beautiful spot," I said, grasping her hand.

"And you're a big fat ham," she responded.

We spent thirty dollars on a kite and a large spool of kite string at a little shop off of Thames Street. I couldn't help but recall when paper kites in the dime store cost a quarter, and I made some noise of that fact. Trisha ignored my sarcasm and handed the clerk her credit card.

A short time later, we were zipping along Ocean Avenue—past Hammersmith Farm where Jackie Kennedy spent her childhood summers, and past Fort Adams, a one-hundred-acre, Civil War-era fortress nestled on the shores of Newport Harbor. We followed the road to the park and pulled into a crowded lot.

Sitting on a green slope overlooking the water, Trisha twitched with excitement as we assembled our thirty-dollar kite. I loved it when she showed that young, schoolgirl spirit; it was one of her many endearing qualities.

We had little trouble getting the kite airborne in the stiff, on-shore breeze. In no time, our red, white, and blue-striped nylon Delta and its eight-foot spinning tail joined a dozen other kites darting across the baby-blue skies above Brenton Park.

With the warm sunshine painting our faces, we spread out on a blanket—Trisha with her head on my stomach piloting our new toy, me with my eyes closed, gently massaging her head.

Trisha talked and I listened. She went on about our future. I caught a glimpse of the old Trish I remembered—the woman in charge. There was little wonder she had become so successful in the business world. She was assertive, yet possessed a soft, gentle side—a helplessness that begged for comfort and protection. I was determined to give her just that.

Two hours later, we watched the dazzling blue eyes of a set of nearby six-year-old twin girls, bug with delight when we handed them control of our soaring kite. Trisha spoke to the excited girls' mother for a few moments while I rolled up the blanket.

"Have fun, kids," Trish said as we left.

"Thank you," they said in unison, their tiny voices nearly blown away by the wind.

"Aren't they adorable?" Trish said. She kept checking the twins over her shoulder until we lost them on the other side of the hill.

I glanced at her and grinned. *Maternal emotions.*

She poked my side. "They were so cute."

On our trip back to town, we visited two museums, the Newport Art Museum and the Artillery Company of Newport.

The "American Painters in Water Colors" exhibit at the Art Museum mesmerized Trisha as we moved slowly from piece to piece. I found the exhibit a real yawner. We were there a long hour-and-a-half.

The military museum was more my style, especially the display of bronze cannons cast in 1798 by Paul Revere. Ancient armaments were not her cup of tea, and Trisha rushed me through the place in twenty minutes.

Later, we dropped a bundle feasting on chicken-fried lobster and polishing off a bottle of Pinot Grigio at Zelda's, a great little café off of Thames Street.

After a long dinner, we strolled the streets, capping an early evening with a pair of large Margaritas at Gringo's, a busy bar on the harbor with outdoor seating.

By the time we spilled out of Gringo's, we were noticeably tipsy. The combination of wine and tequila had us laughing and acting foolish all the way back to the Victoria.

As soon as our suite door latched, we were all over each other. A shirt or blouse button, I'm not sure which, ricocheted off the wall with a sharp crack. We tugged and pulled clothes off one another, leaving a path of hastily discarded garments from the door to the fireplace.

Minutes later, we were clumped in a naked, tangled mass atop the thick, white, woolen rug, hearthside a flickering gas-fired flame.

Sometime after midnight, we stumbled our way to bed, collapsing on the heavy down comforter, wholly and completely spent.

Confused and frightened, I awoke trying to figure out where I was and how I got there. My eyes shot around the room, trying to get my bearings. It took a good fifteen seconds for my head to clear.

I'm at the Victoria in Newport with Trish.

I propped myself up on one elbow and took several deep breaths, waiting for my heart to slow. Within a minute, I was fine, except for the dull pounding at the front of my skull—a hangover. It had been a while since I'd experienced one. It felt no better now than it did way back when.

Trisha was already up. I smelled coffee. Wrapping myself in my robe, I hurried to join her.

"I sure hope you brought a bottle of aspirin. I think I'm going to need it," I said, stumbling into the living room.

Rounding the threshold, I froze in my tracks. Trisha, clad in her nightgown and robe, sat hunched in one corner of the sofa with her feet tucked beneath her, gazing at her cradled coffee mug as if it were life-sustaining. She looked dazed and ashen. Her eyes were red and swollen, her cheeks tear streaked.

I gave her a bewildering stare. "What is it? What's wrong?"

Trying to speak, her jaw trembled.

I rushed over and sat with her. Stroking back her hair, I asked again. "What is it, Trish? What's wrong, baby?"

She squeezed her eyes closed for a second and swallowed hard. "Matt," she squeaked, "I'm losing you."

I looked deep into her worried eyes.

"It's starting again."

"What, Trish? What's starting?"

Her reply dropped the bottom from my stomach.

If I'd held her any tighter, I would have crushed her to powder. With her face buried in my chest, Trisha sobbed in gasping, shuddering breaths at the truth. Tears ran to my chin, falling into her fine auburn hair.

I told her everything; I had to. My worst fears were coming to fruition. The half-doses of AU-811 were failing. I was, she said, slowly slipping back.

Her story sickened me. Friday night, she said, I woke her, my screams warning someone to stay away from my family. She shrugged it off as a nightmare, but still it gnawed at her all day Saturday. At three this morning, she found me sitting on the edge of the sofa, arguing with my father, threatening to kill him if he ever touched my mother again. When she tried to intervene, I shoved her to the floor. I didn't remember any of it.

Horror and an indescribable despair coursed through me. My strength seemed to seep away. I didn't want to open my eyes and let the monster in. I held tight to Trisha and prayed. *What else could I do?*

39

Six Weeks Later

Eric Forsythe sat in his office, surrounded by a gallery of silver wall etchings cast from a lone, state-issued desk lamp.

His gaze lingered on the flat-screen monitor that displayed his final AU-811 report to Portland Pharmaceuticals, but his mind spun elsewhere.

He opened the Nicorette drawer, removed a pack of Marlboros, tapped out a single cigarette, and lit it with the gold Zippo that had lain dormant for months. The stress of everything had forced a relapse.

Drawing in a long haul, he exhaled a white stream across the desk and picked up the framed photo. His girls: Christy, Jenny and his beautiful wife, Jill. How he loved them. In a heartbeat, he'd lay down his life for his girls. He did it all for them, and would do it again without a moment's thought.

He considered himself a good father. His daughters were now assured the good life. Thanks to him, their future would include the best private schools, summers on the Vineyard, and an Ivy League education. But they could never know the truth. Tonight, the lies stopped. Tonight, a new life would begin.

He regretted the deaths. No one was supposed to die.

Lou Fischer, his contact man and a former Jupiter Pharmaceuticals marketing exec, had set the whole thing up. But Lou got greedy and threatened to blow it wide open if his palm wasn't greased with a little of Forsythe's take. That was unfair. Hell, Jupiter was paying the man a small fortune for his part. But still, Lou felt entitled to more; money meant for Eric's girls. The thought of Lou Fischer taking food from his girls' mouths enraged Forsythe.

He couldn't let one man's avarice destroy everything he'd worked so hard for: his years of research, his prominent station in life, and most importantly, his girls' future.

Fischer had to go, and Neil Jones turned out to be the perfect patsy, a paranoid schizophrenic easily swayed by the right combination of drugs and suggestive therapy sessions.

Their meeting that night in the dayroom was no coincidence. Fischer was there to collect his first extortion payment and Jones, convinced the administrative assistant was about to sign his transfer to Building Two, a place he believed steeped in untold horrors, lay in wait.

Forsythe looked off to a dark corner of the office and thought of the paradox. He had devoted three decades of his life to seeking cures for the mentally ill. For years, his specialty, schizophrenia, had responded feebly to drug therapy. Load them with Thorazine and Haldol and lock them away. But then, ten years ago, the Atypicals hit the scene. Clozapine, olanzapine, quetiapine, and the most remarkable of them all, Jupiter's manrazipine, soon had patients unresponsive to conventional schizophrenic therapy, discharged and functioning outside institutional walls.

None of the Atypicals, however, showed the prospect of Portland's AU-811, an agent that reversed schizophrenic catatonia so completely, it was as if the patient had never suffered a day of mental illness. And this was only Phase One of the first clinical trial. Who knew what promise the drug held in subsequent trial studies? AU-811 was a miracle drug, and it scared the living daylights out of the executives at drug giant, Jupiter Pharmaceuticals.

Matt Tracy stood among the lucky fourteen—fourteen of the clinical trial's original forty patients who had benefited from AU-811 therapy without untoward renal effects. But even fourteen successes proved too much a threat for Jupiter's top echelon. If ever approved, AU-811 would take an ugly chunk out of Jupiter's manrazipine sales and their 1.1-billion-dollar-a-year grasp of the psychotropic market. Portland's investigational wonder drug had to be derailed, demonized, and stopped at any cost. Eric Forsythe provided Jupiter the perfect hatchet man.

Altering Matt Tracy's lab results proved simple. A security hole large enough to drive a truck through existed in the hospital's computer system. Lowest bid software, a scourge of the political indifference toward the state's mental health budget. Not only were doctors able to pull up lab values with the faulty program, but they could actually change the reported numbers, a feature few were aware of, most notably the hospital's IT department.

Fortunately, Tracy's consult report from Mercy Hospital came addressed directly to Forsythe's office. Matt's battery of tests proved normal, of course, but the report never found its way into his record. It somehow became misplaced, lost among the endless sea of paperwork flooding this and every hospital. Thank God for shredders.

Matt's feigned renal insufficiency increased AU-811's failure rate to more than two-thirds, a figure that would in itself raise serious safety doubts among the governmental reviewing agencies and much of the medical community.

AU-811's death knell had begun, and to ensure the drug's demise, Dr. Eric Forsythe, the renowned and distinguished, Harvard-educated research psychiatrist planned on devoting the next twelve months to writing journal articles and making presentations at medical conferences and symposiums, stressing the unfortunate and unacceptable renal-damaging effects of AU-811, a risk that he'd passionately argue trumped the study's thirty-two percent therapeutic success rate.

Using Matt Tracy as the perfect example, he'd start by penning letters to the FDA and NIH calling for the immediate halt of all current and future plans for clinical trials of the drug. He'd call in favors from other prominent colleagues, garnering support. Employing an array of impeccable credentials and formidable influence, Forsythe, well oiled with corporate cash, planned on bringing Portland Pharmaceuticals to its knees. His relentless attack would force the fledgling drug company's stock to plummet. Investors would cut their losses and run. The single-drug pharmaceutical company, despite other promising agents in the pipeline, would never survive the onslaught.

But first, Eric Forsythe planned to take his girls on vacation. He'd earned it, and they deserved it. No more cookie-cutter Disney World, wait-in-long-lines-under-a-blistering-sun vacation for his gang. Thanks to Jupiter, he was a rich man now. This time, they'd see Paris, Rome, and then the Greek islands. They'd rent a villa overlooking the Mediterranean, and shop in the finest European shops. A taste of the good life.

Forsythe forced his mind back. The final report had to be dispatched to Portland headquarters tonight. He gave the document one last read.

RE: AU-811 (atrazipine)
Principal Investigator: Eric R. Forsythe, MD
Progress Note – Final

Subject Patient Mathew Tracy – Application No. 38

Patient is a 47-year-old WM in day 38 post-discontinuance of AU-811 (atrazipine) due to drug-induced, acute bilateral glomerulonephritis with creatinine and BUN reaching 3.5 and 60, respectively, on sub-therapeutic half-dose of 4 mg every other day.

Renal function remains normal since day 7 post discontinuance: Creatinine 1.2, BUN 12. Unfortunately, patient has regressed to prior catatonic stupor status since day 10. Patient remains unresponsive to established phenothiazine and atypical psychotropic protocols.

Patient's medical team remains concerned about long-term effects from AU-811-induced renal toxicity.

It remains this investigator's opinion that the devastating potential of this agent's renal toxicity and its unknown long-term toxic effects to other organs deserves serious scrutiny before present clinical trials are allowed to continue.

As it is my professional obligation, and in accordance with their Adverse Drug Reaction (ADR) reporting policy, I have notified the FDA of the damaging effects my patient suffered while under treatment of AU-811.

I further contend that my patient's significant other (girlfriend) has been placed under undue emotional strain in observing her boyfriend emerge from a two-decade stupor and assume normal mental lucidity, only to witness his deterioration back to catatonia when this investigator was forced to discontinue the agent.

Based on my observations, I am forced to conclude the investigational agent AU-811 (atrazipine) poses an unacceptable risk that clearly outweighs its therapeutic benefit, and recommend all trials be immediately terminated.

Eric R. Forsythe, MD

Forsythe hit the *Enter* key, sending the document on its way.

He checked his watch. The girls knew he'd be late tonight, but still, he hated to miss tucking his daughters in and kissing their darling foreheads goodnight, tickling them and hearing their sweet, innocent giggles. He looked forward to pecking their sleeping heads when he got home, but first one piece of business remained, one last loose end.

Forsythe snuffed out his half-smoked cigarette, threw the pack into the open drawer, adjusted the girls' photo, turned off the desk lamp, and headed to the elevator.

The Best Western motel sat next to a McDonald's and across the street from a shopping mall about a mile before the entrance to the turnpike. Forsythe pulled his midnight-blue Toyota Camry into the fast-food lot, drove to the rear and parked next to a large green Dumpster.

He sat for a minute waiting for the drive-through window to clear before getting out and slipping along the back McDonald's lot, through a row of thick shrubbery and over to the rear of the Best Western.

Using a side door to avoid the lobby, he dashed up the carpeted stairs to the second floor. Room 230 was at the end of the corridor, diagonally opposite the stairs.

Forsythe lightly rapped the door twice, stared at the peek hole fish-eye lens, and waited. Moments later, a latch released and the door swung open. She stood there barefoot in white shorts and a navy-blue Champion T-shirt, wearing an impish grin, holding a can of Bud Light.

"Well, hello there, Doctor."

"Kimberly," he said. "Or should I say, *Trisha*."

"Whatever gets you off," she said stepping aside.

Forsythe brushed past her. The small room bore typical seventy-dollar-a-night motel furnishings. Inside, the TV was on but muted, magazines lay spread on the king-sized bed and two empty beer cans sat on the table next to the remains of a six-pack.

"Beer, doc?" she said, holding up the one she was working on.

"No, thanks."

Forsythe hated this former patient. She stood for everything he feared for his daughters. Kimberly Chase, a manipulating man-hater who had been through four husbands in her thirty-nine years.

She was grossly materialistic, and, being nearly incapable of remorse, a borderline psychopath.

Her lust for money and a twenty-year drama background made her the perfect candidate for the ruse—Matt Tracy's subliminally implanted former girlfriend. The real Trisha had never existed.

A year ago, he had read an online article from *The German Journal of Psychiatry* about moderate success by Dutch psychologists to reach certain catatonic patients through subliminal messaging. To the best of his knowledge, it had never been attempted in this country. Not until now.

After a series of e-mail exchanges with the Amsterdam researchers, he was able to obtain a complete copy of their protocol and research notes.

With a few protocol modifications to fit his patient's particular condition, over the course of six months, Forsythe implanted a complete history of the fictitious Patricia Kelly, along with a past-life that never existed, into the vulnerable mind of Mathew Tracy. The outcome exceeded his wildest expectations.

"I believe you have something for me." Kimberly placed one hand on her swayed hip and held out the other, palm up.

Forsythe removed the envelope of cash and handed it to her. He watched her eyes light up. More greed. How he hated it.

"Easiest twenty grand I ever made," she said, opening the envelope and running her thumb across the wad's thick edge. "I wish you could have made the gig last a little longer. I was getting used to that apartment and the Lexus, not to mention Matt. He turned out to be a pretty nice guy and a *great* piece of ass." She snorted. "Coop a guy up without sex for twenty years and then let him loose. Whoa, baby. Look out."

Forsythe's contempt for this unrepentant woman seethed. The damage she could cause if she so chose. He recoiled at the thought of one of his girls turning out this way. It made his stomach wrench.

"Sure I can't talk you into a beer? A little celebration?" she said, with a foxy shake of her hips.

He looked at her and revealed the slightest sliver of a smile. "Why not?"

She tapped his chest with a closed fist. "That's the spirit, doc."

Kimberly turned to the table, but before she took a step, Forsythe slipped a stainless steel letter opener from his pocket, wrapped his hand around her forehead and with one violent tug backward, buried the steel blade into the base of her skull. With surgical precision, the instrument ripped through the cerebellum and into the medulla of her brainstem.

Kimberly immediately stiffened. He felt her eyes bulge beneath his hand. She never cried out. He knew she wouldn't. He eased her to the floor, removed the weapon, wrapped it in a handkerchief and slid it back into his inner jacket pocket.

Forsythe picked up the envelope and tucked it away. He stood over Kimberly, gazing down at her lifeless green eyes, froze open at the moment of death. A gratifying sense of relief swarmed through him. It was over, the lies, the deceit, the greed. *Tonight it ends here.*

Making his way out of the room and down the stairs, Forsythe carefully wiped the brass doorknobs and handles with a clean handkerchief. Stepping into the cool night air, he quickly weaved his way across the lot, through the shrubbery and back to his waiting car.

Tucked safely inside the Camry, he scanned the area for curious eyes. There were none, not a soul. He sucked in a chest full of air and slowly released it. He felt good. At that moment, he decided to stop smoking again. *Back on the Nicorette first thing tomorrow. A new life.*

He turned the key, backed out of his spot, and drove home to his girls.

About the Author

Richard Leverone is a registered pharmacist and has practiced hospital pharmacy in Boston for over thirty years. *Loony Bin* is his third novel.